MODERN MYSTERIES

Contemporary Productions of
Medieval English Cycle Dramas

MODERN MYSTERIES

Contemporary Productions of Medieval English Cycle Dramas

KATIE NORMINGTON

D. S. BREWER

First published 2007
D. S. Brewer, Cambridge

ISBN 978-1-84384-128-9

D. S. Brewer is an imprint of Boydell & Brewer Ltd
PO Box 9, Woodbridge, Suffolk IP12 3DF, UK
and of Boydell & Brewer Inc.
668 Mt Hope Avenue, Rochester, NY 14620, USA
website: www.boydellandbrewer.com

A CIP catalogue record for this book is available from the British Library

This publication is printed on acid-free paper

Designed and typeset in Skia and Adobe Warnock Pro by
David Roberts, Pershore, Worcestershire

Printed in Great Britain by
Anthony Rowe Ltd, Chippenham, Wiltshire

Contents

List of Plates

The plates appear between pp.114 and 115

For my mother, Dorothy
& grandmother, Marjorie

Acknowledgements

This book has been made possible through the support of the Arts and Humanities Research Council and the Arts Faculty, Royal Holloway, University of London. The Anthony Denning Award was given by the Society of Theatre Research to support this publication.

Earlier versions of some chapters of this book have appeared as journal articles, and I am grateful for the permission of the journals concerned in releasing these. Chapter 3 appeared as 'Reviving the Royal National Theatre's *The Mysteries*', *Research Opportunities in Renaissance Drama* 40 (2001), pp. 133–48; chapter 4 as 'Little acts of faith: Katie Mitchell's *The Mysteries*', *New Theatre Quarterly* 14.2 (May 1998), pp. 99–110. Ideas to be found amongst other chapters appeared as 'The actor/audience contract in modern restagings of the mystery plays', *Research Opportunities in Renaissance Drama* 43 (2004), pp. 29–37. Helpful in shaping these ideas has been the response given to papers delivered at the Medieval English Theatre conference, the Leeds International Medieval Congress, and the University of Wales, Aberystwyth, the University of Kent and Royal Holloway.

I am grateful to the generosity of those involved with the mystery plays and the keeping of records of performance: Andy Brereton, Bill Bryden, John Paul Cherrington, Greg Doran, Bill Fisher, Jane Hytch, Hilary Jones, Robert Leach, Mick Martin, Peter Meredith, Katie Mitchell, Jane Oakshott, Matthew Pegg, Keith Ramsay, Richard Rastall, John Retallack, Pawel Szkotak, archives of Poculi Ludique Societas, Julian Wroe, Kimberly Yates, York Theatre Royal.

Thanks to colleagues for their constructive criticisms: David Bradby, Philip Butterworth, Helen Nicholson, Liz Schafer. Any errors that remain are my own. Special thanks go to Zena Sargent and David Thurlby for their efficient help with pictures.

The enthusiasm and patience of Caroline Palmer at Boydell & Brewer and the generously detailed comments of the Readers have made this book possible.

Finally, thank you to my family: Tim, Beatrice and Oliver.

Preface

Since the 1950s it has become increasingly popular to stage medieval drama. It is noticeable, however, that during the ten years that surrounded the Millennium the vogue for reproducing early English drama reached a hitherto unsurpassed height. It was possible to view different productions of the 500-year-old cycles on an annual basis. (During the year 2000 alone there were over half a dozen productions.) The plays were produced by professional, academic and amateur groups throughout this period.

Modern Mysteries investigates the reasons for the popularity of the mystery plays at the turn of the Millennium. It does this by analysing a selected number of productions and posing a series of questions. Why were these mystery plays produced? What features of the plays attracted the modern-day director? Why was staging 500-year-old plays so popular? What can the mystery plays offer today's producers, directors, participants and audiences?

In order to answer these questions it is necessary to go through a number of stages. First, the book begins by examining what is known of the original staging conditions of the mystery plays in order to establish what the plays may offer to today's theatre. Second, it discusses some of the reasons that emerge for staging the plays today; in doing so it begins to develop a structure through which to analyse groups of productions. Last, a series of case studies is analysed in order to determine what features of the mystery plays made them so popular at the turn of the Millennium.

The methodology used to analyse modern-day productions centres on the examination of a number of resources: interviews with the directors and producers, observation of rehearsals, attendance at performances, viewing videos, studying reviews, photographs and programmes from the productions.

But, as ever, the study of performance is difficult. Performances are particular to the space and time in which they are executed. As director Peter Brook points out, 'theatre is always a self-destructive art, and it is always written on the wind.'[1] Performance is a live moment; the moment it ceases it is blown away and no authentic record of it remains. When I write about Katie Mitchell's production of *The Mysteries,* I am discussing an event that I witnessed ten years ago; even if I turn to the video evidence of that performance I can never capture the sense of what it was like for the audience to experience that event. Similarly, how far can my experience of witnessing an event be anything other than subjective? How can I use reviews and eyewitness accounts to construct notions about a performance I haven't seen? How can this material form the basis of an objective account of the performance? How does a reader who has seen many of these performances equate their memories with the accounts that I have rendered? Performance is never capable of a single interpretation. Theatrical systems used to develop meaning within a performance cannot be strictly controlled. A symbol may mean one thing to one audience member and something different to another. It is for this reason that I approach the productions analysed here within a wider framework by considering their intentions, factors that surround their production, and often the cultural milieu in which they were produced.

This study faces another problem. As Edith Hall notes, it is not easy to analyse productions from the recent past, but that we should 'at least try to make sense of it, while acknowledging that the eye of history in fifty or in a hundred years from now will see causes, consequences, contexts, and patterns as yet invisible to us.'[2]

A few previous studies have documented modern productions of medieval theatre. It is some twenty years since John Elliott published *Playing God: Medieval Mysteries on the Modern Stage*, which traces the history of the revival of religious drama from its demise during the Reformation to the Victorian enthusiasm for the modern-day Passion play at Oberammergau. Within the context of modern Britain, Elliott's study focused on the resurrection of the York Cycle in 1951 to mark the Festival of Britain, and he completed his work by tracking the playing of religious drama until 1980. Elliott concluded that the story of more recent stagings 'must of necessity be written by someone else.'[3] This book is a response to that challenge.

There are many differences between this book and Elliott's *Playing God*. His methodology relies on the study of the plays as historical and religious artefacts; *Modern Mysteries* considers the performative aspects of the plays. In analysing the performances that have been selected, this book investigates the reasons for the popularity of staging medieval drama. It does not seek to compare and contrast the differences between the Middle Ages and modern-day stagings, but rather it asks why contemporary producers choose to stage medieval dramas. It attempts not to address what the producers or audience may have learnt about medieval drama (since authentic reproductions can never be achieved), but rather what the plays, often presented in very loose 'versions,' have offered to modern drama and culture.

Specific criteria have been used in selecting the productions for analysis. These productions were produced around the turn of the Millennium, and have mainly been professionally directed. Often they form part of a localised continuing tradition of performance of medieval drama. In order to offer the scope of documentation and analysis that is needed for this study it has been necessary to be selective. For every production included, several have been excluded. The analysis offered within this book is often contextualised by referring to productions that altered the shape of subsequent interpretations; so while historical narratives of the development of modern-day playing are evoked this is not presented so as to construe a comprehensive history of staging, but to examine the facets developed by certain productions.

I hope that this book will be of interest to those who study the plays, those who watch them, and those who produce them.

Overview

Section I (chapters 1 and 2) examines the historical background and the reasons for staging the mystery plays today. Chapter 1 investigates what is known of the performance conditions of medieval England. Chapter 2 gives a brief account of the history of production of the mystery plays in twentieth-century England, and discusses how modern-day popularity of the plays derives from the way medieval dramas articulate pertinent concerns for contemporary theatre makers.

Section II (chapters 3–5) investigates how modern-day productions have experimented with stage space through the mystery plays, and in doing so have articulated dynamic spatial relationships.

Chapter 3 focuses upon academic re-creations of the York cycle using processional pageant waggon staging. The cycle has been produced in this manner on several occasions: in 1975 by Leeds University, at Toronto in 1977 and 1998, and at York since 1998. This chapter compares these productions.

Chapter 4 examines the differences between outdoor and indoor playing, using the productions in York as a case study. In particular, it contrasts the outdoor playing in the Abbey gardens with the way in which Royal Shakespeare Company director Greg Doran's York *Millennium Mysteries* utilised the indoor space of York Minster to celebrate the city of York at the Millennium.

Chapter 5 analyses alternative spatial configurations used at Chester, Lincoln and Lichfield. Productions have been commonplace at Chester, and their playing from 1951 to the present day reveals an interesting interplay between the act and the audience. During this time the plays have been staged in the cathedral, on the green and in a big top tent. The performances at Chester exemplify a changing relationship with church and community spaces within their production.

The Lincoln Mystery Plays Trust Limited has presented versions of the

N-Town plays in the cathedral cloisters every four years since 1981. The N-Town plays are significant because the Passion and Mary Plays appear to have been designed to be played on a series of 'loci' or stages set around the *platea*, the common playing ground.[4] In order to accommodate this style, the Lincoln productions have used a type of place-and-scaffold configuration comprising multiple playing stages.

Lichfield has staged a version of the cycles every three years since 1994. The performance text is based upon fragments of the 'Lichfield plays' (actually the 'Shrewsbury Fragments', surviving liturgical drama texts rather than cycle dramas), and has been constructed by amalgamating material from other cycles. The Lichfield production provides the atmosphere of pageant waggon staging through the actors' procession around the corporate city spaces.

Section III (chapters 6–8) examines three professional productions to show how the plays have been used to articulate various conceptual threads.

Chapter 6 examines Bill Bryden's direction of Tony Harrison's version of *The Mysteries* for the Royal National Theatre, London, performed from 1977 to 1985 and revived in 1999–2000. Central to his vision of the dramas was the concept of workers putting on the plays; in other words, a type of play-within-a play whereby the audience witnessed workers staging the history of salvation. This chapter also discusses the problems of reviving the production twenty years after the original staging following major changes in the social, political and cultural climate of the country.

Chapter 7 investigates Katie Mitchell's 1997 production for the Royal Shakespeare Company at Stratford-upon-Avon. She believed that in the 1990s it was impossible to create the political plays that Harrison and Bryden had produced, and she sought to create a version that would speak to contemporary society. These contemporary mysteries, which significantly omitted the Resurrection, suggested there was no sustained community within society, but that altruism and a type of personal responsibility and spiritualism were the modern equivalents.

Chapter 8 focuses on the Millennium co-production at Coventry between the Belgrade Theatre and the Polish street-theatre group Teatr Biuro Podrózy. The production attempted to find a contemporary 'faith' relevant to a multicultural war-torn city in the throes of urban regeneration.

Section IV (chapters 9–10) looks at the use of the cycle dramas as a celebration of community. The popularity of such productions owes much to the growth of the community-based theatre movement in Britain in the 1970s and early 80s. Two productions are investigated: those of Chichester and Worsbrough.

Chapter 9 analyses productions of the mystery plays as a Millennium celebration by the education department of Chichester Festival Theatre. The plays offered parts for 130 young people aged between ten and twenty-two. Adrian Henri's 1988 two-part adaptation of *The Wakefield Mysteries* was used to examine various concerns such as the nature of responsibility and morality.

Chapter 10 examines cycle drama at Worsbrough, begun in 1977 by the Head of Drama at the local high school. The plays have since been presented outdoors in a local churchyard every three years. Since 1995 a 'definitive' Worsbrough script has been performed, which is amalgamated from the York, Towneley and Chester cycles, but also incorporates 'local material and personalised pieces that have crept into previous performances'.[5] The production demonstrates the considerable draw of the cycles as a celebration of community identity.

Section V (Chapter 11) focuses on the timeliness of these modern productions of medieval drama, and argues that the search for community identity is an essential feature of the New Millennium, and that this found expression in numerous productions of the mystery plays. A common feature of many modern productions of the plays is that they emphasise a belief in the importance of community (either within the concept of the production or within the composition of the participants).

List of Abbreviations

METh *Medieval English Theatre*
REED *Records of Early English Drama*
RIDE *Research in Drama Education*
RORD *Research Opportunities in Renaissance Drama*

SECTION I

Introduction

SECTION I ~ Introduction

The use of the past is contentious. How do we remember things from the past? How much do we remember? How accurately do we remember? How authentic is the past that we conjure up? How do we articulate things that pre-date living memory? Why and how do we use that past? The presentation of drama from the past is no less complicated. And while plays from the past can often be seen to be 'different' from contemporary culture, their re-enactment in modern-day society does not necessarily create a binary opposition between these two worlds.[1] In presenting versions of the medieval mystery plays at the turn of the New Millennium, the meeting of modern and medieval were forced to collide, and as a result 'the modern is not characterized as simply different from the medieval but is touched by the medieval, and the medieval is touched by the modern'.[2]

In *Getting Medieval*, Carolyn Dinshaw looks at interchanges between medieval and modern cultures and argues that contemporary society is 'touching in this way the past in our efforts to build selves and communities now and into the future'.[3] She sees the possibility of using medieval culture within modern-day society to build community values. This interplay between the medieval and modern is important, for the contemporary productions analysed in this book often reveal as much about modern concerns as they do about medieval culture.

This section begins by setting the context for the examination of modern performances of the mystery plays. Chapter 1 is an investigation of what is known of the performance conditions of medieval England. This general overview is presented so that readers who are less familiar with medieval staging are offered a broad contextualisation for the discussions that follow. It is beyond the scope of this book to offer a detailed investigation into the nuances of the contemporary debates on medieval staging practices. However, recent scholarship is increasingly focusing on the variety of staging used and the importance of localised tradition. This means that establishing a set model for mystery play performance is difficult, and consequently the practices that follow are based primarily on those from York.

Set against a context of the history of production of the mystery plays in twentieth-century England, Chapter 2 discusses how modern-day popularity of the plays derives from the way medieval dramas articulate pertinent concerns for contemporary theatre makers. The format of the mystery plays offers interesting challenges for modern-day directors and the production of the plays has resulted in some fascinating staging practices and conceptual realisations. The plays have also become important as a tool for establishing community identity, and the subsequent chapter will establish definitions of shared identities and look at how post-industrial communities have sought to define community through cultural expression.

CHAPTER 1

Playing the Drama: Mystery Plays in Medieval England

The most startling feature of the mystery plays is their longevity. Evidence suggests that performances might have started from as early as 1376, and shows they continued for 200 years.[1] Given this unique production history, it is clear that the plays must have successfully maintained a significance for their community. Part of the reason for their long life is that they were not the work of a single author, and were not limited to the lifespan of that playwright, but instead were fluid and transitory texts that could respond to changing cultural demands. The authorship of the mystery plays is largely unknown, but the method of their production, at cities such as York, interwove the triad of heteroglossic voices of church, civic authorities and guild crafts, and provided a fluid form of cultural expression which remained relevant to its society for an unsurpassed period.

The mystery plays represent only one facet of the complex dramatic and cultural activities that comprised the medieval world – a world very different from modern-day society. Not only was England a Roman Catholic country, but many members of society in the late Middle Ages were illiterate; their communication and understanding of the world was expressed through oral and visual media.[2] Church services were conducted primarily in Latin, which was not accessible to the lower ranks of society.

However, ornate stained glass windows and wall paintings in churches related biblical stories and the lives of saints through series of panels that could be read in a manner similar to the chronology of a book.[3] This suggests something of the importance of visual symbols to the medieval world. Given levels of illiteracy, the mystery plays provided another avenue through which the general populace could learn of the biblical tales, although this was only one of the functions that the plays served.[4]

These plays were not the only cultural form of dramatic expression in the late Middle Ages. The medieval world was marked by a host of entertainments and celebrations that delineated moments within the year. Celebrations marked out New Year, Easter, midsummer, harvest festival and Christmas, as well as individual saint's days. Drama was enacted in numerous locations: on the street, in the fields, on village greens, in churchyards, private houses, churches and so on. The mystery plays were not a separate and distinct part of medieval culture, instead the traditions they drew on were part of a complex and multi-faceted social fabric.

It is necessary to sketch out a broad model for mystery play performances. At York the extant play texts comprise around fifty separate pageants that make up the whole drama; it has been argued that these pageants were performed as an entire sequence covering the Old Testament to Doomsday, and thus formed a cycle which could be performed over the duration of a day.[5] Of the four extant mystery play texts, two are associated with cities (York and Chester), and two have less stable connections to a place of performance (Towneley and N-Town), though these have been associated with Wakefield and East Anglia respectively.[6] Fragments of other mystery plays survive, for example at Newcastle and Coventry.

The model of mystery play performance discussed here is based on evidence from York. This is where the most detailed records of civic organisation and production originate. By piecing together this material it has been suggested that on the feast of Corpus Christi[7] (a movable holy day – the first Thursday after Trinity Sunday – usually between 21 May and 24 June) at around 4.30 a.m. pageant waggons sponsored by guilds gathered at Toft Green (close to the edge of the city walls), and that each waggon was then pulled by men around the city, stopping at between ten and sixteen locations to play their guild pageant.[8] However, this broad model of performance is questionable, and it must be noted that in medieval England the mystery plays may have been an exceptional style of performance. Scholarly research collected and published by the Records of Early English Drama project since the 1980s has unearthed evidence of many parish entertainments and smaller dramatic events which has thrown into question the previous critical use of the mystery plays as a dominant mode of medieval drama. In addition, recent scholarship has suggested that the Towneley plays are in fact a collection of plays, and have no cyclical structure.[9]

This chapter is concerned with investigating what is known of the original performance conditions of the mystery plays. It will achieve this through applying contemporary performance theory in order to align the experience of medieval drama with contemporary sensibilities. One helpful system of analysis is that developed by Richard Schechner. He has explored the way that performance operates as a type of ritual and has declared that: ‘Performances – whether in the performing arts, sports, or everyday life – consist of ritualized gestures and sounds.’[10] Schechner suggests that ritual performance can be understood from at least four different perspectives.[11] He advocates that an analysis of the structures, functions, processes and experiences of ritual engenders a useful critical approach. It is worth looking more closely at these categories.

'Structure' is defined by Schechner as the dramatic techniques that a performance employs, 'what rituals look and sound like.' 'Function' means how the performative practice serves its participants, while 'processes' includes the mechanisms through which rituals are performed and the changes they may bring to bear on society. Schechner's final perspective through which to analyse ritual is that of 'experiences'; by this he means 'what it's like to be "in" a ritual.' His categories provide an interesting framework through which to discuss the mystery plays, although the paucity of evidence concerning the plays means that an analysis of some of the categories is difficult. There is very little evidence that can be drawn on to understand the 'experiences' that a participant had while performing in the plays. However, the other avenues that Schechner suggests – processes, function, and structures – are a helpful device through which to analyse the plays in their original medieval setting and to suggest how these relate to contemporary concerns.

Processes and functions

The two categories of processes and functions are grouped together because the mechanisms through which the plays operated are inextricably linked to how the plays served their community. In analysing the processes and functions of the plays I will draw on scholarship concerning the mystery plays undertaken during the last 100 years. Scholarship has shown considerable change during that time. The earliest analysis, undertaken by E. K. Chambers, reflects a belief that the primary function of the plays was as religious drama; the second wave of analysis in the 1960s, led by theatre historian V. A. Kolve and continued in the 1970s and 1980s by social historians such as Mervyn James and Charles Phythian-Adams, was concerned with the social dimension of the plays. Work undertaken by Miri Rubin, amongst others, in the 1990s examined the dramas as festive rituals, and was followed by that of Sarah Beckwith and Claire Sponsler, who studied the way in which the cycle dramas operated as devices of social exclusivity.[12]

Writing in 1903, Chambers was greatly influenced by anthropological models of scholarship based on Darwinian-influenced notions of evolution and the romantic ethnology of J. G. Frazer. Such an approach led Chambers to assume that each form of drama progressed from the previous one, and that the mystery plays developed when church drama moved outside to the streets and was consequently secularised. Such thoughts about the origins of the plays suppose that the primary function of the dramas was one of religious didacticism and devotion. This view was modified when other functions, such as the civic practices that the plays articulated, were identified by later scholars.

In the 1970s Charles Phythian-Adams examined social and festive practices in Coventry, and concluded that dramatic celebrations and enactments played a large part in shaping the status of guild and civic structures.[13] Seen in this light, it is clear that the mystery plays were important not just for their religious status, but also for the part they played in shaping social structures. For example, the productions of the plays created a hierarchy amongst the guilds, whereby the power of the Mercers, producers of expensive textiles, was affirmed by their production of the final and most spectacular pageant, *The Last Judgement*. The work of Mervyn James undertook a similar sociological angle, but noted that in the performance of the mystery plays the 'opposites of social wholeness and social differentiation could be both affirmed, and also brought into a creative tension with one another'.[14] He argued that the production of the dramas afforded a mechanism through which a new ideal order was placed against the real hierarchy, and that through this tension social stability was negotiated.

More recent scholarship has assessed other functions that the plays may have held. Part of this re-examination has come about because of renewed investigations into their origins. Miri Rubin noted that the plays may have developed from the feast of Corpus Christi, established by papal bull in 1311. She observed that at this point eucharistic parades were established in Europe to mark the new festival. The first celebrations of Corpus Christi in England date from the mid-fourteenth century, but Rubin has noted the variety of parades, some of which included tableaux with spoken words, that developed across the country.[15] Rubin's reading is important because it placed the origins of the mystery plays under the custody of festive, civic and sacred forces. The work of Sarah Beckwith and Claire Sponsler has analysed the intersection between religious and festive practices and the society that viewed these dramatic events. Beckwith, drawing on the work of cultural theorists Pierre Bourdieu and Catherine Bell, noted that social tensions that were released through the production of the plays in medieval York were not monolithic, since the space of production was polysemous.[16] For example, the essential meanings of the plays were forever shifting; Beckwith noted that the playing of *The Last Judgement* or the *Crucifixion* had differing resonances at the various stations where it played. Sponsler has examined how various deviant readings of the plays are possible. She analysed how the image of the violated body, expressed in the mystery plays through moments such as the Slaughter of the Innocents and the buffeting of Christ, expose the commodification of the body in late medieval England and set up a 'contrapuntal ideological work, even while in the service of a dominant religious message and a civic power-structure'.[17]

Records of the production methods of the mystery plays provide further evidence as to the function they may have served in medieval society. At York it is clear that the producing guild was frequently associated with the subject of the pageant it brought forth: for example, the building of the ark was sponsored by the Shipwrights, and the Crucifixion (with its nails) by the Pinners. This suggests that the plays served as a type of advertisement for the trade and skills of the corresponding guild.

Many of the reasons why the mystery plays are popular in contemporary society arise from an interest in the social, festive and religious functions that the dramas served in medieval times. For example, the original reinstatement of the plays at York in 1951 to mark the Festival of Britain drew on all aspects of the ritual functions that marked the original medieval production of the plays. The plays were seen to celebrate a sense of place (York and Britain), time (the Festival of Britain, a mark of post-war rebirth, the anniversary of the Great Exhibition) and community (the citizens of York).

Dramatic structure

The third category in Schechner's analysis of ritual is structure, which he defines as how a ritual may look. The structure of the mystery plays in medieval England was in effect created by the dramatic techniques utilised in their production: these included the use of processional playing, the structure of small episodes that comprise the entire cycle, as well as issues such as acting style, use of rhythm and time. How the plays were performed is, of course, uncertain. There are no eyewitness accounts of the acting styles used in performances of the mystery plays; indeed, there are very few that pertain to drama from this period at all. Similarly, there is no clear evidence as to how the mystery plays were staged, and this has been the subject of much scholarly dispute.

Many of these questions concerning production style are open to speculation. However, by examining fragments of records which pertain to the mystery plays, and through comparison with techniques used for staging other forms of medieval drama, it is possible to formulate some hypotheses as to how the performance of these dramas may have worked in medieval times. Consequently, the rest of this chapter will look at how the mystery play performance was structured through the use of space, actor/audience relationships, acting styles, and rhythm and time. The chapter will also observe some of the differences that exist between the original staging of the mystery plays, and dominant forms of theatre practice in the New Millennium.

Pageant spaces

The model of mystery play performance suggested by extant records from York is that of processional playing, in which the waggons were pulled around the city and stopped at various stations to perform. However, Alan Nelson, writing in the 1970s, postulated that this form of processional playing was never used in performances, but that at York the waggons stopped at each station to show off their tableaux, and the full enactment of the pageants occurred only at one final destination.[18] Nelson's idea neatly avoided the issue of how such a complex form of staging might have worked in practice. How could nearly fifty different pageants be performed so many times in one day? Since the pageants were not identical in length, did traffic jams of waggons form? As Chapter 3 notes, the academic restagings of the mystery plays have tried to elucidate these points. Surprisingly, the modern producers found that the processional form of staging operated in a fluid manner, although it must be noted that modern-day reconstructions have occurred on a smaller scale than the original dramas, and do not, therefore, form solid evidence.

The form of outdoor processional playing undertaken at York raises a number of issues about this spatial practice. The relationship between performance space and the audience is a complex one: not only do the waggons process from one playing point to another, but the spectators are also capable of moving. This model of outdoor procession allows the audience to choose what they watch; they can see some pageants twice or omit others entirely. Consequently, few spectators would have the same experience of watching the plays, and this method of production in effect empowers the establishment of independent viewpoints amongst the audience.

The articulation of space in the production of the plays does not limit itself to the relationship between the act and the audience. In fact the issue of space is expressed in a number of ways. These include the use of space on the pageant waggon,[19] the passage of the waggon through the space of the city, as well as the spatial relationships between the actors and spectators, which includes the notion of the audience's proximity to the waggon and the use of playing on the street level.[20] I will begin by examining the relationship between the processional space and the city, its host.

The French theorist Henri Lefebvre advocates that all space is the product of a series of relationships, and that there is no such thing as neutral or natural space. He suggests that 'Space is social morphology: it is to lived experience what form itself is to the organism.'[21] David Wiles draws on Lefebvre's approach to analyse how 'a linear movement through the streets defines the shape and order of the town and of its processing inhabitants.'[22] He notes that medieval cities were encompassed by walls and that outside these lay 'anarchy and poverty' and inside 'regulation, hierarchy and relative affluence.'[23] The processional route at York emphasised the divide between the boundaries created by the walls. The waggons assembled at a point close to the city walls and then processed past various city institutions, but avoided the margins of the city walls. This is true of the pattern at York, where the pageant route adopted the traditional city processional route from Micklegate Bar, across the only bridge over the River Ouse, towards the Minster, and finished on the Pavement, a market and public gathering space. The city thus became legitimised through a process which exemplified Lefebvre's analysis.

The pageant waggon itself articulated a spatial dialogue between the production and spectators. The waggons were most likely no more than about 2.5 metres wide, between 3 and 4 metres long, and about 1.5 to 2 metres above ground level. They resembled something like modern-day carnival floats. The 1433 Mercers' Indenture reveals that their waggon was double-storied and possibly included a pulley system via which God could ascend to a heaven that comprised blue clouds and golden sunbeams.[24] But it is still unclear as to how the waggons were used during performances. Was the action played predominantly from one side of the waggon (and if so, which?), or staged so that the audience might crowd around three sides? Did scenic cloths enclose some sides of the waggon?[25] Which parts of the waggon or ground were used for performance? Were extra platforms used to stage some of the action?

Meg Twycross has suggested that the physical structure of the waggons created a type of frame through which the action could be observed, and that the effects of this were similar to the picture sequences to be found in stained-glass windows or Books of Hours.[26] The framing of the stage action in this manner probably had several consequences: the acting appeared more formalised; the visual components of the plays were enhanced and lastly, the episodic nature of each pageant was highlighted in the frame.[27]

Two other aspects concerning the use of space have not been examined here, and that is because they form an integral part of other systems that are yet to be analysed. These include the relationship between the use of the pageant waggon space and the proximity of the audience, and the issue of actor proxemics – the use of space between performers.

Actor/audience relationship

Bim Mason noted that when performing outside, 'the dramatic enactment is as much for the participants as it is for the spectators. Indeed there will be a less clearly defined separation between the two.'[28] Mason saw modern-day outdoor theatre as providing an immediacy and intimacy for the audience; this is also a condition that was created by the original performances of the mystery plays. I have outlined above how outdoor performance conditions provided an interaction between the plays and the city, but this form of playing also created a dynamic relationship with the audience. Modern-day theatre usually occurs indoors, with fixed staging on which the actors perform, and fixed seating in the separate auditorium from which the spectators watch. This spatial configuration separates the actors and audience; that contract is laid down for the entirety of the performance. Many contemporary avant-garde productions attempt to challenge this division, but this was unnecessary in the original staging of the medieval plays, where the street formed both the stage and the auditorium, and provided a flexible area where at times, such as Herod's raging in the streets, the actor and audience spaces were not differentiated. Susan Bennett, writing about reception in the theatre, cites the traditional model of audience spectatorship established by Dayan and Katz:

> Spectacle implies a distinction between the roles of performers and audience. Performers are set apart and audiences asked to respond cognitively and emotionally in predefined categories of approval, disapproval, arousal or passivity. Audience interaction with the performance may enhance it, but it is not meant nor allowed to become part of its definition.[29]

This model of audience behaviour is antithetical to the original street theatre of the mystery plays.

The staging of the original plays established an informal relationship with their audience through a variety of methods. Many of these had to do with control of the performance space. The open-air staging promoted an informality which enabled audiences to pass comments with their neighbours, to eat and drink, and come and go.[30] These are all modes of behaviour which are disallowed by contemporary mainstream theatre. The separation of performance and audience space was also less formal in medieval pageant staging than contemporary mainstream theatre. For example, records show that the ground space in front of the waggon (a space occupied by the audience) may have been used during parts of the performance. A stage direction from the Coventry Shearman and Taylors' play indicates that 'Here Erode ragis in the pagond and in the street also.'[31] The potential of this interaction shifts the spatial divide between the actors and the spectators; instead of occupying two disparate and separate spaces, it is possible that there was an interaction between the two groups. Contemporary versions of the plays have frequently replicated this fluid actor/audience relationship. For example, informal audience conventions were in evidence during the outdoor performance of the Worsbrough plays in 2001. During the performance audience members chattered and commented on the stage action. Even though the seating and stage were fixed, the outdoor location provided informality, and allowed audience members to comment on the action and narrate the plot to one another.

Another factor that affects the relationship established between the actors and audience in the mystery plays is the perception of distance. The traditional model of theatre viewing, outlined above, in which the stage and auditorium are separated emphasises the distance between the act and the voyeur. But many of the techniques employed by the mystery plays create a more elaborate relationship with the spectator. The plays use direct address to the audience (for example, when the Towneley Mr and Mrs Noah in turn address the audience to bemoan the opposite sex),[32] which has the effect of breaking the boundary between audience and character. So while the audience are clearly voyeurs for some of the formal action, when a direct address occurs they are more directly implicated as confidantes. The audience are required to switch between these various modes: at one moment sharing a direct encounter with a character, at another distanced by more formal spectacular scenes. It is through oscillating between these various modes of reception that a dynamic relationship is created with the audience.

Acting style

Modern-day discussions on acting styles are dominated by references to the actor-training system conceived in the early twentieth century by Russian director Konstantin Stanislavski. At his theatre, the Moscow Art Theatre, Stanislavski developed techniques for imbuing a sense of truth into the naturalistic performances of his actors. Through drawing on the given circumstances that surrounded the text they were performing, his actors were required to find objectives for their characters (and thus created a fully rounded biography for them). They also kept their attention firmly fixed on the stage during performance through applying a technique he called 'the circle of attention'. This technique maintained the convention of 'fourth wall' drama whereby the actors made no acknowledgement of the audience. Stanislavski's ideas laid the foundation for actor-training methods, and were subsequently adapted and adopted by British and American theatre schools; they consequently dominated film and theatre acting during the late twentieth century. Stanislavski's techniques are for the most part antithetical to those that are useful for performing medieval drama. His theatre placed the audience as fourth-wall voyeurs and encouraged his actors to find through-lines in the action for their characters, so that character development in a drama was logical and seamless – a far cry from the episodic structure of the mystery plays.

If Stanislavski's ideas are of little value to modern-day productions of the mystery plays, there is another contemporary practitioner whose ideas are of help; those of German director and writer Bertolt Brecht. Writing about the use of masks in medieval drama, Meg Twycross and Sarah Carpenter observed that acting during the Middle Ages was not primarily understood as an identification between performer and role, and that 'Brecht may offer more useful tools than

Stanislavski for modern understanding of medieval performance techniques.'[33] Brecht's work with his company, The Berliner Ensemble, focused on creating an epic theatre that utilised episodic narratives, presented the action specifically knowing an audience was watching, and asked that the actors demonstrate their characters (who were largely based on types rather than crafted individuals) rather than become them, as in Stanislavski's theatre.

The parallels with the mystery plays are clear: the pageants were sponsored by differing guilds, so that each character was performed by a number of different actors; for example, numerous actors played the roles of Christ, God, and Mary throughout the day. This conceit avoided the audience identifying with the character and provided an automatic *Verfremdungseffekt*, the distancing from the action which was advocated by Brechtian theatre. A number of other factors in the mystery plays help form this distancing effect. The characters in the plays are generally regarded by scholars as 'types' rather than individualised personas, and therefore readily offer themselves to be read as proto-Brechtian devices. The sense of distantiation was further increased in the original production of the mystery plays, as the actors would frequently be known to the audience. This probably prevented audiences from believing that the players were doing anything other than pretending to be the characters they portrayed. This would be somewhat similar to the use of famous personalities in Christmas pantomimes in modern-day Britain. Although a well-known actor may represent a character, there remain many moments when the character's mask slips and the actor's own personality is allowed to come through.

Many scholars have noted the similarity between medieval drama and Brechtian theatre. For example, Donna Smith Vinter observed that the playing of the dramas comes close to Brecht's use of *Gestus* (defined by Colin Counsell as 'performance signs capable of indicating social positions and relationships'),[34] and that the use of this device enabled the medieval plays to present divine and human elements simultaneously.[35] In other words, the stage could present at the same moment both Mary the mother of Christ, and Mary the poor donkey-rider. Vinter analysed the characterisation of Abraham in the Towneley plays, and concluded that the play is structured in order to create a series of *gests* which allow insight into Abraham's response to God's commands to slay his son. Vinter noted that 'As a character he manages both to call forth a certain empathy from the audience and to impress them with a magisterial distance.'[36] But this sense of empathy is engendered, Vinter suggested, not through the development of psychological depth, but via a horizontal connection of dramatic *gests*: 'Abraham himself does not merely 'live' his reactions but like a helpful narrator indicates them to us, the spectators, at key points in the action.'[37]

Though it is possible to utilise such textual evidence to hypothesise about the stylistic acting required, there is little evidence to suggest exactly how these plays were performed. Records from York in 1415 show that players were required to be well presented and speak clearly, and that they could be fined for breaching this order.[38] Meg Twycross has drawn on evidence from Beverley to discuss the way in which male actors portrayed women characters on stage. She noted a record which observes a male actor 'arrayed and robbed in the manner of a Queen and in the likeness of St Helena', and argued, by drawing attention to the phrases 'in the manner' and 'in the likeness', for a representational style of performance.[39]

Perhaps a clue to the performance style used lies in the adoption by Vinter and others of the notion that the mystery plays are types of 'speaking pictures'.[40] Through this technique the plays are aligned with medieval painting, and the pageant waggon is read as corresponding to the panels of such art. Seen in this light, the waggon acts as a type of frame which captures the actors. The composition of the actors in the stage space then becomes important in echoing medieval iconography and forming a stylistic device through which to communicate the plays.

The framing of time

Anthropologist Edmund Leach employed the cultural theories of Émile Durkheim to suggest that two distinct and contradictory laws govern the English understanding of time.[41] The first is concerned with the notion of repetition; the second with the idea that things grow old and die – in other words, that life is irreversible. Leach argued, though, that in primitive societies time is read as oscillating between polar opposites: for example, day/night, winter/summer, drought/flood.[42] Within this oscillating pendulum of time we can witness a Durkheimian temporary shift from normal, profane time into abnormal or sacred time.

Leach's ideas on English temporal governance provide many ways in which to read the mystery plays. First, the use of cyclical time is shown through the very subject matter of the plays: they are concerned with the Passion of Christ, and chart the birth, death and resurrection of Christ. The structure of the cycles also emphasise temporal repetition; for example, many events, such as Abraham's near-murder of Isaac, reflect God's later sacrifice of his Son. This creates the sense of a cyclical time.[43] The mystery plays also encompass a sense of irreversible time. The play time or narrative time – the time covered in the dramas is, of course, epic – it spans the Old to New Testament, and each pageant as a separate episode can be read in this linear conception. Placed against these articulations of repetition and irreversibility is the actual time that passes while the audience watch the event – in other words, the duration of the performance. This would be individual to each spectator, since there were no fixed rules regarding the viewing of the plays. Attitudes towards the duration of the event have changed considerably from medieval to modern times. Though the original mysteries were performed over a period of one day or more (depending on which city produced them), modern productions have usually shortened this in order to satisfy today's audiences. The Bill Bryden/Tony Harrison production at the Royal National Theatre was divided into three parts, and these could be viewed over three evening or as a single day on Saturdays, but even so they were made palatable for a modern audience by having clear meal breaks between each part.

Leach suggested that the English conception of time is contradictory, and this is clear in modern stagings of the mystery plays. As Richardson and Johnston stated: 'The Mystery Cycle plays focus on the present, showing the past of the biblical events to be integrally connected both to the present of the audience and actors and also to their future in terms of salvation or damnation. The cycle plays work within "God's time" which is universal and contemporaneous.'[44] Past, present and future converge in the plays; we as an audience witness God's time, biblical time, and a sense of the plays in the present time; indeed, the plays are intended to provoke thought about future time – salvation.

It is interesting to see how far the mystery plays extend beyond Leach's definition of English time, and utilise temporal rules that he identified as belonging to primitive societies. Leach noted how such societies use oscillating time – in other words, they operate between polar notions of time and rhythm. This is a key notion for the mystery plays, since they were originally performed on a holy day, a holiday. This, then, is a sort of time-out-of-time; a festive time, a time away from the 'real world'. And it is also clear that festive time has become important to modern-day stagings of the plays. E. Martin Browne's resurrection of the York plays accompanied the 1951 Festival of Britain, the celebration of 100 years since the 1851 Great Exhibition which paid tribute to industrialisation, invention and the British Empire. Equally, the Millennium produced a host of performances: in York Minster, at Coventry, Chichester and Lichfield, and the revival of the Bryden/Harrison version at the National.[45]

Although Leach's ideas provide one way to examine the use of temporal aspects in the mystery plays, contemporary performance theory offers other avenues.[46] I shall examine how the notion of durational time, encountered through the performance of Happenings in the 1960s, might be applied to uncover a fruitful examination of time in the mystery plays. Allan Kaprow's 1966 essay 'The Happenings are dead: long live the Happenings!' discussed the use of durational or event time in Happenings. Happenings, inspired by modernist practices such as Dada and Surrealism, were informal performances which took place as one-off events where the audience formed an inseparable part of the action. Kaprow developed a number of rules for Happenings, one of which was that: 'Time should be variable and independent of the convention of continuity';[47] in other words, things should happen in their natural time – if people perform varying tasks then they would take different times to complete. To see the playing of each pageant under these terms dislodges our often difficult-to-shift twenty-first-century sensibilities that search for the progression of time in drama. We are more used to seeing plays, films and events that have a beginning, middle and end. Instead, in this light, each pageant is seen as a durational event that will conclude without reference to the pageants that are being performed on either side (at the station before or after).

Other aspects of Kaprow's analysis are helpful in reading the relationship between time and space; for example: 'The Happening should be dispersed over several widely spaced, sometimes moving and changing, locales' in order to avoid the static limitations of a single performance space.[48] Again, his thoughts offer an interesting light through which to see the processional playing of the mystery plays. The progression from station to station in medieval York, or even between the four stations in modern-day Toronto, clearly overcame the limitations of a fixed performance space, and many of the eyewitness accounts from Toronto emphasise the difference between the first station, against the steps of a building; the second, an open space in front of the library; the third, in an enclosed passageway between two buildings; and the last, in an open street.

But there are obvious ways that the mystery plays cannot be read as a Happening. Kaprow's rules meant that such an event had a fluid line between daily life and the Happening; the composition should be artless, formless and unrepeatable; and that there was no audience – everyone was a participant. However, the mystery plays are strikingly form-based (they utilise a clear structure and fixed material), and there are distinctive and separate spectators (although they are often implied within the action as a crowd).

There is one final way in which to explore the idea of time in the plays and that is through a notion suggested by Guy Claxton in his book *Hare Brain, Tortoise Mind*. He proposes that the mind works in three ways: the first is faster than thought – our reflexive response to taking our hand away from a hot gas-ring; the second is what he calls d-mode, conscious deliberation; and the last is slow thought, contemplation or rumination – a type of unconscious thinking.[49] Claxton argued that we need the tortoise mind just as much as the hare brain. Does this way of placing thought and time together offer any thing of worth to the mystery plays? One of the scholarly discussions that surround the plays is whether the pageants maintained any unity as a cycle. Some proponents see a unity within the whole cycle, while other academics have argued that there is a lack of any grand schemic unity in performance. It is interesting to turn to eyewitness comparisons of the Leeds 1975 and Toronto 1977 productions of the

York plays, where some academics believed that the productions demonstrated no unity in the event.[50] But then Betsy Taylor, writing about the 1998 production in Toronto, noted that seeing the whole cycle gave her opportunity to recognise the groupings of pageants, and she found 'patterns of correspondence' across the whole cycle.[51] She drew on Peter Meredith's article on fifteenth-century audiences to note that the effect of the cycle is like a story one has heard over and over again. This suggestion seems to acknowledge that the cycles may tap into an unconscious part of our response system. Perhaps, then, it is helpful to apply the hare and tortoise theory. Although watching each single, episodic pageant may provoke a hare-like response, our spectatorship through the entire cycle is mindful of the plodding tortoise, and in our unconscious, contemplative thought patterns we construct a type of unity for the cycles.

CHAPTER 2

Playing the Plays Today: Staging, Concepts, Community

In 1987 John Elliott concluded that there were five reasons why revivals of the cycles were so enjoyed by contemporary audiences.[1] First, they offered a religious content and were 'our chief dramatic statement of the Christian myth'.[2] Second, the nostalgic values of the plays were attractive to an audience, and he used evidence of the appeal of medieval fairs or Victorian evenings to substantiate this view. Third, there was an 'historical importance and dramatic interest' for directors in unearthing and staging medieval drama, though of course this could be applied to the reconstruction of any drama from a past age. Fourth, there was an aesthetic appeal of the pageants in offering a different production style from the conventions of West End theatre in London. Finally, local pride (an important part of the production of the original cycles) encouraged the modern-day staging of the plays. He argued, for example, that the corporate identity of contemporary Chester and York, which have regularly produced their own cycles, was enhanced by the public staging of their city pageants.

Some twenty years after Elliott was writing, it is clear that the priorities for staging medieval drama have changed. This chapter addresses the issue of why directors choose to produce mystery plays today. What drives them to stage versions of 500-year-old plays? What are they searching for when they stage the mysteries? Moreover, how have modern-day directors at the turn of the Second Millennium been affected by the heritage of productions of medieval drama staged in the twentieth century? How have shifting patterns in modern-theatre practice affected their decision to produce medieval drama?

The main impetus to produce mystery plays today comes from three central dynamics: the desire to challenge the predominantly fixed staging forms which dominate modern-day theatre practice (Elliott identified this as the 'aesthetic' challenge offered by the plays); the opportunity to present a strong directorial vision of the plays in order to find a relevance for religious dramas today; and lastly, a desire to use the plays to develop a sense of community identity amongst the participants and spectators. (This function is somewhat akin to Elliott's identification of the importance of local pride and nostalgia.) It may be surprising that, unlike Elliott, I have not suggested contemporary productions are staged for their religious functions, but few of the productions studied here, for reasons that will be outlined below, have undertaken performances of the mysteries for that reason. This is not to say that directors have ignored the religious scope of the plays, but that by the New Millennium Elliott's perception that the mysteries are 'our chief dramatic statement of the Christian myth' is more problematic. In the multi-cultural society of present-day Britain the assumption that society can share a myth in this way is tenuous. It is true, though, that many productions in this book were undertaken for reasons that had spurious links to Christianity. It was repeatedly felt by the directors that one way to mark the beginning of the New Millennium was to celebrate the birth of Christ, and that the mystery plays were a means of doing so. This notion led to the revival of the Royal National Theatre production, and productions by Chichester Youth Theatre, at the York Minster and Coventry and Lincoln cathedrals.

It is also noticeable that a large proportion of the productions outlined in this book took place in cathedrals (or outside the fronts of cathedrals). However, these locations were often chosen not to align the production with the notion of its being 'our chief dramatic statement of the Christian myth,' but had more to do with aspects of decorum, distinction and city identity. The plays as ancient, biblical episodes carry with them a sense of importance through their association with heritage. This association has been drawn on by directors in order to achieve status, funding and encourage participation in their production.

Cathedrals remain popular sites for staging such plays, partly because of the false assumption that the material was originally performed there, but also because they often form part of the distinctive identity of a city: they are large, public buildings of stature: these are qualities seen by directors as helpful to the production of the plays. So while contemporary productions are often associated with religion, it seems that at the turn of the New Millennium the reasons for the production of the plays are more associated with secular concerns.

Staging the plays now

Edith Hall, writing about the performance reception of classical Greek theatre, noted that, 'Greek tragedy has proved magnetic to writers and directors searching for new ways in which to pose questions to contemporary society and push back the boundaries of theatre.'[3] Though Hall chose classical texts to argue her case, her point is applicable to the contemporary production of medieval theatre. For example, a norm of theatre practice can perhaps be seen in West End plays, which are performed beneath a proscenium arch and are frequently acted in a naturalistic mode, whereby the actors and audience behave as if there were a fourth wall separating them. In this mode of performance the actors aim to portray the characters in the most truthful and convincing manner possible, and seek to engage the audience's empathy for the situation of the drama. The mystery plays, however, challenge these staging aesthetics through their manipulation of space, use of acting style and structure of drama. The plays utilise a series of episodes which oppose the accumulation of action offered by traditional three-act dramas. In West End theatre the dominant form of performance is based on naturalism, whereas, as has been noted in the previous chapter, medieval drama requires a high degree of stylisation, such as the Brechtian 'alienation' suggested by Donna Smith Vinter. Fixed-seat auditoriums in the West End separate the action from the audience, whereas contemporary productions of the mystery plays often stress the more dynamic actor/audience relationship that they offer. For example, the texts allow the audience to be implicated as the crowd for some scenes, thus breaking any sense of the fourth wall, and, although critics are in dispute about the point, the original pageant waggons may have afforded the opportunity for playing on both the stage and at street level, and enabled the audience to develop a less formal relationship with the spectacle.

Perhaps the demands made by staging these two different styles (naturalistic drama and medieval theatre) can be further highlighted by the writings of twentieth-century theatre practitioner Peter Brook. In his seminal work, *The Empty Space*, Brook classified theatre into four categories: deadly, holy, immediate and rough. His definition of deadly theatre embraced many of the conventions displayed by traditional West End drama. As he stated, 'It is most closely linked to the despised, much-attacked commercial theatre.'[4] Deadly theatre is defined by Brook as lifeless theatre. This is theatre where the performances are repeated night after night and spark no real relationship with the audience. He contrasted this with the categories of immediate and rough theatre, which seem to owe much to a twentieth-century popular interpretation of medieval drama. For example, he defined rough theatre as that of 'Salt, sweat, noise, smell: the theatre that's not in a theatre, the theatre on carts, wagons, on trestles ...'[5] Similarly his notion of the importance of immediacy to theatre is one which aligns itself with the staging practices of the mystery plays. For Brook, one of the crucial aspects of immediacy is shown through the importance of liveness to theatre; demonstrated by the fact that a live act always operates in the present. The most vital modern-day stagings of medieval drama have worked with a sense of immediacy through developing moments of close interaction between actor and audience in order to engender a sense of experiencing the 'moment'. One of the strengths of the Bryden/Harrison version at the Royal National Theatre was that it emphasised the importance of the 'liveness' of the theatrical event. As the audience entered the auditorium the actors were already in the open promenade space. The actors chatted with the arriving audience members; this made for a strong bond between the two for the rest of the performance. Much of the subsequent action evolved from within the space where the audience looked on, with actors clearing the audience so that each new scene could occur in a new location. This technique created a real sense of immediacy that permeated the entire production.

The opportunities afforded by the staging practices required of medieval drama offer a clear reason why contemporary directors have chosen to produce mystery plays. However, a secondary factor for this choice concerns the chance for them to engage with a conceptual reading of the plays. The plays are interpreted as a framework through which to discover contemporary resonances. In unearthing such resonances directors frequently create a vision that articulates the stories comprising the cycle. All the productions produced by professional playhouses that are analysed in this book developed strong conceptual readings of the mystery plays. It is as if these directors were unconfident that the religious nature of the plays could provide enough association for an audience today; instead the plays were directed so that contemporary parallels could be created. This desire to develop a 'director's concept' is not limited to the staging of medieval drama, but part of an aesthetic change in the nature of theatre direction developed since the late twentieth century.

The penchant for strong directorial concepts in theatrical productions arose in Western theatre from the increased fascination with creating a whole theatrical language; an interest developed from the rise of cultural theory which identified the importance of semiotics. By the late twentieth century directors were not merely concerned with elucidating the text, but also with manipulating a spectrum of sign systems on stage. This is evidenced by many directors: for example, in the late 1980s Arthur Bartow interviewed a number of professional theatre directors in the United States; time after time their views expressed a concern with creating a total form of theatre, particularly one that stressed the importance of visual languages. One such case was innovative theatre and opera director Peter Sellars, who noted that future directors would need to pay attention to 'the vocabulary of stage language, of what a set looks like, how lighting behaves, how sound works, how video works, how all of these things go into creating a total work of art.'[6] Similarly, Robert Woodruff observed that the process of directing 'is a journey into another "studio", where you have text *and* you have visual elements.'[7] Given this trend in directorial practice, it is hardly surprising that professional productions of the mystery plays have found themselves to be part of the growing practice of conceptual theatre whereby strong interpretations arise from or are placed on the dramatic text.

One professional production of the mystery plays to undergo such interpretive treatment was Bill Bryden's *The Mysteries* for the Royal National Theatre. Bryden and his team developed a strong concept for the production, drawing parallels between medieval guilds and contemporary workers' unions to produce a piece that offered at the same time both a nostalgia for a bygone utopia and a critique of the diminishing power afforded trade unions by the then British Prime Minister, Margaret Thatcher. Bryden's production, examined in detail in Chapter 6, demonstrated how design and music could be brought together. William Dudley and John Tams (respectively, designer and composer) were a central part of Bryden's team. Bryden and Dudley turned the Cottesloe Theatre into a promenade space. As Bryden noted,

> All of the Cottesloe team wanted to offer a popular, accessible theatre experience. Bill Dudley discarded the notion of a proscenium arrangement in favour of a flexible promenade space, in which the audience can contribute directly to the vitality of the performance.[8]

Bryden's comments, as well as revealing the concept of the production, reflect Brook's belief in the necessity of the immediacy of such performance material.

Katie Mitchell, directing for the Royal Shakespeare Company some twenty years after Bryden's initial foray into medieval drama, observed that it would no longer be possible to address the plays through a political concept such as the one he raised. Instead she used the plays as a way to explore altruism. As will be discussed in Chapter 7, this was reinforced by the visual templates which the production used, as well as through a concentration on developing intimate connections between the actors and creating a strong sense of an ensemble amongst the company.

The Millennium production of the mystery plays at Coventry was directed by Polish director Pawel Szkotak, whose approach to the texts was distinctively European, in that he used the mystery texts sparingly, and prior to rehearsals created a *mise-en-scène* for the entire production. Szkotak's vision brought his customary stilt-walking and stick-fighting to the Coventry *Millennium Mysteries* in order to conceptualise the dramas as street theatre. Chapter 8 shows how Szkotak attempted to make the plays more globally relevant by including images of tension which found resonance in the site of the bombed cathedral in Coventry.

While the mystery plays have lured contemporary directors with the opportunity to engage with alternative staging practices and conceptual approaches, the major reason for staging the plays today is the potential they offer for the expression of community identity. Directors see in the plays both an opportunity to involve a large-scale cast (with many small speaking parts which are ideal for a community cast) and a text which embodies values pertaining to Christian notions of community. Contemporary productions often involve large sections of the local community and seek to build on local pride and identity through the production of the plays. As has been noted above, productions often revolve around the cathedral of the producing city since it offers a landmark of the city's distinctive identity and is usually located at the city centre.

Such a discussion of 'community' raises the question of how to define that term. Raymond Williams noted that 'community' is a 'warmly persuasive word' and that 'it seems never to be used unfavourably, and never to be given any positive opposing or distinguishing term.'[9] Williams observed that, although use of the word in the fourteenth century stemmed from a reference to common people (as opposed to those of rank), from the nineteenth century, due to the influence of the ideas of the German sociologist Ferdinand Tönnies, the notion of community arose as something that was directly experienced and local; this was contrasted with that of formal or institutional structures. Williams noted that by the mid-twentieth century 'community' began to be used as a term to reflect concerns with local identity and neighbourhood issues.

Other definitions of community question the very existence of any identifiable local community. For example, Jen Harvie, in her examination of British identity and contemporary performance, noted Benedict Anderson's work. Anderson suggested that actual communities do not exist, but that shared cultural practices create a sense of identity which leads to the notion of 'imagined' communities. In other words, through the sharing of events, participants create an illusionary sense of communality; the participation in cultural life thus leads citizens to construct a community for themselves, even though it might not constitute an actual geographic community. Anderson argued that participating in shared cultural practices such as watching national television, reading newspapers etc., created a sense of national belonging. Using Anderson's definitions it is possible to argue that a community is constructed when the mystery plays are performed today, even if some members of the performing group come from outside the immediate locale.

I have argued above that there are three main reasons for the performance of the mystery plays today: the potential to challenge dominant staging methods, the opportunity of the material to allow strong directorial interpretations, and the chance to develop community identity. The case studies in the later parts of this book investigate these notions further. However, in order to establish why the mystery plays are performed today it is important to ask two further questions. How far does the history of twentieth-century productions of the plays affect the decisions to stage the dramas in the New Millennium? In what ways have shifting patterns of theatre practice also affected the decision to stage those plays?

Heritage of modern performances

The starting point for the revival of medieval religious drama is usually ascribed to William Poel's production of the morality play *Everyman* in 1901 for the Elizabethan Stage Society, performed in the private courtyard of the London Charterhouse.[10] Poel's production was undertaken as part of his determination to unearth the theatrical past and from an interest in historic re-creation. His outdoor production of *Everyman* engaged with many theatrical devices which challenged the dominant theatre forms at that time, such as the rising social realism of playwrights like George Bernard Shaw and the popular melodramas offered by theatres such as Drury Lane. Poel instead showed a concern with how an alternative to the proscenium arch might be developed. He decided on a symbolic representation to portray heaven, earth and hell through the use of staging rostrums of various heights. This interest in the way in which medieval drama might challenge staging form was attractive to other directors. In 1920s Europe the German director Max Reinhardt tackled medieval drama with imagination and flair. Reinhardt, with a reputation for staging huge crowd scenes, initiated the Salzburg Festival in 1920 with an epic version of *Everyman* outside the cathedral square.[11] He built a series of broad steps to the front of the magnificent Baroque cathedral and had banks of audience seating erected in the body of the square.

Another director who found inspiration in medieval drama was Irish innovator Tyrone Guthrie, who discovered that Early Modern texts offered him the chance of working with possibilities that extended beyond those of mere 'dramatic illusion' which were created on the proscenium stage. Working on a production of *Ane Satyre of the Thrie Estiatis* (*c.* 1540–1552) for the 1948 Edinburgh Festival, Guthrie noted: 'It began to dawn that here was an opportunity to put into practice some of the theories which, through the years, I had been longing to test.'[12] These theories threw aside the configuration of the proscenium arch and realised a more dynamic actor/audience relationship.[13]

Early innovators such as Poel, Reinhardt and Guthrie discovered that medieval drama could provide a vehicle with which to challenge dominant modes of staging. In particular, aspects such as the use of stage space and the resultant effect that this had on the audience/actor relationship were of interest to early directors. However, other practitioners such as the actress Sybil Thorndike showed an awareness of how the issue of theatrical form and community may intersect. Thorndike addressed a 1934 festival of religious drama organised by George Bell, the Bishop of Chichester, and E. Martin Browne, his director of religious drama, in a lecture called 'The Theatre as a Service to the Community'. She declared that:

> The beginning of the downfall or perversion of the theatre was when the Church let it go ... The theatre had become an excrescence instead of an integral part of religion and life ... The proscenium was the beginning of something that made a division, a gulf between actor and spectator and stopped the theatre from becoming the common art.[14]

Here she recognised an essential bond between life and art, and space and immediacy. In commenting on this relationship, Thorndike, like Peter Brook some forty years later, identified the intersection between performance space and the notion of 'immediacy'.

Although Thorndike's evocation of the Church and its relationship to medieval drama may not be strictly true (in particular the idea that the Church 'let go' of the possession of drama), her comments do demonstrate the importance in the rise of religious drama in Britain in the 1920s and 30s in leading to the eventual establishment of a tradition of playing the mystery plays. The formation of the Religious Drama Society in 1929 under the auspices of George Bell and E. Martin Browne was pivotal. Kenneth Pickering has noted the influence that they held: 'Between them, Bell and Browne ... were to determine largely the development of verse drama in England for the next decade.'[15] Alongside dramatic performances, Bell and Browne arranged conferences on religious drama, and events to accompany the festivals they arranged, such as the one at which Thorndike spoke. Perhaps Bell's most public contribution to religious drama was the commissioning of *Murder in the Cathedral* from T. S. Eliot, which Browne directed at Canterbury Cathedral in 1935. Browne's influence on religious drama also extended to include the formation of the Pilgrim Players, a group dedicated to performing religious drama to civilians and soldiers during the Second World War. But it was in 1951 that Browne made his greatest impact on the public production of religious drama when he directed a full-length version of the mystery plays at York.

The factors leading to the establishment of the production of the York plays are outlined by Elliott in Chapter 4 of *Playing God*, and are re-examined in Chapter 7 of this study. It is worth identifying here how the performance was initially aligned with the production of religious drama. In an informal meeting between Keith Thomson, the director of the York Festival Board and the archbishops of York and Canterbury, it was agreed that they would support the plays if the production focused on the playing of religious dramas rather than the theatrical experience: in order to achieve this they demanded that the plays were performed on a religious site and directed by Browne. There were many other ways in which the production of the plays was aligned with religious concerns: the text was adapted by Canon Purvis, a member of the clergy, and the identity of the actors who played God and Christ was kept anonymous at Browne's request, so that their personalities would not interfere with their representations of the holy figures.[16] Keith Thomson also requested that the actors were Christians.[17]

Although the establishment of the York plays was aligned with the playing of religious drama, it was clear that the notion of community was also central to the re-establishment of the plays at York, since they formed part of the Festival of Britain celebrations in 1951. Sarah Beckwith has outlined the way in which these celebrations 'told a story about the continuity of Britishness, the unbreakable and profoundly informing link between Britain's landscape, arts and people'.[18] Established to commemorate the centenary of the Great Exhibition of 1851 and to boost national morale after the depression of the post-war years, the Festival of Britain provided a fitting platform for the reinstatement of the mystery plays. Beckwith has noted the relationship between place, people and culture in establishing a notion of national identity. The presentations of the mystery plays in 1951 at York were able to do just that. John Marshall observed that the production managed to 'fulfil one of its original purposes in bringing together a community of participants and spectators in celebration of both God and City'.[19] But as well as being a reflection of and celebration for York city, through being part of the Festival of Britain, the plays also expressed national identity; the then Archbishop of York noted how the mystery plays were like 'a silver thread' that bound the separate events of the festival together.[20] He saw them providing coherence for the national celebrations.

The development of the heritage of performing medieval drama was shaped in the 1960s and 70s by the rise of university drama. The preoccupation with how the space of the original plays may have worked fuelled a large degree of academic experiment and research. In 1969 Neville Denny produced the Cornish *Ordinalia* for Bristol University in an authentic Cornish round. In staging medieval drama Bristol University followed earlier experiments by Martial Rose in directing twenty of the Wakefield (Towneley) plays in 1958 at Bretton Hall, Wakefield.[21] Later, in 1967, John Hodgson directed a complete version of all thirty-two of the Wakefield (Towneley) plays at Bretton Hall. However, it was the events of the 1970s which were to shape contemporary productions of medieval drama by universities. The first, in 1972, was an experiment in processional playing by Phil Butterworth at Bretton Hall, where he produced the passion sequence of the Wakefield (Towneley) plays (Conspiracy, Buffeting, Scourging, Crucifixion), plus the fragment of the Hanging of Judas. This production was processional, using different locations and roofs of buildings in the grounds at Bretton Hall. Both the cast and the audience formed the same procession, with action taking place *en route*.[22] Another of these events is outlined in Chapter 6, and concerns the pageant staging of the York cycle at Leeds University in 1975. This production experimented with processional staging of the dramas and firmly established the notion that modern staging could be a genuine method of researching issues related to medieval performance. This production laid the way for larger reconstructions, such as those at Toronto, which are covered in the following chapter. Other significant academic reconstructions were undertaken by Meg Twycross in 1988 and 1992, when some of the York pageants were staged in their original place of performance on the pageant route at York. The legitimacy of the study of modern-day performances of medieval drama was helped by another academic development evidenced through the cataloguing of records of performance from early English drama. Established in 1975 by the University of Toronto, Records of Early English Drama (REED) has collected and published evidence of early performance from parishes, households, guilds, and civic documents for each county in Britain.[23] The success of academic experiments from the late 1950s and the accessibility of the REED project have ensured that modern-day productions of medieval drama have been widely staged at the universities of Lancaster, Oxford, Durham and Toronto, and at Bretton Hall.

The heritage of staging productions of the mystery plays is grounded in the notion of celebrating Christianity, unearthing theatrical convention and exploring community. I have argued above that the latter two functions have remained in currency in the New Millennium, but it is interesting to see how far changes in theatre practice, that date back to the 1920s, have also influenced the production of medieval drama today.

Changing theatre practice

The development of the theatre practices which I claim have affected the restaging of medieval drama today are linked to the avant-garde movements of the early 1920s. The practices, expressed in such movements as Dadaism and Surrealism, afforded a challenge to dominant forms of theatre representation by establishing movements that were deliberately 'anti-art', abstract or assembled by chance. In turn, modernist theatre practitioners such as Meyerhold, Craig, Appia and Brecht destroyed a reliance on mimetic practices and developed new languages of theatre which were more concerned with displaying the mechanics of theatrical representation than developing naturalistic modes. Many of these practitioners turned to texts that offered them alternative approaches and away from three-act plays; often they worked with montages created from a number of allied texts. By the late 1960s this dynamic exploration of text, and acting style (often alongside inspiration taken from the radical politics of that time), gave birth to a whole theatre movement of alternative practice which sought to question many of the practices established by traditional playhouses. A vast array of experimental touring companies were developed in Britain, Europe and the United States during this time, many of them devoted to specific political, performance or community agendas. Many of these practitioners adapted versions of the mystery plays and biblical stories, since they found the material provided a vehicle through which to develop more interactive and theatrically innovative productions. For example, in the 1960s The Living Theatre produced *The Mysteries and Smaller Pieces*, and *Paradise Now*; Polish director Jerzy Grotowski made an ensemble piece, *Apocalypsis cum figuris*; and Italian writer, performer and political activist Dario Fo produced a comic version of the mysteries entitled *Mistero buffo*.

Part of the alternative theatre movement of the 1960s and 70s also saw the rise of the community play, another dimension of the radical theatre movement which has affected the production of the mysteries today. A community play, according to Helen Nicholson, 'is characterised by the participation of community members in creating a piece of theatre which has special resonance for that community'.[24] In Britain, the model was initiated in the early 1960s by the work of director Peter Cheeseman, who worked first at the Stephen Joseph Studio in Scarborough and then the Victoria Theatre, Stoke-on-Trent, to produce community documentaries.[25] This was followed by the development of the community play by Ann Jellicoe; in the 1970s she worked in Lyme Regis with local residents to create a play called *The Reckoning*.[26] The model of community involvement that she established involved hundreds of people in a creative process which took over two years. Her example was followed by other notable playwrights, such as David Edgar, who worked in Dorchester to produce *Entertaining Strangers*. The upsurge of interest in community theatre was also reflected in the development of the Theatre-in-Education movement which arose during this time. The first company was founded in 1965 at the Belgrade Theatre in Coventry, and was accompanied by radical politics which were often reflected in the social issues that the work depicted.[27]

Although the notion of the community play has doubtless influenced large-scale productions of the mystery plays, performances of the mystery plays by communities do not fall into this definition of community theatre in a straightforward manner, since the participants rarely mould their own materials, but instead perform a pre-existing script. However, this is not to say that participating in these events does not provide an expression of communality or local identity; indeed, the community-based productions that are included in this book usually make much of their specific location. Many productions deliberately utilise the landscape of their performance to emphasis a local identity and enjoy the opportunity to ad-lib local references.

Millennium rebirth

So far this chapter has focused on reasons why directors are attracted to mystery plays; however, John Marshall has outlined a number of problems that face the contemporary director, and it is important that these are acknowledged. One of the primary challenges he identified was the difference between medieval and modern societies: 'What distinguishes medieval drama from that of our own time as much as anything else is its religious sense of festive occasion.'[28] Though the results from the 2001 Census in Britain show that 71.6 per cent of the population claim to be Christian,[29] the nature of Christian belief has changed dramatically since the Middle Ages. Perhaps the disparity between practices can be seen in the issue of worship: while this formed part of the backbone of medieval life, less than 3 per cent of the population attended the Church of England each Sunday by the New Millennium.[30] As Marshall suggested, modern-day productions can often attempt to overcome this change in religious belief by humanising issues, placing the plays in a contemporary setting, or overemphasising comic interpretations.[31] The productions that are discussed in this book for the most part did not choose to stage the plays because of their Christian material, but rather because they offered opportunities to connect with some of the themes they saw reflected in the plays: issues which relate to notions of community and celebration. It is perhaps for this reason that the mystery plays found such popularity at the turn of the New Millennium, for it was an occasion that called for the recognition of these values.

There are other hurdles that a modern-day director faces when directing the plays. These concern the issues of modernising the texts, cutting or unifying the cycle structure, and securing funding for the epic productions. Although some modern-day productions have observed the pageant structure and maintained separate episodes (mainly those performed in processional or promenade style), others have changed the dramatic episodes that comprise the cycle of plays into a coherent two- or three-part play. There are understandable pressures that cause companies to do this, most notably the duration for which contemporary audiences are prepared to watch an event. Most audiences will only give a performance two hours. The creation of essentially a two-act play, with the first act covering the Old Testament and the second act the Passion, has many implications, since the consolidation of the cycle structure means that frequently one actor will play a single character. Paula Neuss has commented that this practice in turn produces a flawed attempt to try to find characterisation which does not really exist.[32] This problem is compounded by the influence of post-Stanislavskian actor-training systems, which encourage performers to try to find the motivation for their character and construct a through-line which makes psychological sense of their actions. This reading of the roles in medieval drama is flawed. As John Marshall noted, the plays require an acting style that defines the roles as 'acts of presentation rather than identification'.[33]

Neuss noted that the texts of the mystery plays must be modernised for contemporary performances. The modern-day versions that are presented in this book have all sought to overcome the challenges presented by updating the texts in a variety of ways. Usually productions draw from the four extant groups of plays to create a composite version. The dramatists of the modern plays are, however, driven by a wide range of priorities. One of Tony Harrison's main desires during his preparation of the texts was to keep the northern idiom of the York and Towneley texts, a decision that reflected his own identity as a poet. On the other hand, Edward Kemp's texts for the Royal Shakespeare Company (discussed in Chapter 7) were prepared through focusing on modernising the representation of God and obliterating politically incorrect references. Adrian Henri's version of the plays, used in Chichester Youth Theatre's production, was constructed to emphasise issues of the parent/child relationship. A noticeable facet of the production of the plays is that most directors feel compelled to create their own modernised version of the texts; they clearly wish to establish their group identity through such an exercise. The texts are often used to determine a distinctive local identity for the production. This is evidenced by the fact that many writers have copyrighted their versions; for example, in 1995 John Kelly copyrighted 'The Worsbrough Mystery Plays'.

The issue of funding these large-scale productions has been a major concern. Although the examples analysed in this book are often performed by amateur actors the staging demands are considerable: a fact often felt by the medieval guilds, who levied fines on their members to create pageant silver through which to fund the productions. Today the cost of the staging, costumes and seating for audiences is enormous, and many companies have struggled to find sponsors and arts funders to support their plays. The occasion of the New Millennium provided some financial support for mystery play events: for example, the Lincoln Plays received £26,000 from the Millennium Commission.[34] The York Millennium plays were also supported by the National Lottery through a grant made by the Arts Council. However, as is acknowledged in Chapter 4, the precarious financial position of the York Mystery Plays has considerably affected the history of their production, and the continued playing of a large-scale event remains undecided.

The large cluster of productions of the mystery plays that occurred around the Millennium demonstrates that the cultural conditions in Britain at that time were able to support such an enterprise. Contemporary theatre scholar Jen Harvie has outlined the changes in cultural identity in Britain that inspired her to write her examination of British performance at the Millennium, *Staging the UK*. She noted the changes that occurred in Britain around that time which affected the expression of cultural identity. For example, 1997 saw the election of a Labour government after eighteen years of Tory rule. A number of other shifts occurred: 1997 also saw the symbolic end of the British Empire, when the sovreignty of Hong Kong was transfered to China; in 1999 devolution of power, in which independent governance was granted to Scotland and Wales, further affected the alignment of power in the country; and a further shift occurred in 2002, when Britain stood outside the European Union and failed to adopt a common currency.[35] As Harvie suggested, these factors led to a redesign of the cultural identity of England.

In 2000 the government launched Panel 2000, a collaboration between the Foreign Office, the Department of Trade and Industry and others to rebrand the image of Britain abroad and to boost the export of its culture. The emphasis on culture as a commodity and the use of the term 'creative industries' displayed a new arts policy in which the wider benefits of creative practice were emphasised. As Harvie remarked, this policy was not without its flaws; it risked over-commodification and the loss of a sense of importance for artistic agendas.[36]

However, it is possible to see that the wider context of enthusiasm for the creative industries at the turn of the century in Britain provided a platform which reinvigorated a passion for the mystery plays. The conditions which sparked the seminal productions at York and Chester in the 1950s were replicated. In both cases Britain was suffering from post-depression: displayed by the effects of the post-World War conditions in the early 1950s and the aftermath of extended Tory rule in the late 1990s. Britain at the Millennium was, for the reasons outlined above, a place of shifting identity, and, just as the Festival of Britain had renegotiated national identity, the Millennium reconstructed the complexity of an identity that was now 'hybrid, multiple and produced in diverse ways'.[37]

The productions of the mystery plays examined in this book frequently show an awareness of the importance of their production in shaping contemporary identities. Projects such as those at Coventry, Lichfield and Worsbrough provoke debate about contemporary community, while those undertaken by the major national theatre companies, the Royal National Theatre and the Royal Shakespeare Company, offer more wide-ranging reflections on the nature of a nation driven by secular experience. These expressions of identity are important, and, taken together, this cluster of performances offers an insight into how cultural representation can explore and shape local and national identities.

SECTION II

Playing Spaces

SECTION II ~ Playing Spaces

One of the most important features of medieval drama was the manner in which it utilised its performance spaces. Unlike modern-day theatre, many performances occurred outdoors. In addition, the variety of staging configurations employed was enormous, so that the audience were placed in a number of different relationships with the action being performed. Chapter 1 outlined how some medieval mystery plays, York, for example, were performed on waggons processing through the city. It is likely that parts of others, such as the N-Town plays, were performed in a fixed place-and-scaffold configuration. Interlude drama was probably performed indoors in banqueting halls, while other outside performances included a host of festive celebrations linked to the calendar year, such as harvest festivals and midsummer dances, where the actant and spectator could occupy the same space. The streets of the city provided a stage for civic processions such as the entry of a monarch or an elaborate funeral parade.

The mystery plays as processional dramas held an important relationship with not only their spectators, who could process freely between the sites, but also with the site itself. The York plays processed to between ten and sixteen stations around the city. Meg Twycross has traced the likely stopping places of the pageant routes, and they are notably close to many parish churches.[1] This processional form of performance offered a complex intersection between play, person and place.[2]

The differences between spaces used for performance in medieval England and those used today is colossal. It is not just the physical properties of these spaces that are so diverse, but also the ideological and aesthetic characteristics. Medieval city space was more clearly delineated with cities bound by walls designed to keep out intruders and protect citizens. The medieval city placed less importance on personal and domestic space than modern-day society does. Instead the streets themselves were central to the performance of everyday medieval life. Teresa Heitor has commented that 'In the medieval urban space the street is a structuring value: it established directions, site hierarchies and functions as a space for the discrimination and staging of social order.'[3] The streets, then, were a place where medieval life was negotiated, defined and lived: a concept which is not necessarily shared by modern-day experiences.

This alternative method of experiencing or 'living' space is contiguous with the ideas of theatre historian David Wiles, who has explored the development of perceptions of space. Wiles has discussed theorist Henri Lefebvre's approach to space, in which it 'is not "read" but experienced by means of the body which walks, smells, tastes and in short lives a space.'[4] This sense of space being a 'lived' entity maybe foreign to today's experience, but it provides a useful framework through which to analyse the spatial conventions utilised in outdoor medieval drama. In medieval times the performance spaces of the streets of York were where the body literally lived. The streets were the places that contained markets, trade and the livelihood of merchants. The streets also hosted the civic and church buildings that formed another important aspect of medieval experience. This notion of the city and the importance of the streets is a far cry from Britain at the New Millennium, where city centres have increasingly lost their importance, with the development of out-of-town shopping centres and business parks. If medieval experiences of space fit with an approach suggested by Lefebvre, then modern-day spatial experiences seem more akin to the fragmentation suggested by the ideas of the seventeenth-century French philosopher René Descartes. Descartes maintained that there existed a dichotomy of body and mind; mind and body were able to exist separately and were formed of distinctly different matter. This notion can be applied to an understanding of modern-day spatial experience: for example, the city centre and the retail parks are two dichotomous experiences.

David Wiles has applied the notion of a Cartesian dichotomy to theatrical space, and reads this as being emblematic of the separation of the stage and auditorium.[5] This is a separation that has occurred on stage since the development of the proscenium arch and the use of perspective in the seventeenth century. Meanwhile, it is possible to see Lefebvre's 'lived' space reflected in medieval processional playing. Here, as the spectators walked the streets to view action from various stations, they experienced the city, which formed a dynamic part of their response to the plays.

This section examines a number of productions that have articulated a particular relationship with space. Chapter 3 focuses on academic reconstructions of the York cycle using pageant waggon staging. These productions are discussed in order to assess how far they illuminate historical staging practices, and to assess what has been learned from these experiments.

Chapter 4 looks at the staging practices that have been used at York during the past fifty years. The York plays were initially played outdoors in the ruins of St Mary's Abbey, before moving to the indoor space of the Theatre Royal in 1992. In 2000, to mark the New Millennium, the plays were presented for the first time inside York Minster. This chapter examines the effects of the changing spaces on the productions of the York plays, in particular the way in which a different audience contract has been established through the shift in location. For reasons outlined in the chapter, the move from the outdoor space to inside venues has changed the nature of the audience experience from one of collectivity to individuality.

Chapter 5 utilises Lefebvre's spatial analysis to investigate how a selection of other productions used space. For example, the history of the productions at Chester shows a gradual passage of the control of the plays from Church to the city. In doing so, a new set of spatial practices were engendered. Similarly, the Lichfield plays demonstrate a complex interrelationship with the space of their performance. They utilise a form of processional drama in which the players parade with their props to a series of fixed spaces which represent the market, the Church and recreation. Finally, the Lincoln Mystery Plays, which use the N-Town play texts (part of which were originally written to be performed using place-and-scaffold staging), have experimented in using both a fixed, single stage and multiple playing stages. They have found ways in which to explore spatial practices in the fixity of an indoor space.

CHAPTER 3

Pageant Staging: Experiments with the York Cycle

The first 'full' production of cycle drama, at Leeds University in 1975, is often cited as a response to Alan Nelson's questioning of the likelihood of the accuracy of medieval pageant performance.[1] Nelson argued it was impossible in medieval England that each pageant played at every station, and that instead the waggons simply processed around the city and then played once at the end of the route. However, when his study was published in 1974 preparations for the pageant drama at Leeds were already well under way. In actual fact the intentions behind the production of the York Cycle at Leeds were more to do with an investigation into the validity of medieval staging practices than a direct response to Nelson's hypothesis. Peter Meredith, one of the co-organisers observed that: 'When we started on a grand scale at Leeds in 1975, it was with the intention of testing medieval staging techniques.'[2]

The impetus for the 'Leeds Experiment', as it was known, came from Jane Oakshott, then a post-graduate student of medieval drama and a professional theatre director. Oakshott's fatigue with the condensed, fixed playing York cycles, reinstated on a three/four-yearly basis since E. Martin Browne's production to mark the Festival of Britain in 1951, was largely responsible for her desire to produce a pageant version of the cycle.[3] She was keen to investigate whether the plays were more effective when staged using the practices that were originally intended. She objected to Browne's treatment of the York cycle:

> By placing the drama on one fixed stage, in a statuesque mode of performance with a single cast and seated audience, he completely changed the relationships between text, actors and audience: and by reducing a full day's drama to a mere three hours he lost the enormous vitality and dramatic scope of the cycles as originally conceived.[4]

Oakshott suggested that the turning point in the staging of medieval drama came for her in 1969 with the full-length outdoor production of the Cornish *Ordinalia* by Bristol University. This notion of the epic, full-scale, outdoor performance is what inspired her to attempt a large-scale production of the York plays at an outdoor location.[5]

This chapter examines academic reconstructions of the plays which have been undertaken in order to elucidate information about the staging practices that medieval drama utilised. The productions assessed here were all produced in order to reveal how the mystery plays offer a unique staging form.

Leeds 1975

On 17 and 18 May 1975 the York plays were staged in the Leeds University precinct as part of the University's centenary celebrations. It is estimated that more than 4,000 people saw the production, and that about 250 people aged between four and seventy participated.[6] In all, thirty-six of the forty-seven extant York pageants were played at three stations on a pageant route of about 400 yards. Groups from Leeds town produced twelve pageants and the University staged twenty; colleges outside the city produced the remaining four pageants. The project utilised a modernised version of the text originally commissioned from Canon John Stanley Purvis for the 1951 York performance.[7] As was the case in medieval England, a group that had an association with the subject matter was assigned to the pageant. For example, the Department of Physics performed *The Creation of the World*, Chemistry the *Transfiguration*, and a local church group, St Mary's Church, Whitkirk, *The Death of Mary*.[8] While Oakshott maintained responsibility for the overall organisation and direction of the event, each individual group had a separate organiser and director and they were responsible for providing costumes and properties for their own pageants, again much like the original events, where staging responsibility laid with each producing guild. Unlike medieval times, there were a limited number of pageant waggons. Only eight waggons were utilised, which meant that they were recycled throughout the performance and each group had to set up and dismantle its set. Pageant waggons were provided with a basic dressing, so that if required three sides of the waggon could be curtained.

The 'Leeds Experiment' was important in proving several points about the nature of pageant playing. These findings related mainly to the nature of processing with and playing on the waggon, the relationship between the actors and audience in processional drama, and the importance of both the site and context of the presentation of the dramas.

Previous academic studies by Alexandra Johnston and Margaret Rogerson had attempted to defend the possibility of pageant playing against Nelson's scepticism. In a hypothetical reconstruction of playing conditions, it had been postulated that the setting up of the waggon at a site, or station, might take as long as five minutes. Oakshott's experiment found that it took only a few seconds.[9] Additionally, prologues at the beginning of each pageant could be delivered from the ground or *platea* to cover up the set-up. (This device was used liberally when Johnston produced her own version of the cycle at Toronto in 1998.)[10]

Photographs from the production show that the waggons were presented in a variety of states of dress.[11] At times only a backdrop was used; at others the back and three sides of the waggon were enclosed. One pageant, *The Road to Calvary* employed no waggon, and the action was successfully played on the street. The hard surface of the road provided no cushioning for Christ's fall, and added a harsh reality to the play.[12] Some waggons utilised a roof cloth; while one, lent by Bretton Hall College, had two storeys.

The use of waggons revealed few problems with managing the restricted playing space. The waggons used varied in dimension from between 15 by 6 feet to only 6 by 4 feet. The question over whether Christ and twelve disciples would fit on a limited stage space for the playing of the Last Supper was easily dismissed. In fact, as Peter Meredith pointed out, the playing on the waggons was more successful when they were used as a focal point and frame for the action:

> Using the waggons as a center-piece for the action, rather than seeing it as a limitation of the action seems to me right – it certainly works. The plays which used additional pieces of set – thrones, hellmouths – tended to destroy the focus of the action, quite apart from making it difficult for the audience to see.[13]

The largest waggon seemed cumbersome, and dwarfed the players, whereas the smallest focused the attention on the actor and meant that anything more than a few gestures was superfluous; the limited space also acted as a control for the amateur actors and discouraged extraneous arm movements.[14] The discipline that the small stage provided for the actors came as a surprise to the producers. The success of playing on a single waggon also dismissed previous academic suggestions that an additional waggon or platform was present at each station and was used as part of the staging.[15]

Both Oakshott and Meredith remark on the considerable power of the spectacle of the waggons being pulled from one station to another.[16] In fact, Oakshott's community productions at Wakefield in 1977 and 1980 further proved the importance of the procession of waggons. At Wakefield the groups processed between three fixed stages; Oakshott felt that the focal point provided by the waggon was absent from the productions. Indeed, the movement of the waggons at Leeds was like a 'magnet'; their arrival at a station commanded the audience's attention.[17] It is evident from Oakshott's account that the procession of the waggons provided a sense of grandeur and added to the ceremonial feel of the event; already present because of the occasion of the University's centenary. The sense of ceremony was highlighted by the candlelit procession that accompanied the final pageant; a ritual undertaken by players and audience alike.

The context of the event of the centenary celebrations provided only part of the necessary atmosphere to support the plays. Alongside the plays, a medieval fair was hosted in the pedestrian precinct. The stalls were useful in defining and restricting the playing space and created a more in-depth relationship between the actors and the audience. Performances by 'itinerant' players such as tumblers, a dancing bear, wandering minstrels and a Punch and Judy show added to the ambience of entertainment. As Oakshott pointed out, the stalls at the fair served a number of functions beyond defining the processional route for the waggons.[18] They drew an audience that would not have been attracted by the plays; they enabled some groups to raise money to support their pageant; and they provided refreshments and souvenirs. One must assume that the stalls also offered a break from the plays, for, as John Marshall pointed out, the relationship between the audience and these street dramas is 'non-compulsory'.[19] Audience members have the choice of whether to watch the next pageant or take a break. Unlike indoor entertainment, the audience is not contained by fixed seating (see Plate 1).

The relationship with the audience proved to be a complex issue at Leeds. The three differing stations (two of them with fixed seating for some of the audience), demonstrated that these dramas have a shifting relationship with the spectator. Oakshott noted that the actors responded to the differing demands of the audience and the specifics of each site, and that the proximity between the players and the spectators shifted for each pageant.[20] This dynamic interplay is, of course, something that a fixed-seat single-space playing of the pageants can never achieve. The standing audience viewed the plays from the sides of the waggon and sometimes formed a circle around the action. However, even at the second station, where the audience were closest to the waggon, they were easy to control and backed away if the space in front of the waggon was needed to serve as a *platea* for action on the ground.[21] Questionnaires completed by the groups that performed the pageants testify that they felt each audience was different, and that this added to their enjoyment of the repeated performances.[22] This notion is interesting, for it suggests that for performers the issue is not that they are repeating the pageant at each station, but instead are aware that each performance is a new experience.

The final issue raised by the Leeds Experiment concerned the unity of the whole performance. Both Meredith and Oakshott observed that processional pageant performance emphasised the individuality of each play, but that this approach released a form of limited unity. For Meredith the real dramatic unity lay within each pageant: 'What unity there is in the whole cycle is simply the story, and that is left to look after itself. It is within the individual pageant that the dramatic unity lies.'[23] Oakshott used the metaphor of a piece of jewellery: each pageant is a jewel in a string that makes up a necklace.[24]

The team that steered the 1975 York cycle at Leeds got a further opportunity to investigate pageant staging in their production of twenty-five plays from the Chester cycle in 1983. This production visited Chester, and was thus the first time that a series of pageants had been played on a former pageant route. This time the event ran over a three-day weekend provided by the public holiday in May. For this performance special emphasis was placed on the authenticity of the costumes. The production was notionally set in 1553, and theatre historian Meg Twycross undertook costume designs. Importance was again placed on the context of the presentation of the plays; this time they were accompanied by a Renaissance Festival. By this point Oakshott had experience of directing other versions of medieval drama, such as the community Wakefield plays in 1977 and 1980. The team was also able to draw on the lessons learned by another large-scale academic performance: that of the York Cycle at the University of Toronto in 1977. There is a similarity of experience here, for both the York Cycle of 1977 and the Chester version at Leeds in 1983 had to be moved indoors for part of the performance because of adverse weather. Although deeply regrettable for the productions, this occurrence did provide an opportunity to compare outdoor and indoor performances of the pageants.

Toronto 1977

The production of the York cycle at Toronto consciously credited the influence of the Leeds Experiment.[25] The event was co-produced by Poculi Ludique Societas,[26] a university group set up to undertake the performance of medieval drama, and Records of Early English Drama, with Alexandra Johnston as the Chair of the Planning Committee, and David Parry the artistic director. Like Leeds, the Toronto production used the modernised text version of the York cycle by Canon Purvis.[27] The production staged forty-seven of the pageants and played at three stations utilising eleven waggons, which as at Leeds were recycled between groups. The use of the waggons confirmed many of the findings at Leeds: the 12 by 6 foot playing space allowed plenty of room;[28] the waggons were easily moved by four to five people, and it took only 20–30 seconds to set up the waggon, which could be covered by the use of the prologue.[29] At Toronto experiments were also undertaken to investigate supporting the corners of the waggons, as they tended to become unstable when pageants required larger numbers of players.[30] This additional propping potentially added to the length of the changeover times, but Parry argues that the changeover could be reduced by having the next waggon waiting a few yards away. He claims the attention of the audience was easily diverted away from the awaiting pageant when it was located even a few yards outside the playing area.[31] Part of the reason why the audience readily entered into this 'suspension of disbelief' was that the playing of the cycles, as Sheila Lindenbaum has pointed out, required them to enter what Kolve defined as 'a special game world':[32] the audience must be willing to recognise the rules of the performance and let their attention leave the world as they know it and enter the game world. When the waiting waggon falls outside the boundaries of that game world, the audience ignore its presence.

The waggons used at Toronto were significantly developed from those at Leeds. Here there was the opportunity to customise the basic structure, which meant that documented staging devices such as a rising trap could be tried out.[33] According to original staging records curtains were often used to conceal the wheels, which means that the deck of the waggon must overhang them. (It is this overhang that created the instability problem referred to above.)[34] The majority of the waggons were a single storey with a box-like frame on top of the deck from which curtaining could be hung. One waggon, built specifically for *The Creation*, *The Last Judgement* and *The Harrowing of Hell*, had two storeys and a lift. Parry played God in the *Last Judgement* and utilised the rising lift; he testified that its use could be 'quite controlled, and quite smooth'.[35]

Although the Toronto production enabled a further testing of the conditions of waggon playing, the adverse weather and the chosen site prevented other spatial experiments. The pageants were played around an open area called King's College Circle; a medieval fair was to be hosted in the centre. In the event, the poor weather forced the stallholders inside and sodden grass meant the audience were forced to stand a long distance from the front of the waggon. However, the unfavourable weather did confirm the importance of playing the pageant dramas in close proximity to the audience and in a site that was surrounded by buildings. As Peter Meredith observes, 'Leeds had the advantage of a more enclosed setting; the streets of the University Precinct already partly filled by bustling rows of stalls for the fair created a sense of festivity and everyday life and an intimacy which I found lacking at Toronto (1977)'.[36]

After the first ten pageants the production moved inside to a 2,000-seater auditorium, Convocation Hall. Because poor weather forced half of the pageants indoors it was not possible to test the idea of whether the whole cycle could be played in one day. It would take the full outdoor playing of the cycle twenty-one years later to test this. Inside Convocation Hall one waggon was erected on the proscenium stage. The changeovers between each pageant were noticeably longer, as each group had to reset the same waggon with their set and props. Despite the anticipated difficulties of moving waggons from one station to another during outdoor performances, it was shown to take longer to perform the pageants inside.[37]

Indoor playing also changed the contract between the actors and the audience.[38] Sheila Lindenbaum noted that during the outdoor performances the audience often saw a pageant for the second time, and that, 'the line that separated the actors from the audience was therefore constantly shifting.'[39] For some outdoor performances the audience's spectatorship formed an important part of the concept of the drama. During the *Crucifixion* the 'crowd responded by forming a circle around the playing area as if to give the sacrifice a sacramental quality.'[40] Other eyewitness accounts indicated that outside the audience had the opportunity to watch players set up and dismantle their waggons, to see the players switch from playing their character to being themselves, and even to help push the waggons so that the performers and audience were totally integrated.[41] Inside the audience occupied fixed seating and were less able to come and go. This increased formality was highlighted by the presence in the auditorium of a dog, whose behaviour demonstrated the difference between indoor and outdoor playing. Whereas interventions such as a dog barking or crossing the stage would seem to be part of the risk of outdoor playing, inside this became an uncontrollable moment, and was 'funny in the wrong sort of way.'[42] Lindenbaum noted that 'a greater professionalism also seemed required indoors' since the plays were now performed against the demands of a proscenium stage and no longer needed the boldness of outdoor playing, which had redeemed some clumsy performances.[43]

As Gail McMurray Gibson pointed out, the mystery plays are 'consummately visual.'[44] The use of the pageant waggon with its box frames and curtaining has reinforced scholarship undertaken since the 1920s which has linked the original medieval staging with contemporary visual art.[45] Indeed, the analogy with visual forms extends further. Parry noted that the structure of the waggon provided a visual framework through which to view the action: 'there is often action spilling out of the frame, but the frames are always there.'[46] The link between the tableaux of medieval art and the acting style of medieval theatre has led some scholars to believe that the original method of performance was one based on stillness. Interestingly, Lindenbaum's analysis of *The Harrowing of Hell* pageant at Toronto identified that the most successful mode of performance was when stylised gestures were linked together to form more fluid and expressive movement. Lindenbaum noted that it was not only the actors' gestures that helped to create this fluid expressivity, but also the dynamic flow between the spectators and performers formed part of this process:

> The fluid quality of the performance was instructive, in view of the point scholars often make that staging a series of pageants on waggons places each pageant in sharp focus, as if it were a single compartment in a narrative series of manuscript illustrations or stained glass windows. But at least outdoors the pageants differed from the compartmentalised scenes in art as a result of the shifting line between actors and audience and the movement of the waggons within the ebb and flow of the procession.[47]

One of the criticisms raised against the Toronto 1977 production was that an emphasis was placed on the didactic and devotional aspects of the plays, and that the ceremonial and civic was somewhat displaced.[48] Of course, it is impossible for a modern-day audience to respond in a similar manner to their medieval counterparts, but it appears as if the Leeds medieval fair and occasion of the University centenary was more successful in providing a sense of the ceremonial as a background for the staging of the plays.

Toronto 1998

The 1998 staging of the York cycle at Toronto was the first opportunity to fully test whether the cycle could have been played over a single day. The production, once again organised by Poculi Ludique Societas with different groups performing each pageant, embraced the full forty-seven plays, and the weather on 20 June 1998 enabled them to be played outside. The specific purpose of playing the whole cycle was identified by the organising committee as two-fold. First, to test whether it was possible to play the whole cycle in one day, and second, to undertake a practical exploration of how the pageant waggons might have been used, specifically in relation to end-on or side-on staging.[49]

The 1998 Toronto plays were performed at four different stations which spanned Victoria College; each station offered differing performance conditions; this was useful in testing the relationship between pageant playing and site. Like its predecessors at Leeds and Toronto, these plays were accompanied by a fair which provided a sense of context and occasion for the performances, and succeeded in attracting to the event audiences who might otherwise not have attended.

It is evident from the pre-planning that the organisers were concerned that the pageants would not fit into one day. Producers were instructed to ensure that the plays were 'very tight and relatively quick in pace', that extra dramatic elements such as music be kept short, and that where possible the prologues be used to cover the set-up of the waggon ('for many plays it works quite well indeed and saves quite a bit of time').[50] As the event drew closer it became apparent that the organisers had been over-zealous in planning a 4.30 a.m. start, so this was duly switched to 6 a.m. The meticulous planning paid off, and pageant producers were surprised to find themselves assembling their actors far earlier in the day than had been scheduled.[51] In the event, the pageants finished at the final station at about midnight. Johnston asserted that: 'Whether all forty-eight pageants were ever done at one time remains an issue but we demonstrated that it could be done.'[52] However, there were some aspects of the Toronto experiment that were not fully watertight in proving the case. The Toronto performances played at only four stations, whereas records indicate that at York in some years the plays could have been performed up to sixteen times. Any minor delays at Toronto could easily be dealt with, but would have been magnified with more stations. However, it must be pointed out that the original York cycle would have benefited from some time-saving devices. Medieval staging conditions meant that each company owned its own waggon. At Toronto, as with earlier experiments, the waggons were recycled between groups and this led to some delays.

Another question which concerns the issue of a full playing of the cycles on one day is that of actor stamina.[53] Experience from Toronto showed that trained actors and singers believed they could have performed the pageants only a couple more times due to the voice strain of playing outdoors. As Johnston points out: 'The actors must either have been phenomenally well trained in the use of their voices or the situation of the original production was such that they never had to shout to be heard.'[54]

An enormous amount has been written on the Toronto 1998 York Cycle; the development of electronic sources means that the Internet has been appropriated as a place where further accounts and photographs can be accessed. Special attention has been paid to the production in volumes 1 and 3 of *Early Theatre* (1998 and 2000 respectively), in volumes 38 and 39 of *Research Opportunities in Renaissance Drama* (1999 and 2000), and in volume 19 of *Medieval English Theatre* (1997). It is not my intention to survey that material here, but to develop some of the arguments that are appropriate to the focus of this book. One of the most useful papers on the Toronto production is Alexandra Johnston's, 'York cycle 1998: what we learned'. Alongside her assertion that the experiment demonstrated that a full playing of the whole cycle may have been possible in one day are a number of other pertinent points. Johnston's arguments relate to the use of the waggons, the varying stations, and the effect of the time of day on performances.

Although one of the aims of the production was to test the validity of end-on or side-on use of the waggons, this aspect was to be proven irrelevant.[55] As David Bevington pointed out, the issue of playing end-on or broadside was exemplified by *The Temptation of Christ*, where it was apparent it 'was less important than the fact that one could see through the set from any angle, encouraging acting in the round'.[56] There were other moments when the audience were encouraged to view predominantly from one side, such as *The Remorse of Judas*. Such pageants rely on hidden stage devices, in this case the hanging. Although the spectacle worked best when viewed from the broadside of the waggon, many of the audience were tempted to circle about the waggon to see how the trick worked. Bevington noted that the use of the broadside playing did 'reduce flexibility of movement and reinforced the pictorial dimension'.[57]

It is no surprise that the Toronto 1998 production found the issue of which way the waggon faced to be irrelevant. Academic experiments in England had reached the same conclusion a few years earlier. In 1988 Meg Twycross directed a selection of pageants at York along part of the route of the original plays (a section which still held the original building lines). In 1992 she produced a further five pageants in the streets of York. Part of the context of this production surrounded the hypothesis she had put forward in the 1970s, suggesting that in the York pageant route the stations were all on the left-hand side, and that in order to avoid unnecessary manœuvring of the waggons, each played broadside with its right-hand side facing the audience.[58] Further research into the pageant route in the 1980s and early 1990s questioned this theory by showing that some stations had been on the right-hand side. Indeed, Twycross's 1992 experiment with end-on staging demonstrated that playing in such a direction was possible and sometimes preferable. But, like Toronto, it proved that such arguments are merely academic and not of practical importance. Phil Butterworth, who directed the *Crucifixion* pageant, discovered that the most successful form of staging was the three-dimensionality created by playing in the round – thus arguments about which was the front, side or back of the waggon were irrelevant, as the audience could crowd round a waggon which ever way it was facing (unless, of course, it was curtained).[59]

Some other aspects of waggon playing were elucidated by the 1998 experiment, although these elements had been present in the earlier Toronto and Leeds productions. For example, at Toronto it became evident that the use of the *platea* severely limited the sight-lines for the audience, and that acoustically the street space was less strong than the platform of the waggon. The audience were also aware that when the actors moved too far from the waggon the action and focus became dissipated.[60] But this issue of the use of the waggon or the *platea* is one that is possibly affected by twenty-first-century sensibilities. The suggestion is that the use of the waggon was more effective both visually and vocally than playing at street level. But how far is this the product of an expectation of theatricality that has been developed by the dynamics of a fixed-seat indoor theatre? Megan Lloyd draws on research undertaken by David Crouch to suggest that the conditions for the majority of medieval spectators meant that they had only a 'fleeting view of the plays from awkward angles, or simply heard the dialogue' and that there was little room for the audience to move within the 'clogged and heavily policed street' of York.[61] It is perhaps, as has been suggested of Shakespearean theatre, that audience members went to hear rather than see a play.

The Toronto production raised several other issues regarding the use of the waggons. One of these was whether the waggons had roofs. The main reason for suspecting that they did was the acoustic benefit. Johnston remarked that:

'Certainly those without roofs were effective as set pieces. If the set designers had provided a back for the waggon, as many did for interior scenes, the back served as a sounding board and there was no need for a roof.'[62] But Johnston further noted that the Mercer's indenture of 1433 for their production of *The Last Judgement* suggests that their waggon had a roof.[63] However, Johnston observed that the last four pageants in the York cycle (which includes *The Last Judgement*) require a more sustained use of sound or staging mechanics and may be the only pageants that actually had roofs in medieval England.[64]

Playing the pageants outside through the duration of a day helped to highlight other issues. Some productions, such as *The Last Judgement* used an awareness of the anticipated performance time to inform their production decisions. Knowing that darkness would descend, they used artificial lighting to highlight aspects of their interpretation of the pageant. In fact an awareness of fitting a pageant to its performance time is one of the most neglected aspects of research into the staging of the mystery plays.[65]

The individual characteristics of each station revealed further information about the possible conditions of medieval pageant staging. Bob Potter described the four differing stations like 'succeeding holes on a golf course' designed to test the skills of the actors.[66] The first station played to the steps of Old Victoria Hall, and therefore offered raked seating for the audience, but the backdrop for the performance was unfocused (see Plate 2).[67] The second station backed onto Knott Library and the widespread grassy area of the quad in front meant the audience was dispersed. The effect of the heat of the day drove the audience further back into the shade and produced an even greater distance between the performers and spectators. The fourth site received the most varied reviews from spectators. While some found the closed public street distracting as it was subject to modern ambient city noise, for others it was a favourite as it offered good acoustics and an open but manageable scale.[68]

It was at the third station that the most interesting observations were to be made. The third station, wedged between two buildings, 'formed an intimate, voice-friendly meeting point for audience and actors that most closely resembled the narrow streets of ancient York' (see Plate 3).[69] For some this site had the feel of a private open-air theatre,[70] and the effects of playing at the station made Alexandra Johnston radically reconsider the mode of performance and reception in pageant playing. As she pointed out, we usually consider that the majority of the audience watched the plays from ground level, below the height of the waggon. However, at Toronto many of the residential bedrooms were in a building overlooking the third station. From here Johnston remarked that the spectators had 'superb acoustics and sight-lines – especially if the waggons had no roofs'.[71] Evidence from York and Chester bears out that the most important townspeople viewed the pageant from above. At York the mayor and council viewed the pageants from the first floor of the Guildhall overlooking Coney Street, the site of the eighth station. At Chester tenants leased their rooms so that the plays could be viewed.[72] Johnston went as far as to state: 'I have become convinced that the audience to whom the plays was directed was the one seated above.'[73] If this is the case, then the relationship between pageant playing and the audience comes close to resembling something more akin to Inn-yard playing.[74]

I would like finally to focus on the acting styles used at Toronto and the reception these received. As outlined in Chapter 1, it has been argued that the acting style of the original pageants achieved a type of Brechtian *Verfremdungseffekt*. Each episode was presented by a different guild and featured a new cast.[75] During the course of the York cycle the audience would witness performances by numerous Christs, Gods, Marys etc.[76] At Toronto this experience was further heightened by some groups using two casts. The Universities of Birmingham and Toronto both utilised double casting of some figures; under the arch that separated stations 2 and 3, Mary Magdalene's costume was hastily switched from one actor to another. As Barbara Palmer pointed out, in assessing any critical report of the plays we must be aware that the audiences did not necessarily see the pageants at the same station, or indeed with the same cast.[77]

The Toronto production allowed reflection on other aspects of the acting in performances. In many of the productions women played men's roles. Most notable was Hillsdale College's production of *Christ's Appearance to Thomas*, where the apostles were predominately played by cross-dressed women. This is, of course, a reversal of medieval staging practices where men played all the female characters. But it is worth noting the reaction to this gender reversal: 'This was swiftly accepted as convention ... these bearded women simply became what they played because they drew no attention to anything other than that.'[78] Such acting conventions were easily accepted.

While the Toronto production reinforced the necessity of clear projection, maintaining a speedy pace, and the like, the genuine lessons to be learned about the acting style seem to be sparse. This is perhaps because the pageants were prepared by an international spread of producers and, despite the organisers' bulletins, it was difficult to control the productions at such a distance. The problems of co-ordinating a series of pageants that are produced and presented by different groups was one known during medieval times, and perhaps explains why such a number of edicts are documented.[79] Records from medieval England show that the authorities were concerned with controlling, amongst other things, the arrival time of the actors, their line-learning, costume, and the number of pageants they performed in.[80]

It has been left to smaller-scale modern reconstructions to provide an insight into both the acting style that might have been deployed in medieval times and that which can be used by modern actors to successfully play medieval texts. Meg Twycross's 1977 pageant version of the York *Resurrection* at Lancaster University demonstrated the framing effect of the waggons,[81] while her earlier experiments with medieval texts at Oxford were noted by John Elliott for their use of stylised gestures which he saw to be akin to Noh or Kabuki theatre.[82] Meanwhile practical work by Phillip Butterworth on the York *Crucifixion* in 1992 has shown the importance of direct forms of address to the audience when performing medieval texts.[83]

The audience's reception of the Toronto experiment revealed other issues relating to the dynamics of pageant staging. Of course, it is impossible for any reconstruction of medieval audience's experiences to take place,[84] but the reactions of the modern-day spectator do raise aspects worth considering. Bob Potter reflected on the way that the children experienced the plays by 'following the stories raptly one moment, and asking blunt cosmic questions the next, issuing inappropriate demands, yawning in the inevitable dull moments ... frightened by devils then laughing at them, learning to mimic and harass them back.'[85] Potter's focus on the reactions of child spectators highlights the multiplicity of the spectators and the lack of homogeneity of their response; a fact which presumably was just as true in medieval times.

Megan Lloyd's eyewitness account of the Toronto plays is mindful of another aspect of audience reception. In medieval times the guild members who performed in the plays would have been known to many of the spectators. This was also true for some of the audience at Toronto. Lloyd records that the experience of seeing familiar faces on stage at once brought her into the action on stage and separated her further from the drama as she focused on the players rather than their roles.[86]

Much of the experience of the audience at reconstructions of pageant dramas is formed by the spatial relationship between the waggons and the spectators. Since neither the audience nor the stages are static, these dramas form a very particular actor/audience dynamic. This dynamic is achieved by the informality of outdoor playing; the ebb and flow of the pageants as they process through the town, and the audience as they move from stalls to stations. Megan Lloyd noted that at Toronto the intermingling of the actors and audience (as they processed from station to station and when the actors used the ground level as a playing space) broke down the barrier between reality and fiction, and often caused the audience to become part of the play.[87] She observed that while the York plays started as a collective experience, they soon became an individual one;[88] although members of the audience began by watching the same pageant and sharing the stories of the Passion of Christ, in the end the individuality of personal response to issues such as religious belief and the Crucifixion became stronger than any group reaction. In raising these issues the notion of the expression of community in reconstructions of the plays is highlighted. As the producer Jane Oakshott noted, 'Processional staging by its nature is more broadly based in the community at large.'[89] While it might be argued by such commentators as Benedict Anderson, whose views were cited in Chapter 2, that community itself is absent, or imagined in our experience of contemporary living, the notion of 'community' still seems to be evident amongst both participants and spectators of medieval drama. For example, a participant in the Toronto 1998 production documented that in her participation for Hillsdale College she was 'carrying on both a family and a college tradition.'[90] It was the third time a member of her family had appeared at Toronto.

York 1998 and 2002

Peter Meredith's extensive spectatorship of modern stagings of mystery plays has led him to have an acute awareness of the importance of community in the plays. He has suggested that the future of reconstructions lies with smaller community productions and not large events like Toronto, events where there is 'a sense of growing out of the local situation rather than being imposed upon it.'[91] He reported that, despite the success of the Toronto project, it did not provide a sense of community, but rather one of multifariousness. Instead he pointed to the success of another production of the York pageants that occurred in 1998: a playing of eleven pageants around the streets of York. It was here that he found evidence of 'a community in action.'[92]

The 1998 York pageants were presented as part of the York Early Music Festival, and were the brainchild of Jane Oakshott, the producer of the 1977 York plays at Leeds. Her dream over those twenty years was to produce a version of the pageants that were played, or at least sponsored, by some of the remaining York guilds. Where possible, guilds took plays for which they originally had responsibility. In other instances more modern guilds, like that of the builders, took plays that enabled them to utilise construction skills. So the York Guild of Builders took *The Creation of the World to the Fifth Day*, and built a waggon with speaking tubes for God and various levers that portrayed creation as a type of child's pop-up book. The Merchant Adventurers, the oldest surviving guild in York (in fact the renamed Mercer's Guild), sponsored a glorious production of the Doomsday play, complete with trumpeter and angels in ornate wigs, from the Settlement Players, a highly regarded amateur group in York. Richard Rastall noted of the production that, 'In effect, this was not so far away from the kind of involvement found in the sixteenth century, and all the guilds concerned found that they had, and were proud of, a sense of ownership of their plays and the preparation and performance of them.'[93] The exercise owed nothing to a historically accurate notion of the guilds or the plays, since the lineage of both is flawed, but instead demonstrated how a notion of heritage was popular amongst the participants.

The 1998 pageant plays in fact built on a tradition of performing a pageant on a waggon in the streets. In 1954, to accompany Browne's Museum Garden production, Stewart Lack produced a single pageant on York streets. This tradition continued for many years with students from Bishop Holgate School performing. Other waggon stagings have occurred at York, such as the previously mentioned 1988 and 1992 university plays, and in 1994 Oakshott had directed community groups in nine pageants which played at five stations in the city. The 1998 project was on a larger scale than previous productions: it became, in Oakshott's words, a 'deeply-rooted community event.'[94] This statement is validated by the fact that at a subsequent York Early Music Festival the guilds were able to produce and support their own plays: 2002 saw a reprieve of the event on a more substantial scale, and the performance continues to be played every four years, with another in the summer of 2006 (see Plate 4).

It is worth reflecting that the reason why the 1998 pageants at York were deemed to be such a success is that, unlike many of the other reconstructions, they were not staged as part of an academic experiment. Instead these plays became about issues that were still living: the city of York, its guilds, its people. As one of the members of the Guild of Butchers remarked: 'To be able to participate in the live production within the City streets was quite an extraordinary personal experience. Everybody involved wants to do it again.'[95]

In 2002 the participants were given a chance to do it again. This time the guilds took full responsibility for their pageants, and the event expanded to two weekends. Director Mike Tyler reflected that the eventual pageant route marked 'a series of compromises between safety and aesthetics.'[96] The route included mainly pedestrian areas, and somewhat ironically the last station was close to St Mary's Abbey – the site of E. Martin Browne's 1951 production. Tyler notes that the choice of locations affected the design and playing of some of the pageants. Side-on staging was chosen to aid ease of manœuvrability of the waggons.

Margaret Rogerson's review of the 2002 production highlights the issue of spectatorship of pageant drama:

> In the stands in the Museum Gardens I found myself conscious of a temptation to view the plays as if they were an outdoor version of the proscenium arch production. At large around the town, I was troubled by the various discomforts of standing or sitting on the ground or on the steps of the Minster. Perhaps in suffering discomfort, and in not always seeing a

> particular play in its entirety or not always seeing the plays in their proper order, I was moving more towards the experience of a medieval audience that did not have our cultural expectation of 'theatre'.[97]

These remarks are a useful reminder that the viewing conditions, and thus the relationship between the spectator and performer in pageant staging, are far removed from the cultural expectations of modern-day spectatorship.

The productions that I have examined provide valuable insights into the success of pageant waggon staging. They have shown the importance of creating a whole context in which to present the occasion, of the site, of the community, and of maintaining a fluid relationship between the actors and audience. Modern reconstructions have shown us the shortcomings of such academic exercises – we cannot reproduce a medieval audience, or acting style. They have also highlighted the sheer irrelevancy of some of the academic speculations that have taken place, such as the direction of the waggons – but perhaps more than anything they have stressed the importance of the procession. Unexpectedly, all the reconstructions have shown that moving large waggons through small spaces, stopping them, playing the play and moving them is extremely easy. The procession is central to the audience's involvement. Julia Smith, writing about the 1998 York plays, noted that 'Talking with people gathered in the street convinced me of the success of the processional method of performance. Being so close to the actors the crowd becomes almost a part of the action.'[98] Finally, as Meg Twycross observes, one of the main features of cycle drama is the processional quality, 'a sense of marvel following upon marvel.'[99]

CHAPTER 4

From Outside to Inside: Fifty Years of the Plays at York

Anthony Dawson, writing about the nature of play-going in Shakespearean England, noted that the audience's role in creating the theatre event develops both a sense of social collectivity and one of individuality.[1] For a moment 'a (temporary) collective is constructed out of an array of separate persons'.[2] The dramatic intent of the piece, and the audience's response to it, creates an event which either reinforces cultural and social practices or challenges them. Dawson argues that the act of viewing directs the audience's gaze back upon themselves. In interpreting an event the audience not only views the play, but also reveals its own preoccupations. If this is the case, then the contract between the spectator and the theatre event reveals as much about the nature of the audience as it does about the play. The act, the spectator and the producing society are irrevocably intertwined.

It is important to think about the demands that the medieval audience brought to performances. There is, of course, a methodological problem here. As has been explored in Chapter 1, there are few eyewitness records of medieval drama, and fewer still that pertain specifically to the mystery plays.[3] One methodology that could be usefully employed to gain insight into the performance of the mystery plays would be to look at records pertaining to other forms of medieval performance. It is difficult, however, to read such medieval records with any sense of confidence about their meaning. For example, Sheila Lindenbaum demonstrated that the Venetian ambassador's eyewitness account of the 1521 London Midsummer Watch interpreted the event as unifying the community, but the Drapers' records show the spectacle was to honour the Mayor and Sheriffs; a celebration of oligarchy.[4] This draws attention to the fact that each member of the audience interprets a performance differently. It is difficult to speak of the reception of meaning as a homogeneous response.

Records from outside Britain offer further evidence concerning audience behaviour, but provide little detail. For example, the evidence of French dramatic records pertains mainly to requests that the audience be silent, avoid displays of rowdy behaviour, and not climb upon the stage. While this provides little insight into the detail of audience response, it does show something of the physical and vocal proximity of the actors and audience. Another source, the *Cambridge Prologue*, an early fourteenth-century fragment of unknown provenance, reveals, through a character's direct address to the audience, something of the nature of the behaviour expected of the audience:

> Now sit still and all pay attention, to make sure that nothing unpleasant happens to you here! Sit well apart from each other, so that folk can pass between you. You who are gathered together in this crowd, don't talk too loudly – it would also bring great disgrace on you to impede our entertainment. Moreover, I swear by this day and by the law of Mohammed that if anyone is so bold as not to keep the peace the emperor commands his men to seize and hang him, unless it be a child or a lunatic – and he has ordered that even he shall be tied up and soundly thrashed ... Now sit still, that is my advice![5]

This quotation discloses the contract that existed between the actor and audience in this form of drama. There was clearly interplay of voices, action and space. The audience are required to leave enough space for people to pass through meaning either actors or other audience members were bustling around. Clearly, audience members felt that they wanted to interject comments or talk with their neighbours. The contract between performer and spectator was a dynamic one, despite the audience being seated.

This chapter examines how the changing performance location of a play cycle can alter the relationship between the audience and the act. The York cycle will be used as a case study. Reinstated by E. Martin Browne as part of the 1951 Festival of Britain, the plays were initially enacted against the backdrop of the ruins of St Mary's Abbey, in what are now the gardens of the Yorkshire Museum, a central city location between the River Ouse and the Minster. The plays were performed every three or four years between 1951 and 1988. In 1992 the plays moved indoors to the auditorium of the nearby Theatre Royal, the city's main theatre. Then in 2000, to commemorate the Millennium, the plays were produced in the Minster. This chapter focuses on how the changing spatial location of the plays has affected the production of the mysteries. It is not the intention to provide a history of the development of the plays in the city, but rather to examine how the changing performance site has reconfigured the value of the plays.

Outdoor performance 1951–88

E. Martin Browne's 1951 production created a sensational response. It marked the Lord Chamberlain's loosening of the ban on the representation of God and Christ on stage; an event which made way for future productions of medieval drama. The choice of site for the first plays was determined by the necessity of appeasing the Archbishop of York. As Elliott points out: 'The choice of the Abbey setting was originally made, back in 1951, for religious rather than theatrical reasons—

because the then Archbishop of York insisted that the plays be performed on sacred ground as a condition to giving his permission for the revival.'[6] In other words, the selection of a performance site was never made with the notion of theatrical effectiveness in mind. Instead the plays were associated with the sacred, and the ruins notionally provided an opportunity for the establishment of this connection. (In actuality the grounds of the ruins were no longer sacred, but still provided that identification in the minds of the producers.) Margaret Rogerson's research into the revivals of the mystery plays at York has focused on the way in which community and heritage values are augmented by the production of the plays. She noted that, even though the original plays were performed in the streets, 'The sacred location affords a revival performance an additional spiritual dimension which could impact on all members of the audience, no matter what their personal standing with regard to Christian heritage.'[7] The performance of the plays within a sacred site increased their value as sacred objects, but, as Rogerson pointed out, this decision did not limit the plays' effectiveness, as this spirituality is open to a wide audience.

The choice of a central site was essential for the city; from here the production could reflect the importance of the metropolitan centre. The production celebrated the importance of York, its institutions and its people. As John Marshall reflected, the production showed faithfulness to medieval drama, in that it 'fulfils one of its original purposes in bringing together a community of participants and spectators in celebration of both God and City.'[8] York has found part of its modern identity through the presentation of these plays, and has profited from this – the plays have proved to be a huge tourist attraction.

Browne, an experienced producer of religious drama in cathedrals, took on the epic site of St Mary's Abbey. His set designer, Nora Lambourne, reflected the pictorial evidence of medieval staging from Valenciennes in her designs, which created a series of frame-like stages from the upper levels of the remaining architecture of the 150-foot-long ruined north wall.[9] This wall, Browne declared, 'has its own power to stir the imagination, and to produce the Mystery Plays before it would be to add like to like.'[10] The upper level of the clerestory hosted God within the central arch; the lower mansions housed Pilate and internal scenes such as the stable, and the High Priests. This highly pictorial approach meant that the composition of large crowd scenes was a significant feature of the production. A long-time participant in the plays, Ossie Heppell, recalled that the use of the mass of actors resembled a Cecil B. DeMille production.[11] The production of the plays also exploited the environment of the ruined abbey. An eyewitness report of the 1951 event noted that, 'In the gaping stone frames of the clerestory windows we are shown a glimpse of Heaven where God the Father sits.'[12] Other moments used the natural fall of light to mark a moment of metaphorical significance. During the darkness of *The Last Judgement*, 'There was silence, a peculiar stillness that could be felt.'[13]

Browne's production fulfilled the specifications of the York Festival Society. In their report they note plans for the 1954 festival:

> There will be nothing in this York Festival which does not have its proper place and justification. The buildings will not be adapted for the event, the event will adapt itself to buildings and grow in greater strength from that marriage of the site with the artistic creation.[14]

It is clear that the priority for the producing body lay with the glorification of the city, not the plays. The plays were used to celebrate the splendour of York.

The triumph of Browne's production was repeated in 1954. But after the production in 1957 it was felt that Browne's devices were becoming tired, and a new director was sought. The Festival Committee procured the eminent director Tyrone Guthrie for the role. However, he later resigned because of his dislike of the abbey setting for the production. Guthrie's gesture was significant, because the issue of the place of performance is one that has come to dog the plays. While the producing committee and citizens of York revelled in the site, it often repelled producers and critics. For example, Joan Littlewood was invited to direct the plays in 1976, but agreed to do so only if she could abandon the abbey, and instead present the mystery plays on waggons on the street.[15]

The debate over the setting of the plays continued with subsequent productions. For example, Kenneth Cameron blamed the setting of the 1966 production for the 'dullness' which he found:

> At the root of the trouble, I suppose, is the presentation of the York plays in a simultaneous setting for which they were evidently not intended, resulting in such oddities as structures built in false perspective, as if for a proscenium theatre, and the use of the ruins of St Mary's Abbey as a background – an art object in its own right, but not, as it were, in the cycle's right.[16]

The disparity between the needs of the cycle staging and the iconographic status of the abbey ruins were clear to others.

In 1973 John Elliott launched an attack on the values that had become attached to the York plays, 'slow-paced, reverent, dignified and stylishly archaic.'[17] Elliott's review of Edward Taylor's production that year noted that the production had drawn on the influence of Oberammergau, Pre-Raphaelitism and twentieth-century church drama. Although Elliott criticised the manner in which the plays had been fitted to modern ideas of dramatic religious drama, and the lack of dramatic reality of the event, it was the use of the site that he objected to most vigorously. Elliott added that: 'The very choice of the Abbey ruins as a backdrop places the plays in a historical perspective quite foreign to the spirit in which they were originally presented.'[18]

Each subsequent director tried to design a concept that would enhance the staging of the plays. Jane Howell, the first woman to direct the cycle, used two pageant waggons in her 1976 production. These were rolled onto the epic stage and used for the playing of interior scenes. Howell added other touches to create a sense of a 'street' on the set of the abbey, such as using live animals. However, the concept was poorly received by the local audience, who felt that the spirituality of Browne's production had been lost, and that the production pandered to tourist taste.[19] It was an opinion shared by the *Guardian* newspaper reviewer: 'The York Festival is in need of some radical rethinking if it hopes to restore these plays to something of their original life, purposes and meaning.'[20]

Patrick Garland's 1980 production with Christopher Timothy as Christ attempted to bridge the distance between the spectator and the act. The chorus was used in scenes to represent the audience's experience. At times the spectators were encouraged to join in by singing.[21] The playing of the Ascension fully capitalised on the outdoor setting. Timothy was slowly raised into the sky on a CO_2 hoist, with his face spotlit against the darkness.

In 1984 Toby Robertson directed the plays as a 'large-scale, modern, outdoor theatrical event.'[22] Robertson used the scale of the backdrop to magnify the epic nature of the themes of the drama. God was placed on a 40-foot high platform, hell was in a pit 6 feet deep, a hydraulic lift connected the various hierarchies. The set design included tubular steel frames, and the Cross itself was metal. John Elliott remained unimpressed, and noted that, 'Much seems so ingrained in York's attitude towards its plays that even talented directors prove unable to extricate them from it.'[23] Elliott believed that the production lacked any real spirituality, and instead drew on hackneyed ideas.

Stephen Pimlott's 1988 production controversially used an Indian actor to play Christ, Victor Banerjee, who played Aziz in the film *A Passage to India*. A boy actor represented God. Pimlott's production was praised for the inventiveness that a boy God brought to the interpretation. Pimlott also used medieval staging devices to enhance his production. Simultaneous action was played so that one scene could reflect or comment on another. For example, David Mills noted that the Last Supper played at ground level and was counterpointed by the Priest's banquet above.[24] The market scene, in an attempt to draw the audience closer, was played out in the *platea*, amongst the spectators. But the success of these devices did little to prove the overall merits of the York plays. As David Mills points out, the production had a number of obstacles: a playing time of three and a half hours; a huge community cast; the necessity of bringing in a star actor to play Christ; and 'the vast space of the set in the Abbey ruins, with its fixed row of tiered seating.'[25]

Sarah Beckwith has investigated the way in which ruins are associated with notions of memory and heritage. She examined how the plays at York were placed within a nostalgia for the past, and saw the community performances as an attempt to revive the city's identity. She postulates: 'The insistence on the ruins as a backdrop is a longing for and an isolation from a past that is petrified in the ruins.'[26] However, this desire for, and separation from, the historical past is only one function that the site has served.

The ruins of the abbey as an environmental space have affected the style and presentation of the mystery plays. David Wiles's study of performance spaces discusses the importance of 'sacred spaces.' Wiles used the ideas of Henri Lefebvre to argue that the representation of the sacred is tied to the question of power.[27] Indeed, at York the sacred site of the abbey has held a special power over the mystery plays. It has allowed a society to develop a sense of Dawson's social collectivity through the celebration of the plays, and produced a powerful sense of local identity for those involved with the plays. As Alderman Keith Wood commented, 'Perhaps it's in our blood, I don't know, maybe that's one key to it.'[28] The city of York has also developed a power through its international reputation for producing the plays; spectators from throughout the world have visited the plays. But the power of the site has also been limiting. Though the Festival Board demonstrated an ongoing commitment to the site, it has been a hurdle and deterrent for many professional directors.

The site of the ruins dominated the production values of the mystery plays at York. The features of the site led to productions that were staged on an epic scale, with large scenery and massive community casts. This type of staging of the plays required each director to bring a new concept to the event in order to achieve a sense of originality or freshness. But the spatial relationship between the audience and the event was one built not upon intimacy or communication, but on awe and nostalgic sympathy.

The move inside: York Theatre Royal 1992–6

It is difficult to ascertain exactly why after over thirty-five years of outdoor playing the mystery plays moved inside, but a combination of factors was at work. By the late 1980s the finances of the York Festival were less stable, and the plays were one of its largest expenditures. In 1984 the Festival had a surplus of £40,000, but by 1988 they had lost £80,000.[29] Further financial concerns were highlighted by the failure of the Festival to submit its accounts to Companies House in 1991/2.

Preparations for the 1992 York plays also met with problems during the early stages. The first director Kevin West suffered from ill health and had to withdraw.

Increases in health and safety regulations meant that the price of hiring a fixed seating bank for the audience was an astonishing £100,000. The appointed director for 1992, Margaret Sheehy, a director with experience of staging large outdoor community events, laid out plans for a promenade production which would play for six hours over two separate evenings. A text from Scottish poet/playwright Liz Lochhead was commissioned for the occasion. But by November 1991 Sheehy's production had attracted little sponsorship, few bookings and the concept did not satisfy the Festival Board. Six months before the plays were due to open, after recording a vote of no confidence, Sheehy was sacked as director. The *Independent* newspaper reported that her 'grandiose plans became hopelessly at odds with the meagre financial resources'.[30] Ironically Sheehy's concept for the production would have returned the plays to a medieval-style use of space. The promenade performance echoed the actor/audience arrangement of the original plays.

The York Theatre Royal stepped in to bail out the Festival, so in 1992 under the direction of Ian Forrest, with Liz Lochhead's text, the community plays were taken inside. Many of the same criteria applied to the production: a community cast of over 100 people, and performed with a professional actor, Robson Green (best known at that time for playing a hospital porter in the TV series *Casualty*), playing Christ. The concept of Forrest's production centred around a building site; a choice which echoed the maintenance work being done to the theatre itself. In a device reminiscent of Bill Bryden's version for the Royal National Theatre, the production placed God on a hydraulic construction lift. The 1992 production asked how Jesus would fit into today's world; in answer to that he wore denim. The director made full use of the indoor location which benefited from permanent technical theatre equipment. For example, an electronic musical score was commissioned which accompanied the final piece. Other benefits from indoor playing were seen by critics to be the control over visual effects and imagery. The *Guardian* reviewer praised devices such as:

> Noah's ark as a flying gantry swaying above a waving Flood; the Victorian Christmas card street scenes that surround the Nativity; the paramilitary violence of the Slaughter of the Innocents; the stag night feel to the Last Supper; and the stunning stage pictures of the Harrowing of Hell and the Last Judgement. Superb.[31]

But many reviewers did not find that the plays were as successful as the outdoor productions, and there were reports that the Festival Board felt that they did not work inside.[32] The performance, despite vigorous last minute pruning, lasted five hours and proved to be a marathon for actors and audience alike.

Victor Lewis-Smith accurately identified the problems of indoor playing. The plays, once placed behind a proscenium arch, attracted 'a new and more critical aesthetic', contributing to the 'feel of a school play that has mistakenly ended up in the West End'.[33] For Lewis-Smith the problem lay with the fact that the mystery plays are pageants which are attached to the city. He argued that they could not be performed without the backdrop of the city, or more specifically the abbey.

Despite reservations, the plays were performed again inside in the Theatre Royal in 1996. This time under the direction of John Doyle the plays received further adverse attention by the casting of God as a woman. The Archdeacon of York, George Austin, felt this to be inappropriate and decreed that this was 'political correctness gone mad'.[34] One again the benefits of playing indoors were exploited. Doyle's use of medieval and Renaissance iconography provided a rich, visual framework for the production. Liz Lochhead's text had been reworked to reduce the playing time, but maintained both a sense of accessibility and a rich use of rhyme and alliteration.[35]

Given adequate preparation time for the performances, this indoor production quietened some of the previous critics and showed that the plays could still work without the abbey backdrop. However, the dominant aesthetic of an indoor theatre performance was often at odds with the festive nature of the plays. As Charles Spencer noted, the move indoors turned the plays into 'just another show', when they should be 'in a great public arena'.[36] But Sarah Paul argued that the relationship with the audience was not as simple as that of a traditional proscenium arch theatre. The use of nearly 200 local people 'achieves as rare communion for the audience between "spectating" and identifying with the performers'.[37] The use of community players cut through the fourth wall and allowed the audience a more complex relationship with the event.

The indoor playing of the mystery plays changed the relationship between the event and the spectator. The indoor playing offered the chance to develop some aspects of the play production, for example the use digital sound and music. The visual language was more controllable and thus spectacle could develop further. However, the inside playing opened up the acting techniques to closer scrutiny. In effect the proscenium arch of the Theatre Royal replaced the artefact of the ruins that dominated the outdoor playing of the York Mystery plays. One set of problems had been replaced by another. Most importantly, the sense of the plays being an event different from any other piece of theatre had been lost. Many of the participants from the earlier Museum plays were also alienated: 'I've got to confess that since the decision was taken not to perform them in the open air, I went to the first production in the theatre, and said, it wasn't for me, never again, and I don't believe the mystery plays should be ... are effective, as good indoors'.[38]

The Minster mysteries 2000

The beginning of the New Millennium provided the opportunity for the York cycle to rediscover itself. In order to celebrate this event the plays were performed in the Minster. There was a sense (though historically misplaced) that 'The mystery plays have come home at last.'[39] The Festival Board secured the prestigious Royal Shakespeare Company associate director Greg Doran for the event.

Doran's preparation, beginning some two years before the project reached completion, centred around his visits to the Minster: 'In order to present the Mystery Plays in this great building, we would have to respond to both its history and its ongoing development as a place of worship.'[40] But, as critics were to note, it was also 'a space that could overwhelm a theatre performance'.[41] With designer Robert Jones, Doran conceived a production that constructed a giant stage in the nave, with costumes based on the colours found in the stained glass windows. Joshua Abrams noted that:

> Through explicitly drawing on images from within York Minster, the production team was able to take advantage of the sacred nature of this theatrical space, in effect resacralizing the production and the space – achieving an effect possibly similar to that achieved in a medieval production where Corpus Christi attempted to renew the religious bonds of the citizens.[42]

The use of the Minster space provided the opportunity to revitalise the religious function of the plays. The epic scale of the building provided inspiration for the creation of a Cecil B. DeMille-style four-tiered series of stairs and terraces, some 26 metres long, 16 metres wide and rising to 5 metres at the back.[43] The back row of the 1,000 audience seats rose to 8 metres, and was an astonishing 65 metres from the rear of the stage.[44] Margaret Rogerson pointed out that the stage design meant that even at the highest tier the spectators were on a level with one of the acting stages.[45] She argued that this increased a sense of intimacy, but my personal viewing of the performance from this point indicated that the distance was too great to offer any such sense of intimacy.

Doran's production was at its most successful when it married visual spectacle on stage with the pictorial and atmospheric boldness of the Minster. Smoke and a trumpet fanfare accompanied God's triumphant entrance, his back-lit body literally glowing in a white robe. The Creation swamped the stage with the majority of the 200 cast in robes of turquoise, yellow and blue carrying puppets on sticks; Eve's hair was so long it fell to the ground, Satan had a 4-metre tail; a troupe of animals ingeniously made from umbrellas passed onto the ark; during the flood metre after metre of blue silk rapidly filled the entire stage, only the miniature gothic ark remained above the water (see Plate 5).

The fluidity of Doran's choreography of the crowd – so sought after in the rehearsal room – meant that the epic stage could be swiftly filled and emptied. Each pageant seamlessly flowed into the next, with detailed attention to the composition of the stage continuously reflecting the work of the German painter Matthias Grünewald. (Books of his pictures lined the rehearsal rooms.) Scenes such as the Crucifixion showed the influence of Grünewald's compositions (see Plate 6). The attention to the relationship between the chorus and the central characters was evident on stage. Focal action was enhanced by having the crowd relate to significant moments; when Eden was created the whole stage breathed collectively; when Eve sinned, they all sighed. As Doran admitted in an interview with the *York Student Vision* journal: 'In the Minster there's no point in doing a lot of fussy psychological detail ... it's about making sure that the audience can focus on the right bit at the right time.'[46]

But the limitations of the stage arena became more apparent in the New Testament stories. The production easily produced a sense of authority (which as Paul Taylor noted was emphasised by the use of bass and choral music),[47] but found ritual and humour more difficult. The text was well shaped through the concentration in rehearsal on issues like cadence, onomatopoeic language, and the rhythm of punctuation. But on the vast stage action, as opposed to spectacle or speech, seemed to find little place. As Robert Hewson pointed out in his review for the *Sunday Times*, 'The sheer size of the production sometimes robs it of the kind of intimacy achieved by Bill Bryden and others.'[48] Paul Taylor noted that 'The humanising tension between the cosmic creation-to-Last-Judgement subject matter of the plays and their frequently humorous homely tones loses some of its force when the proceedings are transferred to such a monumental setting.'[49]

Deprived of the intimacy, and thus much of the emotional involvement which the mystery plays can evoke, the weaknesses of the production were apparent. This is not a criticism of Doran's production, but rather an acknowledgement that the contract that was set up between the spectator and the act was a rather strange one. Our contract existed primarily with the building. Indeed in an interview the Dean of York stated that: 'We consider this to be the most appropriate way for the Minster to be marking the millennium.'[50] And, as Margaret Rogerson has pointed out, 'For the audience, the stage became the Minster and the Minster became the stage.'[51] Perhaps this was expressed most clearly in the production when during the final moments – the ascension of Christ – the nave was lit in a glorious rainbow. The spectacle belonged to the building. The fixed-seat audience in the gigantic Minster was not offered a contract which allowed for an intimate relationship with the production, but rather one that bound them to the building. However, there were some rare moments when Dawson's notion of 'social collectivity' was present for the audience, for example, when the rainbow appeared in the nave, a collective 'Ooh!' was emitted by the audience, and in that moment they were joined in their response.

The relationship between the audience and the performance space is an important factor in the presentation of medieval drama. The York *Millennium Mysteries* were doubtless the result of much community activity. As well as involving more than 200 people on stage, the production involved hundreds of others through helping with production and design work and through the associated outreach programmes attached to the event. Over 28,000 people saw the plays.[52] The bringing together of the community and the building was emphasised in the production when Jesus was welcomed to the temple in the pageant of *Christ and the Doctors*. Here the text was changed so that the Doctor addressed Jesus with the sentiment, 'Welcome to this Minster.' The celebration of the glorious York Minster resounded through the audience. Here York became a substitute for Jerusalem. The meeting of dramatic celebration, local pride and the site of performance was complete.

Despite the prestige of the York mystery plays, there is something unsettling about their presentation. They have happily settled into part of the heritage industry; they attract a wealth of tourists and signal part of the cultural heritage industry of York. But they never really seem to have found their own space. The performances in front of St Mary's Abbey signalled one set of values, but provided an epic and unmanageable space for the plays. The indoor location of the theatre aided the development of spectacle, but brought the audience no closer to the event; even the glory of the Minster provided a wonderful backdrop, but it failed to allow for the development of any sustained 'social collectivity.' And it is perhaps telling that the plays seem to have no home for the future. At present there are no plans to revive the plays on a large scale again until 2010. The future of the York plays seems to lie instead with the guild pageant versions, outlined in the previous chapter, that are played on the streets of York every four years. Having played in the abbey grounds, the Theatre Royal and the Minster, it is on the streets that the future of the plays seems more secure.

CHAPTER 5

Spatial Practices: Chester, Lincoln and Lichfield

Henri Lefebvre's ground-breaking analysis of how space is used by society provides an interesting framework through which to analyse how modern productions of the mystery plays articulate a relationship with space. Lefebvre postulates that three main spatial models are used in society. These are 'representations of space' (organised and designed controls of space, such as those undertaken by architects and engineers), 'representational space' (the symbolic use of space – this is the spatial function that theatre embraces) and 'spatial practice' (how society forms a relation with space – this is a dialectical space which, for example, iterates a relationship between private space and working places).[1] This chapter examines how modern restagings of the mystery plays have highlighted variations in the spatial relationship between drama and its audience. It begins by assessing the changing spatial articulation of the Chester plays, before considering those of Lichfield and Lincoln. These productions offer an insight into the spatial practices involved in staging medieval drama today.

Chester

Like the York plays, the modern-day performances at Chester are built on a strong tradition of play production which stretches back to the Festival of Britain in 1951, and in the case of Chester and beyond.[2] At York the plays were presented against the spectacular backdrop of the Museum Gardens, while Chester opted for a simple setting of the thirteenth-century refectory hall sited in the cathedral. Perhaps the simplicity of the presentation accounts for the relative obscurity of the Chester production. Although the 1951 production was visited by national media, the event did not receive the same profile as that of York. And even though Chester has produced a version of the cycle every five years, the plays have never established the glamour that is attached to York. This may be partly due to York's geographical location – it is situated on the mainline London to Edinburgh train route – partly to do with the greater success of York in establishing a profile in the tourist culture,[3] and partly because while York created a tradition of large-scale outdoor spectacular playing, productions at Chester moved their playing place. Despite the five-yearly staging of the Chester plays, the shifting location of the event has meant that the production has received a less clear profile.[4] However, the twenty-first century may bring about a change in the fortunes of

Chester, for while the future of the large-scale production at York is unclear, the survival of the Chester tradition seems more certain. The success of the Chester productions relies on the increasing secularisation of the plays, which is clearly reflected in the choice of their location. While the early productions happened within the refectory in the body of the cathedral, the later productions switched to the cathedral green, playing first in front of the west doors and more recently inside a big top in the centre of the green. The changes of location demonstrate society's developing relationship with the plays over the fifty years of their production; in Lefebvre's terms they show a switch from conceptualised space through creating representations of space, to one that is more dynamically fluid and entails developing spatial practice.

David Mills has outlined how the plans for the resurrection of the Chester plays began in 1949 (before those of York were known). Graham Webster, curator of Chester's Grosvenor Museum, suggested a processional production through the streets of Chester, with the specific aims of creating a 'National festival reflecting great credit to our city'.[5] Webster's ideas for such a staging were quashed at the Liverpool Festival of Britain planning committee's meeting, partly because using a professional producer meant ticket prices would need to cover this cost and an indoor performance ensured an easier way of charging entrance. Various spaces for the performance of the plays were considered by the town clerk, Mr G. Burkinshaw, such as the Abbey Green, but in the end the refectory was preferred.

The planning of the 1951 event continually emphasised the importance of the sacred function of the plays. The eventual appointment of Christopher Ede (the grandson of the Dean of Worcester) as producer and Reverend Joseph McCulloch as adapter of the text reaffirmed this position.[6] A further intervention which aligned the Chester plays with sacred purposes came through the Lord Chamberlain's Office. David Mills reports that the Theatres Act of 1843 forbade the representation of Christ on stage; however, plays written before 1700 were exempt from this act.[7] Though Ede argued the plays were written before 1700, there was a debate as to whether the modernised text by McCulloch was akin to a translation, in which case it would fall under the Theatres Act. The Lord Chamberlain's Office, however, concluded that if the Chester Diocese were content with the production then 'all necessity for intervention was removed'.[8] The control of the production was thus placed with the Bishop of Chester, with whom Ede had to discuss his plans. The plays were influenced by religious forces in other ways. The actual production of the Chester plays drew heavily on religious iconography. The fifteenth-century costumes were based on illuminated manuscripts; critics noted that, 'the small stage and quaint settings have a vivid charm of their own.'[9] (See Plate 7).

The plays were restaged in 1952 and 1957, again under Ede's direction, in the fixed indoor space of the cathedral refectory; records show that 5,500 people saw the performances of the former production.[10] Correspondence sent after the 1957 event reveal Christopher Ede's increasing despondency with the formulaic nature of the productions, declaring 'I feel we ought to face up to a new production, by which I mean a new setting.'[11] By this point Ede also faced criticism from the Bishop. A letter sent by Burkinshaw raises three points of concern that the Bishop wished communicated: that the Passion play was too short, Christ was too hirsute and needed more authority, and lastly, that more fun might be included in the production.[12] The need for change was realised in the 1962 production, when the plays transferred outside to the cathedral green.

The change of location was marked by the commissioning of a new text by John Lawlor and Rosemary Sisson, who aimed to make the dramatic pattern clearer.[13] The transfer of the production from the Church to the city or state was also symbolically marked by a royal visit from Queen Elizabeth II's sister, Princess Margaret. The plays involved a larger cast (some 200 people from Chester and the surrounding area: Warrington, Ellesmere Port, Runcorn and Birkenhead), and 12,000 people saw the production.[14] The transfer of the production to the green outside was significant in that it acknowledged the importance of the community and city values of the plays as well as their religious alliance. Such a view is noted in the comment made by J. M. Temple: 'the production ... does great credit to our civic and community authorities.'[15] Indeed, records show that there was much local support from businesses for the 1962 plays. One employee received travel costs from Cadbury's to support his participation in the plays.[16]

Photographs from the 1962 production show an emphasis on creating two-dimensional imagery: the set had painted brick flats and screens, and the ark rose as a flat piece of scenery in front of the stage. For the birth of Christ another painted flat was inserted into the frame of the main stage. The Last Supper included a painted table and cloth. This use of painted and flat settings, along with amateur costumes and the false beard for Christ, gave the production a sense of naivety. This was further reflected in the static and highly compositional use of players on stage.

But despite the local enthusiasm for this production, there were some concerns. Letters from the Town Clerk, Burkinshaw, to the producer, Ede, and the Dean reflect issues with the productions. Ede was told that: 'A body of opinion among those concerned with the last production seems to be that the time had come to make a fresh approach to the plays with a new producer.'[17] There was also discord concerning the open-air venue for the 1962 plays. Consequently, Burkinshaw approached the Dean to request that since there was a 'strong feeling that an indoor performance is very much more satisfactory', the cathedral nave and west steps be used for subsequent performances. Burkinshaw's request was clearly partially successful, since the 1967 production did take place in front of the west steps. Photographs show the strange disparity between the form of the stage and the architecture of the cathedral; a collision in Lefebvre's terms of the representations of space of the cathedral, with the representational spaces of the stage.

A community green

The 1972 production at Chester caused much controversy – but also marked the beginning of a new spatial device there: the tent or big top.[18] Director James Roose-Evans initially discussed having live animals around the perimeter of the tent to evoke a sense of circus, but the impracticalities of working with animals prevented this from happening. Instead Roose-Evans designed a large circular stage with a 30-foot pine tree representing a cosmic tree which Lucifer climbs down to indicate heaven above and earth at ground level. The production attempted to foreground the spirituality of the piece. Roose-Evans records that he was asked to deliberately break with the previous style of production.[19] As a response to this, his production aimed not just to tell the stories of the mystery plays, but also to engage with a sense of developing a community amongst the actors. In order to achieve this, he drew on avant-garde theatre practices of the time which emphasised the collective experience of theatre making. He used the ensemble to develop a chorus that magnified the central action. For example, Eve's biting of the apple was mirrored by all the other couples on stage, so that instead of being an individualised response it was represented as a global one. Within the production the chorus also frequently switched roles and played multiple characters, a device which Stanley Kahrl saw as inspired by production of the musical *Godspell*,[20] but probably owes more to the sway of Brechtian-influenced 1960s and 70s theatre companies. In undertaking this form of character representation, the production came close to the techniques used by medieval drama whereby each pageant had different actors playing each character. Other memorable moments for Kahrl included a Crucifixion that was represented symbolically through the pelting of Christ with mud, an ark constructed from packing boxes, and boy angels on bicycles. All these devices gave the sense of what Peter Brook called 'rough theatre', 'the theatre that's not theatre, the theatre on carts, wagons, on trestles', one that is 'close to the people'.[21] In this sense the production engendered a very romantic view of the mystery plays.

Roose-Evans's production had a very mixed reception. His radical interpretation, like that of Mitchell's Barbican production (discussed in chapter 7), raised the question of what happens when a performance is pushed to the extreme end of the reconstruction-to-reinterpretation axis. In his review of the production Kahrl concluded that: 'The medieval Chester cycle provided Mr. Roose-Evans not a text but a pretext for his own particular preconceptions of what a religious drama should be.'[22] Kahrl argued that the production should be seen as a modern interpretation of biblical material rather than a production of the cycle. However, the production's ability to engage with what Lefebvre described as 'spatial practice' should be seen as a clear success. Roose-Evans's production abandoned the previous representations of spaces that had affected the Chester mysteries; the influence of the Church, seen via the presence of the cathedral was eschewed, and instead a new dynamic spatial practice was discovered. The centre of this practice rested on the metaphor of the big top. The circus tent provided the 'dialectical interaction' that marked Lefebvre's reading of spatial practice.[23] The core of this dynamic relationship between space and inhabitants (both the audience and actors) was primarily achieved through the use of Christ's ministry. The impact of this was clearly effective. Roose-Evans supplemented the mystery play material with the Sermon on the Mount and the bequeathing of the Lord's Prayer in order show a clearer picture of Christ's teaching.[24] The use of this material, and the unusual curtain call where the cast exchanged the sign of the peace of God through either a kiss or handshake with the audience, was deeply affecting; Kahrl reported that the 'applause was sincere.'[25] The tent became a space where experience was shared, and through this spatial practice a new meaning was negotiated.

The production of the Chester plays in the late 1970s and early 1980s set a new tone, and one which returned to reflect the importance of representational space. David Mills noted that a 'dramatic and philosophical conservatism marked the work of Peter Dornford May.'[26] Dornford May, the Chester county Drama Advisor, directed the plays in 1977. The reliance on the use of representational space was inherent in the directing plan. In the programme notes from the Queen's Silver Jubilee production in 1977, Dornford May stressed the religious function that the original plays held, and noted that 'A revolving stage will represent the various pageants, properties will be ornate but everything will, I believe, be pervaded with a spirit of sincerity and belief.' From the late 1980s there was a shift in the tone of the Chester productions as the semi-professional performances became more community centred. Bob Cheeseman, a professional director teaching at Chester College, took over the direction and involved local groups to a far greater extent. Each pageant was given to a separate community group and played on the communal space of the cathedral green. Mills observed that Cheeseman's productions were 'at once a celebration of the community and a festival of different kinds of theatre manifested through the production.'[27] In fact the presentation of the plays drew more from an informal sense of street theatre than other genres of playing. Edward Burns, who wrote a new text for the event, noted that Cheeseman and his designer, Tony Lewery from the outdoor performance group, Welfare State International (WSI), wanted to utilise the large outdoor location and eliminate formal church or high art connotations by creating a sense of a festival.[28] In order to promote this, a figure called Gobbet on the Green, played by local actor and street entertainer David Alexander, was expanded from the original texts to link the individual pageants and to serve as a commentator on the action for the audience. This character symbolised the link between the audience and actors within the space.

The use of a designer experienced in working outdoors created a sense of a 'theatre of the fairground.'[29] Many of the props emphasised this festive aspect of the production. For example, artist Kate Barfield created large animals made of straw, welded metal and willow for the Nativity. The set, an L-shaped four-levelled scaffold made from rustic poles with a 40-foot open-tower at one end for God, was placed facing the green, with its back to the chancel and north transept. The green itself formed the bottom level of the playing arenas. The plays in effect turned their back on the cathedral; this use of the space offered a symbolic image for the production which prioritised the needs of the community over the sacred function of the dramas. However, the symbolic representation of the space placed the cathedral in the distance, but was careful to ensure that the cathedral was still present within the setting – it formed the backdrop to the plays, and the scaffold structure of the set reflected the skyline of the building. Edward Burns observed that: 'The neutral colouring of the set, sympathetic choice of materials and subtle echoing of architectural detail made the plays, and God's presence in particular, seem to emanate from the cathedral itself.'[30] But Burns remarked that paradoxically the building became central to some of the interpretations of the pageant scenes. For example, the ringing of the cathedral bells accompanied Christ's ascension and actually foregrounded the building at that moment. The relationship of the plays to space in Cheeseman's production was one which played fully with Lefebvre's systems, intertwining the triad of perceived, conceived and lived space that form the basis of the thesis of *The Production of Space*.[31]

Back to the cathedral

Edward Burns concluded his review of the 1987 production of the Chester Mystery plays by stating that the forthcoming 1992 production intended to build on the notion of the festive event established in 1987. In particular he saw the use of festive practices in the procession in which the audience paraded behind the crucifix to the town hall before returning to the green. He predicted that for the 1992 production, which marked the millennium anniversary of the Benedictine abbey on the site of the cathedral (though it was actually 900 years), both the inside of the cathedral and the city streets would be used: 'So Chester's cycle will go back into the city itself.'[32] In the event, the 1992 mysteries were 'community spectacle, involving many local participants [some 600], at its very best.'[33] Director Bob Cheeseman signalled his dedication to community performance in the programme. He wrote of the mystery plays: 'Whatever may have been their original conception, they became ... of the people, by the people and for the people.'[34] This notion was evident in the production. David Mills noted the enormous scale used in the design of this production, where a 20-foot-high scaffold enclosed an oval grass playing area from which raked audience seating arose. Mills contended that: 'Almost symbolically, we sat with our backs to the cathedral, which had provided a referential backdrop for the previous productions.'[35] The traces of the previous productions had been removed and for the 1992 production, the space reflected a change from the dominance of the cathedral to the rise of the city – the new backdrop against which the plays now performed.[36]

In order to fill the huge oval playing space Cheeseman used multiple actors to represent personas from the plays, so that a whole group of Rabbis replaced Herod's Doctor. Other choruses filled the stage: gangs of children playing games filled the space before the Crucifixion, and six women portrayed the speeches of the three Marys at the Cross. In a moment that pre-empted the Coventry Millennium plays, enormous stilt-walkers from the Wotan Stilt and Drama Company dressed in black, representing evil, appeared before *The Woman Taken in Adultery* and again at the start of Judas Plot. Herod was depicted through a carnivalesque mode as a giant. The configuration of the space also reflected a medieval place-and-scaffold staging, which is acknowledged by Mills's review of the event. Mills noted how the 'arena,' the oval grass playing area, was filled with various crowd scenes, for example, *The Entry into Jerusalem*, and the animals for Noah's ark. The scaffolding was used to highlight more contained and central scenes.[37] The production kept the successful procession of the audience behind the crucifix to the town hall, which had marked the 1987 version. As Beroud and Maguin pointed out, this device 'was in effect a way of effacing the partition between the stage and the outside world.'[38] This manipulation of the spatial formats was also effectively shown in the final festive dance, where actors and audience celebrated together on the green.

Despite the successful audience reception of the 1992 plays, the production was marred by poor weather. The Saturday afternoon performances were redirected into the cathedral, which ironically, given the history of the Chester plays, proved totally unsuitable; the remaining performances were endured outside, with diminished numbers. In 1997 director George Roman used a big circus tent to host the production and the weatherproofing device increased audience levels four-fold to 800 people.[39]

In 2002 the production was postponed so that more organisational time could be found: the resulting 2003 production repeated many of Cheeseman's earlier uses of space. The set, now played against the backdrop of the cathedral, was multi-levelled but also had a playing area on the grass in front of the scaffold, a type of *platea*, which was used for choral action (see Plates 8 and 9). The audience seating was roofed in order to avoid problems of wet weather. However, the formality of the ranks of audience seating forced a rigidity on the playing conditions and use of space. In effect an indoor theatre was created outside. Such a static relationship with the plays prioritised a representation of space dominated by a conceived notion rather than allowing that space to live – a concept that had been so important in the history of the modern staging of the plays at Chester.

Lincoln

The use of playing space has been one of the most interesting features of the Lincoln Mystery plays, revived by Keith Ramsay and directed by him with vigour since 1978. Ramsay's sustained relationship with the plays and Lincoln Cathedral enabled him to experiment with playing locations within the cathedral precinct.[40] Ramsay's claim that the N-Town plays belonged to Lincoln is somewhat dubious, since the plays were possibly associated with Bury St Edmunds and thought to have toured to parts of East Anglia. However, a sense of historical accuracy has not marred the ownership which Ramsay brought to bear on the Lincoln production. The N-Town cycle is a composite text in which some plays are believed to have been written for place-and-scaffold configuration: a series of platforms set around an open playing area. This method of presentation was used by Ramsay to great effect when he produced the plays in the cloisters in 1985. In actuality his staging fell somewhere between place-and-scaffold and transverse staging, with three platforms under the colonnades and one opposite these, in between a break in the tiers of audience benches. The sense of an enclosed place was completed by other audience members sitting on either side. As Alan Fletcher remarked, this staging configuration allowed for a keen exploration of the typology of the plays; thus the Forbidden Tree was sited in the *platea* before the audience arrived and was later used as the Cross for Christ's Crucifixion.[41] The platforms under the colonnades allowed for many of the Old Testament scenes to be expressed simultaneously through tableau, which Fletcher found 'a pleasing way of condensing a cycle that could not otherwise have been produced in the given time'.[42] Ramsay utilised the cloisters again in his 1993 production, this time in a classic traverse staging with two stages set up in opposition to each other, and two banks of audience sitting along the other two sides of the rectangle. Ramsay's innovation did not stop at the use of spatial configurations, for this production also included a female God.

The longevity of Ramsay's relationship with the plays enabled him to undertake various other spatial experiments. The first production in 1978 was played under the central tower, which Ramsay noted as being visually powerful, but 'The spoken word goes straight up the tower.'[43] In 1981 they were played against fixed platforming in front of the west front, which caused a series of problems: as Peter Happé reports, in order not to be dwarfed by the impressive cathedral front the staging incorporated many steps, which actors would continually ascend and descend;[44] and there were significant problems with audibility since the open playing provided few buildings in which to contain or reflect the sound (see Plate 10). Ramsay noted that the acting area was also too large, and 'especially lacked the intimacy so required of medieval drama.'[45] Another experiment with staging was undertaken in 1994, when Ramsay used the nave to host a traverse production. With spectators placed at either side of the nave, a huge *platea* was created of some 100 feet long; this allowed for the development of symbolic playing areas: Heaven in the east, under the rose window, and Hell in the west. Pamela Brown reports that Hell was comprised of a jungle-gym of pipes, scaffold and platforms, while Heaven was grander, a 10-foot-high platform of 25 feet across which supported God, the Angel Gabriel and eight angels.[46] In Lefebvre's terms this demonstrated a clear mix of representations of space and representational space; the nave demonstrated both of these functions simultaneously.

Ramsay's final production in the Millennium, with the aid of a £30,000 Millennium Commission grant, explored the use of multiple spaces by moving the action around the cathedral. The action started in the familiar location of the cloisters, then in candlelit procession the audience moved towards the nave for the climax of the Crucifixion. The acoustics of the inner cathedral proved less successful than the intimate cloisters.[47] For Ramsay this was an opportunity to explore the various spaces of the cathedral that had been previously used in a variety of productions; here he was able to manipulate the spaces so that differing features could be joined in one production (see Plates 11 and 12). However, despite the experimentation with the fluidity of the space, for Ramsay the one over-riding spatial symbol was the building itself: 'Take away the Cathedral and the production loses a major dimension.'[48]

The relationship between the plays and the space has remained an important feature of the Lincoln production even though the custody of the plays has been passed to a new director, Karen Crow (who had previously played Satan). In 2004 Crow played in the nave using what was in effect a proscenium staging, but resonances of the architecture of the cathedral were reflected in the production. The pageants selected were played against their natural order, thus the production began with the Baptism. Six actors took up the poses of the kings from the west front of Lincoln Cathedral and thus created a sense of the building writing the plays. The rood screen was fundamental in framing the action. The rest of the action chose to take its references from outside the building, with modern-day soldiers in Desert Rats and SAS uniforms, and rock music with Satan on the electric guitar. In these moments the spatial design of the production amalgamated the past and present to suggest an application of the mystery plays for the future.

Lichfield

The final model to be considered here is that of the Lichfield plays, which were initiated by community arts worker Glen Buglass. Buglass began planning the event in 1992 and realised the first production of the plays in 1994; since then they have been produced every three years. He conceived of the production as a way to bring together groups of people, be they friends, work colleagues, or social clubs, to participate in the plays. But as Robert Leach, director of the first event, noted, the expression of *communitas* felt within this production extended beyond the participants to include the May Day Bank Holiday audiences:

> This huge community project attempts to recreate the spirit and the conditions of the medieval Festival of Corpus Christi ... But the recreation is not merely antiquarian. It is calculated to provide spectacular entertainment to large numbers of Bank Holidaying people today.[49]

Leach created a textual compilation from fragments of the original medieval Lichfield plays. (These are actually referred to as the Shrewsbury Fragments and are copies of lines from a Nativity, a Resurrection and a *Peregrini.*) The plays which comprised the modern Lichfield version were taken from an eclectic mix: and included texts from Durham, Towneley, York, Chester and N-Town. Leach divided twenty-five pageants into three sections: the Old Testament, the Nativity and Christ's Passion. Each section was accompanied by a particular visual style so that the Old Testament plays took their inspiration from early medieval art; the Nativity from Brueghel; and the Passion from Renaissance art.[50] The three sections were also coded through utilising dominant colours: blue for the Old Testament, green for the Nativity, and red for the Passion. The idiom of the show was based on the influence of street entertainments such as *commedia dell'arte* and clowning. For example, Cain and Abel were played through a Punch and Judy style of slapstick with a hobby-horse and Punchinello-style costumes; a maypole dance ended the flood sequence; conjuring was used in the Exodus from Egypt and again in the Shepherds' play; and the Buffeting drew on clowning, knock-about traditions and children's games, such as Blind Man's Buff.

The budget for the 1994 production was £100,000, which came from private sponsors such as the Royal Mail (Jesus was played by a postman), with a matched donation by ABSA, Lichfield Council and Sainsbury Art Foundation (to help a specific pageant by Pentabus education theatre group). The event involved over 500 people.

The most enterprising aspect of the Lichfield plays is their relationship with the space. The 1994 production set up a promenade performance whereby the actors walked with their props between three playing stations. (Although the website for the 2000 production stated that this processing was the practice in the Middle Ages, it is not the case.)[51] In medieval pageant playing scenery and presumably often props and even actors may have been transported on the pageant waggon. At Lichfield the actors promenaded, carrying with them their props, which were often symbols or visual pictures of their characters' functions.

The three stages for the plays were carefully chosen to reflect various aspects of the city of Lichfield (see Plates 13–15). As Buglass explained: 'It has a magnificent Cathedral, a well-planned market, and between the two the linear park of trees, grass and open water – reflections of Man, God and Nature in the same place.'[52] The choice of the procession from Conduit Street Market to Stowe Field, and finally to the cathedral reflected the importance of commerce, recreation and religion in the currency of the plays. The use of this concept of procession affected not just the players, but also the audience. A commentator from the local paper noted how: 'The city centre was transformed into a moving community of actors, buskers and neighbours all mingling in a mass of colour.'[53]

The choice of locations was selected in 1994 by Robert Leach and Glen Buglass after many hours of walking around the city.[54] They were immediately certain that they wanted to use the cathedral and to represent the sense of mercantile life through the market. The original choice of location for rural life, or peasantry, was to be a field further away, but this was changed to Stowe Field to avoid the performers crossing a major road. The practicalities of such a processional performance technique were none the less substantial. An elaborate timed rehearsal on the Saturday before the performances on Sunday and Monday allowed Leach to devise a system of timing the promenading of the pageants. The eventual system set off the plays in batches of three in order to both avoid delays and backups.

The concept of the interplay of recreation, commerce and religion was interwoven into the interpretations of some of the pageants. The cathedral as a place of unity was used at the end of the performances for a final curtain call involving 300 performers in a torch-lit procession. Elements of 'folk traditions' found themselves reflected in the plays. Such aspects as the maypole dance that concluded the Flood or the oranges and lemons song at the Annunciation reflected games played in open spaces, such as village greens. The vocabulary of outdoor celebration iterated the importance of the site of Stowe Fields. It must be recognised, though, that the interpretation of the plays was somewhat romanticised. The use of rural games in the performance was incongruous with what was originally an urban text.

The tradition of playing the Lichfield plays was revisited in 1997 but suffered adverse weather, forcing the plays inside to the Guildhall on the second day. In 2000, under the direction of John Paul Cherrington, the final stage was moved inside the cathedral; subsequent versions in 2003 and 2006 have built on this relationship with the cathedral. Though this has offered weather protection and prestige, it is important that the plays continue to offer a dynamic spatial practice and do not succumb to complete indoor performance.

Playing spaces

This chapter has examined how different approaches to the playing of space in contemporary productions have articulated various relationships between the plays and the spectators. Invisible within the process of securing performance spaces are a series of negotiations with the authorities, either diocese or local councils. It is often difficult to determine exactly why certain sites are chosen as performance spaces – the rationale can be obscured by a number of details.

Writing about a performance of the Towneley plays at Toronto in 1985, Martin Stevens asserted that the experimental playing of the production in the round on fixed scaffolds is one that could be applied to any of the extant cycles in order to learn more about the plays.[55] It is true to say that the playing of these productions in a variety of spaces does place them under the scrutiny of a new lens. Stevens argued that although, 'Historical recreation is, in fact, a crucial issue in the performance of medieval plays', this is set against the dynamic that 'The play tells us that history is only meaningful when we bring it into the orbit of our own time and place.'[56] As evidence for this he used the manner in which the original plays seemingly brought characters dating from ancient biblical times such as Adam, Eve, Noah, even Jesus alive in fifteenth-century life. The productions that have been discussed at Chester, Lincoln and Lichfield have all used the interaction with space to bring the medieval plays into modern-day life. They have achieved this through a series of negotiations with space. Henri Lefebvre argued that producers of space have traditionally negotiated the representation of space, while users of the space have had to accept its pre-existing patterns.[57] In producing the mystery plays today, producers and audiences have demonstrated that spaces can be reconfigured in order to rearticulate the relationship between spaces and people and that the qualities of the plays provide a vehicle through which to achieve this.

SECTION III

Contemporary Concepts

SECTION III ~ Contemporary Concepts

The previous section focused on the appeal that the staging practices of the mystery plays hold for modern producers. The alternative spatial arrangements, and consequently the actor/audience relationships the pageants engender, are one reason for the popularity of the plays today. However, that aspect of the plays does not fully account for why professional directors are attracted to them.

During the years surrounding the New Millennium three major productions of the mystery plays were undertaken by professional companies: Bill Bryden's revival of his 1985 production at the Royal National Theatre in 1999; Katie Mitchell's version for the Royal Shakespeare Company in 1997, and the Coventry *Millennium Mysteries*, a co-production between the Belgrade Theatre and the Polish street-theatre company Teatr Biuro Podróżny. Though these productions were ostensibly undertaken for a variety of reasons, the real appeal of the mystery plays to these professional companies was the opportunity that they provided to become a vehicle for the directors' concepts and visions.

The role of the director grew in importance throughout the twentieth century, to the degree that Delgardo and Heritage, writing in 1996, were able to observe that in Britain an audience was as likely to go to the theatre to see a particular director's work as they were because of the appeal of the play or an actor.[1] This suggests that modern-day directors create a particular type of work and become known for that style. It is certainly the case that Bryden, Mitchell and Szkotak brought their distinctive directorial styles to bear upon their productions of the mystery plays. This section will examine what facets of the mystery plays these directors drew on in order to bring them to commercial audiences in Britain. It will ask how these directors sought to make them relevant for an audience today. It is noteworthy that none of these directors chose to stage the plays for religious reasons, and that they were often concerned with the limited appeal of such material for a modern audience. In fact, I suggest that in order to make these plays attractive to today's audiences the directors replaced medieval concerns with faith with their own directorial concepts.

This section details three contrasting approaches that have been taken by professional productions of the plays in the late twentieth century. The first of these, Tony Harrison and Bill Bryden's production for the Royal National Theatre in London, developed between 1977 and 1985 and restaged in 1999, replaced the Christianity of the plays with the idiom of a workers' community. As Sarah Beckwith observed, 'Bryden made the miner's light the central prop of his passion play.'[2] The production aligned medieval guild workers with modern-day trade unions, and particularly with a sense of community that was imagined, somewhat nostalgically, to be found amongst mine workers. As will be demonstrated later, Bryden invented a somewhat idealised version of community.

Katie Mitchell's production of *The Mysteries* was first performed for the Royal Shakespeare Company in Stratford-upon-Avon in 1997, and toured the following year to Plymouth in South West England and the Barbican in London. Mitchell and her dramaturge Edward Kemp began with an interest in Pre-Reformation culture and a notion of wanting to strip the plays back to their original source material. In doing this, the production tried to focus on creating a genuine intimacy between the actors and the audience. Mitchell's production projected her interest in acting onto the plays to create a series of intense relationships between the characters on stage. As a result, a broader sense of religion was replaced with a notion of personal altruism. Beckwith noted, however, that Mitchell's production 'never seemed fully to understand the complex kinds of agencies that had produced the Corpus Christi plays in the first place' to the extent that it was 'no longer a medieval passion play'.[3] The following chapter investigates how far the replacement of the religious underpinning of the plays with late twentieth-century ideologies caused the notion of the plays to collapse.

The last production to be examined in this section is the Coventry *Millennium Mysteries*; a co-production between the city's Belgrade Theatre and Teatr Biuro Podróży. The inclusion of the latter company provided a potentially interesting input to the religious dramas, for Poland still hosts versions of mystery plays (such as those held at Kalwaria Zebrzydowska, ironically seen by Mitchell in the early 1990s). However, this collaboration produced a version of the plays that veered away from tradition. The single faith of the plays was replaced with a display of multiculturalism which is important to Coventry's contemporary identity as a city, and their theatrical form was expanded so that their content was transmitted through elaborate street theatre spectacle. However, I suggest that these overlying themes eventually gave way to another dynamic that lay beneath the production.

These contemporary professional productions of the mystery plays sought to discover ways in which devotional material can be made accessible to modern-day secular audiences. They achieved this through a variety of concepts: a nostalgic sense of community, a commitment to personal altruism, and an expression of multiculturalism. In finding metaphorical resonances these productions have brought medieval devotional drama to life some 600 years after they were first performed.

CHAPTER 6

Bryden/Harrison's *The Mysteries*, Royal National Theatre

The 1999 revival at the Royal National Theatre, London, of Tony Harrison and Bill Bryden's promenade production of *The Mysteries* had an extensive history. A version of *The Passion* was first presented in 1977 outside the theatre on Easter Day. In the early 1980s subsequent versions of *The Mysteries* were revived at the National Theatre, and at Edinburgh, Rome and Cologne. The three-part production was first staged in 1985, playing at both the National Theatre and London's West End before being broadcast on national television by Channel Four; it was then revived as part of a discrete Millennium celebration by the National Theatre in 1999.[1] Such an extensive production history is unique amongst contemporary stagings of medieval drama. The fact that a core company of actors participated in the production during its twenty-three year life-span surely marks *The Mysteries* as a phenomenon in the history of Western theatre. This production was also important because, as Sarah Beckwith noted, it marked the first modern-day London-based production of the mystery plays in a subsidised theatre.[2] With this status it signalled a national platform for revivals of medieval drama, which John Elliott pointed out had only been locally achieved up until that point.[3]

This chapter assesses the reasons for the popular success of Bryden's production in the 1980s and asks how, and if, the production maintained this success some twenty years later. Given that Bryden's original production was acutely tied to the political milieu of Britain at that time, and that those political circumstances had changed by the point of the reproduction, how could a revival possibly succeed?

Bryden's popular theatre

Bryden's desire to direct the mystery plays was born from a commitment to popular theatre; a theatre of the people. Writing in the *Scotsman* before the performance of the embryonic *Mysteries* at the 1980 Edinburgh Festival, Bryden located his production in a tradition he called 'people's theatre':

> The performance is a celebration. A celebration of the stories. A celebration of the plays and playwrights ... but most of all it is a celebration of the working people who created the first performance. These are not religious

> plays, although they tell the Bible story. They are not bound by any creed or denomination. They are, instead, the declaration of the simple faith of the working people of the time.[4]

Bryden's views of the origins of the mystery plays are extremely romanticised; he incorrectly places the original dramas at the hands of medieval 'workers', seemingly ignores the Christian bias of the plays, and overlooks the importance of any civic or guild structures in the productions of the dramas. If Bryden showed little concern for historical accuracy, then what vision was behind his production of the *Mysteries*? Perhaps the answer lies within the same article. There he put forward the view that: 'the theatre must be progressive so I see no point in trying to recreate what a performance was like then. A performance in the theatre is always in the present. Now.' Bryden's concerns with the plays are quite clear: as a contemporary theatre director his responsibilities lay in making a theatre piece effective and enjoyable for an audience today. Given the difficulties that face modern-day directors of the plays and Bryden's decision to overlook the proper origins and functions of the mystery plays, it is clear that he had an enormous task in creating a performance for 'now'.

In his quest to produce a version of the mystery plays that emphasised the notion of a 'people's theatre' Bryden had a firm starting point. In 1975 Peter Hall, the director of the National Theatre complex, established three resident companies within the building, and placed Bryden as artistic director of the smallest and most experimental, the Cottesloe. At the Cottesloe Bryden gradually developed what he referred to as 'a creative "family"', an ensemble of performers, designers and technicians who frequently worked together.[5] This tight-knit group meant that there was a sense of 'community' amongst the team; this doubtless helped to create a sense of citizens working together, a central concept of the final production.

Other keys to the vision of the production came from the development of the text, design and music. Tony Harrison, a poet and dramatist with a reputation for preserving regionalism and blending old forms with contemporary idioms, had initially suggested the project to the National Theatre. His adaptation of *The Mysteries* was distinctive for two reasons: first, much of the text was developed from workshops with the actors; this led to the ensemble basis of the piece (in publicity material the company was credited as authors alongside Harrison), and second, the adapted version frequently used Northern expressions and idioms, a facet which was particular to Harrison's work to reclaim regional poetry. (Harrison selected material from across the extant texts, but a large proportion of the material was from the York cycle; it is that sense of regional identity that he captured in his modernised version.) Given these two distinctive features, an ensemble developed text and a strong sense of regionalism, it is clear that Harrison's adaptation fitted well with Bryden's category of 'people's theatre'. In an interview Harrison noted the importance of the original performance conditions in shaping the verse:

> remember alliterative verse is an outdoor medium, designed to command the attention of drunken holiday crowds. In verse speaking, you usually stress the vowels. Here, you must stress the consonants: the energy is in them.[6]

Like Bryden, Harrison showed little understanding of the original context of the performance of the dramas. Given that the plays were performed on a holy day, the reference to 'drunken holiday crowds' is misleading. However, it is clear that a dynamic sense of the popular pervaded Harrison's adaptation.

The concepts underlying William Dudley's designs were also based on the notion that 'These plays were essentially a popular form of street theatre, and that, as in medieval times, it was crucial to incorporate the audience.'[7] Dudley stripped the seating from the ground level of the Cottesloe courtyard-like theatre and utilised the audience balconies like buildings around a town square. The 'square' was then decorated with nineteenth-century trade union banners, in an attempt to draw a parallel with medieval guilds. Though this parallel is faulty on many levels, the use of these modern interventions began to create a style for the piece which 'allowed the medieval and modern notions of story-telling to co-exist, so that the audience were not witnessing an historical reconstruction but were complicit in, and interacting with, a living experience.'[8] The notion of a 'living experience' and the emphasis on the popular forms were further accentuated by the use of music in the production. The Albion Band, led by John Tams, accompanied the plays with live folk rock. However, this creation of a modern-day popular form was difficult. The use of a combination of nineteenth-century trade union banners and folk rock suggest that it was not possible to find appropriate modern-day parallels or popular forms. Instead this led to the construction of a patchwork of ideas. As I demonstrate later on, although the creation of this tone was in many ways false, it provided the backbone of the popular appeal of the production.

The Mysteries and politics

The National Theatre production of *The Mysteries* was particularly dependent on the social, political and cultural climate in which it was first produced. In the 1970s and early 1980s Britain was in crisis: the economy was weak; the strength of the pound fell; industrial output reduced by 11 per cent between 1979 and

1982; unemployment increased from 1.2 to 3 million; and inner city riots were commonplace.[9] In the late 1970s a number of measures were introduced to try to stabilise the economy; these included pay freezes, enforced three-day weeks, electricity rationing and new industrial relations acts. This course proved unpopular and culminated in a head-on collision between the government and trade unions during the 'winter of discontent' in 1978/9 with widespread strikes amongst miners, dockers, car manufacturing industries, and firemen.[10] The manufacturing towns of northern England were the worst affected, and, as Paul Hirst has pointed out, there was 'a marked split between North and South.'[11]

The Mysteries, in celebrating a simulacrum of northern folk culture and trade unionism, struck at the heart of the tensions of Britain at the time. Critics were quick to see the relationship between the production concept and the political climate of England. As one critic rather facetiously remarked, the production had the feel of 'yet another unofficial strike at the National, perhaps over a leaky lavatory or burned-out lightbulb.'[12]

The development of *The Mysteries* between its inception in 1977 and the presentation of the trilogy in 1985 continued to draw on the political climate of England. The election of Margaret Thatcher as Prime Minister in 1979 marked the beginning of an increased battle between government and unions, in particular the miners. The privatisation of national industries in 1982, and the centralisation and reduction of local government spending powers demonstrated the actions of a government determined to bring the country under its control. This climate could not be more apposite for Bryden's vision of *The Mysteries*. The development of the production paid increasing homage to social unrest in Britain, and in particular the plight of northern mining communities.

The Mysteries was also a response to the larger political climate. Many critics saw the 1985 production as an attack on the values introduced by the government, and in particular, 'the arrogant society of Thatcher's Britain, with the highest homeless population in our cities that we've had since the Victorian values she's so fond of quoting. Let her ponder on that next time she kneels in church to worship.'[13] Other pertinent issues were incidentally raised through the production of the piece. In an attempt to achieve central control the Conservative government decided to terminate the body which regulated the capital, the Greater London Council. The GLC, which had become a notorious left-wing organisation, was responsible for much of the public arts funding in London, including the National Theatre. These cuts forced director Peter Hall to close the Cottesloe Theatre for a period, and forced the homeless production of *The Mysteries* to transfer to the Lyceum Theatre in the West End.

Nostalgia

The development of the nostalgic tone was partially created by the way in which the production established a sense of community amongst the spectators. This notion of community, was of course, illusory, but operated on the principles of Benedict Anderson, whereby a group forms an 'imaginary community' through a shared experience. It is interesting, then, that the production focused on the notion of sharing, both among the spectators and between the actors and spectators.

The initial environment established by the production emphasised the importance of a shared experience. On entering the Cottesloe an immediate sense of an 'event' in which the audience would participate rather than just spectate was created, since the production utilised many devices which broke the customary boundaries of theatre-going. The rows of seats were cleared from the space, and the dimly lit auditorium was filled with smoke. Above the open space hundreds of kitchen utensils, such as metal colanders and graters, dangled from the roof like rough shiny stars; these stars were no dreamy constructs but down-to-earth representations made from kitchen tools (see Plate 16). In this atmospheric space the actors, dressed in the costume of contemporary workers such as nurses, tradesmen etc., mingled and chatted with the audience. William Dudley's set design attempted to create a sense of an open street inside the theatre, with some members of the audience at the balcony level where they sat and stood in a manner reminiscent of bystanders around a market square. With Dudley's set an awareness of the theatre building disappeared, and instead a dynamic interactive space was developed, albeit a nostalgic space which evoked a sense of bygone 'community spirit'. The production achieved this further by utilising a promenade style of performance so that action seemingly emerged from amongst groups of spectators, or played on platforms spread amongst the auditorium. This method of playing broke down the traditional actor/audience divide, and indeed the usual spatial proximity between spectators as they nestled close to each other to watch the action; a factor which lent the production a sense of being a 'lived experience'. The sense of community was further engendered amongst spectators by programming which allowed all three parts of the production, the *Nativity*, *Passion* and *Doomsday* to be seen separately or together on a full day. The full-length events bound members of the audience together for a whole day; with many of them crowding into nearby restaurants during food breaks.

The nostalgia of Bryden's production was also developed through his use of characterisation. Presenting the actors to the audience before the official beginning of the plays allowed the modern-day audience to glimpse the notion of a worker playing another character – again, a romanticised interpretation of the medieval conditions since records indicate guilds often hired other actors to perform their play. However, many critics noted the success of this approach. For example, in the 1978 production 'Albert Finney was perhaps mayor of York or Jerusalem' and 'Mike McManus, who played Jesus, began quietly, almost awkwardly – the York worker called upon to act the part and a little self-conscious about it.'[14]

Bryden's depiction of the characters frequently drew on northern idioms: for example, God appeared on top of a fork-lift truck, and had a miner's lamp. Other expressions of working-class culture found themselves in the representation of characters (see Plate 17). Mary at the Crucifixion was in her best coat and handbag; Mak's wife, Gill was complete with 1950s bouffant hairstyle and cigarette hanging out of her mouth.

Other aspects of the dramatic language drew on images of contemporary working life, so that Satan was pursued by street-cleaning equipment; Hell's mouth appeared as a gigantic pair of diggers' jaws, and an enclosed cage with revolving wheel portrayed the bad souls at the Day of Judgement (see Plate 18). Set against this nostalgia for working-class representation was that of folk custom. This was realised through drawing on a mixture of traditions such as the Padstow Hobby Horse, the illusionist's box from which Jesus escaped at the tomb, Morris dances by a row of butchers at the conclusion of the Abraham and Isaac play, a Durham miners' gala procession for Mary's funeral, and slapsticks for the Noahs' fight. Again, many of these customs presented an illusion of folk custom, since the majority of these were of nineteenth-century origin rather than genuine. The choice of customs was also selected in a rather indiscriminate fashion which did not distinguish between urban and rural games; a decision which showed little understanding of the origins of the dramas in medieval life.

The 1999 revival

Bryden's decision to produce *The Mysteries* in the late 1970s and early 1980s was based on his commitment to creating a people's theatre (however misplaced this may have been) and as a response to the political climate of Britain at that time. In reviving the production as part of a discrete celebration for the New Millennium, there was a question as to whether the production would weather the time. How could a production so bound to the political situation in which it was produced be successfully resurrected fifteen years later?

I would like to consider how a production so reliant on contemporary references drawn from the 1970s and 80s could be successfully revived at the turn of the Millennium. Central to this argument is the way in which the notions of communal nostalgia continued to play on the heart-strings of the audience. The 1999 production was revived as part of the National Theatre's Millennium celebrations. In many ways this was appropriate; as one critic remarked, 'I cannot think of a better millennium gift from the National to the Nation.'[15] And, as Michael Billington pointed out, the use of the giant rotating Ferris wheel in which entrapped bad souls were damned to hell during the *Last Judgement* seemed strangely prophetic.[16] A few hundred yards from the Cottesloe Theatre another Ferris wheel, the 'London Eye', had been built as part of the celebrations for the Millennium.

But Britain in the late 1990s was a considerably changed place from the one that spawned Bryden's original production. The coal industry, a central image in the original production, had all but disappeared. Economic recession during the early 1990s was felt nation-wide, and 'The suburbs found out that unemployment was not just for Northern manual workers.'[17] This, and the fact that England was increasingly looking towards the possibilities offered by the development of a more unified Europe, had decreased the sense of isolation felt in the regions of the country. The novelty of dialects from northern England had long since dwindled: regional rather than Received Pronunciation accents regularly delivered the evening national news bulletins. Most significantly, the late 1990s saw the establishment of New Labour in government office. The left-wing values that underlay Bryden's production were now largely superseded in the modernised Labour Party, which had thrown off the vestiges of its affiliation with trade unions and realigned itself with centrist policies.

The political and social shifts within Britain in the last fifteen years meant that Bryden's revival in fact demonstrated an increased tone of nostalgia. As one critic remarked: 'There is a good deal of nostalgia here. The technology is old technology, the assumed values are Old Labour, or perhaps even further Left.'[18] Bryden's original philosophy behind discovering a modern relevance for the mystery plays no longer seemed convincing. As Charles Spencer noted: 'If the production has dated, it is in its vision of a cohesive northern community of full employment. The destruction of mining communities, the decline of the trade union movement and the revolutionary arrival of the computer are unacknowledged in this revival.'[19]

Although Bryden's focus was upon the community value of the pageants, changes in religious belief also altered the revival of the plays.[20] By 1970 church membership had undergone a massive decline since its height during Victorian England. Between 1970 and 2000 overall church membership further declined from 23 to 17 per cent of the population.[21] It would seem as if this might be a major obstacle in reviving productions of the mystery plays; however, Peter Brierley makes an interesting point:

> It is important to realise that this decline in membership parallels the decline in membership of many other institutions in the latter part of the

> twentieth century. Thus while the Christian church membership in the UK may have decreased by 21 per cent between 1980 and 2000, the decline in the trade union movement over the same period was 55 per cent.[22]

Perhaps, then, the decrease in union affiliation was a greater obstacle for the successful reception of Bryden's revival than lack of religious belief. In fact, while church membership declined in the latter parts of the twentieth century, there is no indication to suggest that fewer people now believe in God.[23] Seventy per cent of people say they believe in God; a statistic which has remained unchanged in the past thirty years.[24]

In the rehearsal room for the revival of *The Mysteries* it became apparent that despite Bryden's intention to recreate the production of 1985 there were many factors that mitigated against this. One of the notable features of the 1985 production was, of course, the presence of actor Brian Glover, who played God. Glover, a bald-headed Yorkshireman and ex-professional wrestler, also familiar from many television adverts, played God as 'part gaffer, part old-time mill owner'.[25] Glover's premature death meant that he was replaced by David Bradley. Bradley's God was more melancholic and mournful, as Charles Spencer pointed out, he 'chillingly suggests God's grievous disappointment in man'.[26] I felt that this central change in the interpretation of God provided a more measured tone for the production and emphasised a greater sense of loss during man's fall and Christ's Crucifixion. The interpretation that Bradley brought to the role increased a sense of nostalgia in the production. (This tone was already set by the strong sense of the plays as a 'revival'.) Bradley's God was more understated than Glover's caricatured, larger-than-life God. The more sedate, 'human' tone that Bradley added fell in line with the decision to cut some boisterous moments from the production, such as Noah's ark being constructed by a troupe of clowns, and the use of the 'Aunt Sally' stocks for Mak's punishment (the fun-fair-style throwing of wet sponges). The reduction of the comic, popular moments in the plays, which many critics, perhaps expecting a more sombre tone, found unacceptable in the original production, is curious. Perhaps the music-hall and fun-fair vocabulary seemed too distant in the New Millennium.[27]

There were other changes in the acting ensemble aside from Glover. However, these were minimised, since many of the new actors were apparently selected for their similarity in appearance to previous performers, such as those taking the roles of Christ and the young Virgin Mary. This decision reinforced the notion that Bryden's objective was to recreate the 1985 production of *The Mysteries*, rather than approach them afresh in 1999.

The role of Mary Magdalene had developed since the 1985 production. The appearance of Christ as a gardener to Magdalene was charged with greater sexual tension, and now included physical contact as she touched his feet. In rehearsals Bryden spent a lot of time establishing a dynamic 'electricity' between Christ and Mary at this point. But this moment does little to alter Carole Woodis's charge that 'feminists may freeze at [the] patriarchal bias' of the original mystery plays and that Bryden and the company have done little to alter this in performance.[28] Women were a noticeable minority in the company, and were of little importance in crowd scenes, where, as Katie Mitchell discovered, the limitations of the predominance of male characters contained in the textual moments need be less rigid.

It is not surprising that there were so few changes made to the revival of the production. A close examination of the production history of *The Mysteries* from its genesis in 1977 to its completion in 1985 reveals that actually few major developments were made to the piece. The prompt-books show that the material used for *The Passion* in 1977 remained largely unchanged throughout the evolution of the whole production. Minor musical changes and alterations to Christ's speeches were made, and the entry to Jerusalem was originally accompanied by a section which incorporated the appearance of ten burghers of the city. The alterations made to *The Nativity* between 1980 and 1985 were more substantial. This is perhaps because at the time of the development of that section Tony Harrison was in the United States, and it was adapted by a variety of people, including Jack Shepherd and John Russell Brown. Harrison reworked the material in 1985 when *Doomsday* was added to the trilogy.[29] The changes that Harrison made increased the use of Northern idiom, and consolidated dramatic plotting through the addition of the Abraham and Isaac pageant and a monologue by Death.

Other changes occurred during the process of rehearsing the revival. A key feature of the original production of *The Mysteries* was the ensemble style of playing, developed, as has already been noted, through the creation of a strong team of actors and production personnel who were used to working together. The development of the original production of *The Mysteries* drew on the creative input of the acting ensemble. Tony Harrison bore witness to this, and has frequently commented that the input from the acting company was essential in creating the text. However, the revival of the production in 1999 faced a different challenge. The production drew on an already existing performance, which meant that the creative input of the acting company was less vital. My observations of the rehearsal process were that, while there was a good atmosphere established between actors during rehearsals, there was a considerable difference in the input made between different members. Frequently during breaks Jack Shepherd or John Tams, two members who were important to the creation of the text and music for the first production, approached Bryden and made suggestions about changes. This seemed a privilege afforded to them alone, as other members of the company had less control in shaping the overall piece. This sense of the differing experiences of the company members was felt in other ways too. While the older, long-standing members of the troupe could adapt to the varied performance styles needed, the younger members, brought up on a diet of television and film acting, were less versatile.

The demands made by the acting style had changed little since the first piece, but involved a concept that asked actors to shift between various modes. However, this concept was not uniformly sustained by the acting company, either in the original or the revival.[30] This is hardly surprising, as there was clearly a difference of opinion amongst the production team about an appropriate acting method. For example, Jack Shepherd noted that the alliterative verse style preserved by Harrison from the original medieval texts had been important in order to reach an outdoor audience. Shepherd was keen to preserve the style that this promoted and observed that, in the National Theatre production, 'The text, therefore, had to be spoken rhythmically and the alliteration stressed. No place here for present day naturalism.'[31] By this Shepherd means the use of language that sounded like everyday speech and accompanied a sense of creating a real person on stage. While Shepherd indicated that the production required a broader form of performance than that of naturalism, Bryden's comments hinted that the performers were required to portray 'reality': 'The audience are closer to the actors' energy than in any other kind of production. So you see the sweat, you see the real emotion being produced.'[32] Bryden seemed to suggest that a certain degree of realism was created because of the actor/audience proximity. In rehearsals the tension between discovering a coherent acting style was also evident. Sometimes the actors created stereotypical characters, finding large traits which they signalled overtly to the audience, while at other times Bryden's direction pointed them towards discovering the naturalism within the situation. For example, while rehearsing *The Passion* Bryden asked that the actors use the verse to discover a personal and naturalistic emotion. In particular, he requested that the company respond to Christ's Crucifixion as if the suffering was being undertaken by a human being. While it could be argued that these two styles (Shepherd's anti-naturalism and Bryden's naturalism) can co-exist within a production, and that they did in the original medieval productions, it is evident that these issues were not clearly resolved.

Despite reservations about the lack of clarity of some moments of the playing of the texts, the revival of the plays was a success in many ways. For example, box office sales were very buoyant (often audiences queued for returned tickets), and the production received a good critical response. However, Bryden's production in both its original form and the revival was criticised for its emphasis on the importance of trade unions and lack of 'religious awe'.[33] The production was also censured for its gimmickry and creation of a false portrayal of an England that never existed. Nowhere was this more manifest than in the fact that each part of the trilogy ended with a communal dance shared between the actors and spectators; a moment which reflected the glory of an imagined village green existence. But, as some critics observed, the production never sought to be accurate either in its reconstruction of medieval drama or its portrayal of the current social-political situation: 'The object was not to reproduce medieval theatre nor to update it aggressively, but to allow its openness and communal spirit to infuse a company trained in modern improvisation.'[34]

The very fact that the production relied on nostalgia for a bygone age that never really existed is one of the factors that allowed the Millennium revival of the production to be so successful. Had Bryden's first production been associated with an accurate portrayal of the political landscape at that time it could not have played successfully fifteen years later. Instead it celebrated the notion of camaraderie between the workers and complicity between the actors and spectators, both of which formed part of Anderson's 'imagined community'. Bryden's original production and the revival showed that modern-day productions of medieval drama can portray an image of community as being, in the words of Raymond Williams, 'warmly persuasive'. Bryden's vision of the plays as people's plays was highly successful. His production allowed him to explore a concept in which the medieval plays were 'theatre of the people and for the people',[35] and one in which the audience was central to the production of meaning within the event; they were 'also the participants and the creators of their own theatrical experience'.[36] Bryden's production was less about creating a sense of religious faith than about putting faith in the theatre-going experience as a living experience.

CHAPTER 7

Katie Mitchell's *The Mysteries*, Royal Shakespeare Company

Katie Mitchell's production of *The Mysteries*, which opened in March 1997 at the Royal Shakespeare Company's studio space, The Other Place, continues the debate as to why people are impelled to produce the mystery cycles, and highlights some of the problems in staging them in the secularised society of late twentieth-century Britain. Mitchell produced her versions of the plays in the knowledge that Bryden's production at the Royal National Theatre had been well received. Mitchell's staging of the plays for a large-scale national company occurred some twenty years after the first, and while Bryden found ways to develop a popular theatre style in his production, it was clear that Mitchell needed to find her own distinctive style with which to produce the plays. But the question remained as to how Mitchell would manage to find a concept for the production, given the success of Bryden's approach and her reputation as a director who engaged with realism.

Katie Mitchell's desire to direct the mystery plays dates from five or six years earlier. Edward Kemp, the dramaturge for the Royal Shakespeare Company production, recalls that Mitchell's interest in pre-Reformation England was partly ignited by her encounters with theatre and folk culture through Gardzienice Theatre Association in Poland.[1] When Mitchell became director of The Other Place in 1996 an opportunity arose to stage the mysteries – in fact, she decided to devote the whole of her first season to medieval drama. The mysteries were produced in repertoire with the morality play *Everyman*, and the season was supported by a host of events which celebrated medieval culture: concerts of early music, and platforms which discussed the concept of producing medieval drama in the late twentieth century.

Like Bryden, Mitchell's initial interest in the plays was somewhat nostalgic:

> I was very interested, politically and culturally, in the meaning of the Reformation and the feeling that we'd lost something; we'd lost some connection with the past. In the same way that when we go to Spain and we go to Semana Santas: yes, we don't approve of the Catholic Church's abortion record and so on; on the other hand there is something miraculously wonderful about those processions, the ritual, and that music. It was almost like that muscle in our culture had been chopped off, and I wondered what it meant to us culturally.[2]

Any production of the mystery plays faces the predicament of 'their place on the "reconstruction" to "reinterpretation" production scale',[3] and there is evidence of Mitchell's awareness of this problem before the Royal Shakespeare Company rehearsals began. In 1994, when working with her own company, Classics on a Shoestring (many of whom were later involved with the Royal Shakespeare Company production), she discussed the idea of staging the plays: 'It's a mega-epic – and there are so many decisions to be made: do you do it in the original, do you update it like Tony Harrison, what do you do with it?'[4] In the event, at the beginning of 1996, a year before *The Creation* opened, the concept of the production very loosely followed Harrison and Bryden's model.[5]

Mitchell's reputation is as a director who meticulously researches and rediscovers something of the spirit of the original context of the play she is working on. Her productions such as *The Phoenician Women* and *Rutherford and Son* were notable for the emotional intensity produced by her actors. Unsurprisingly, then, as the team began their period of research, the guiding principles behind *The Mysteries* began to shift:

> I suppose really early on we departed from an analysis of medieval society and culture, and became much more interested in liberation theology. A fantastic biography of God by Jack Miles, the Gnostic gospels, Judaism: they all became much more interesting points of reference. ... We thought that we were going to do medieval mystery cycles, then we realised we couldn't do the medieval mystery plays because we wouldn't subscribe to the ideology at any level.

Mitchell's team found in particular that the plays were too misogynistic and anti-Semitic for use today: so two months before rehearsals commenced, the team began to immerse themselves in recreating the texts of mystery plays for a modern audience by returning to the 'source' material and focusing on the teaching and life of Christ. The production team believed that the Christian content had to be reconsidered, since it was too exclusive, not offering itself to the whole sector of the population. (They were particularly concerned about the attitudes expressed towards women and Jews in the Bible, and were aware that Christianity might exclude some members of the audience for religious or personal reasons.) Instead, the company replaced the Christian myth which forms the mystery plays with a set of more general values and principles which stressed altruism and personal responsibility towards others.

It was inevitable that Mitchell's style of direction would shape the concept of the Royal Shakespeare Company mystery plays. Thus, her methodology of painstaking research resulted in the dramaturge rewriting the texts from the 'source' material to create modern mystery plays. Meanwhile, the audition process had brought to light a problem with the acting style of the production. Originally the cycles were produced by local guild members, some of whom would have acted in the pageant, while other actors would have been hired from outside the guild. Bryden had romantically interpreted this as meaning that in order to re-enact the mystery plays a modern-day actor needs to pretend to be a tradesman acting a role. However, Mitchell's style of direction asks that the actors portray their parts as authentically as possible, and that the actor comes as close as possible to that character. For her actors to play a role-within-a-role would require her to betray the beliefs that she held as a director. So by the end of auditions it had become apparent that the mystery plays, which have traditionally been played in a non-naturalistic style, were now being directed by a person whose directorial mark was to 'combine clarity with intensity of feeling'.[6]

It was inevitable, then, that Mitchell's approach would be one of reinterpretation rather than reconstruction. In the process of bringing medieval drama to a modern audience, in the manner that served Mitchell's directorial style and beliefs, the production team had to overcome several problems: the nature of the text, the question of acting style, and gender representation.

Rewriting the texts

Edward Kemp was originally employed as a dramaturge to be the 'writers' representative in the rehearsal room, trying to get the plays on to the stage in as unhampered a form as was commensurate with comprehensibility and changing theatrical times'.[7] As the project shifted to become a retelling of the gospels rather than an enactment of the medieval texts, his role changed significantly, and he became responsible for writing the performance texts. It is perhaps surprising, given that the team were to abandon the extant texts of the mystery plays, that they ever began working with them. Though it might be argued that they initially chose to use the existing texts because it was safer to stage pre-existing material or that audiences would know them better, it seems as if Mitchell and Kemp embarked on the project with the intention of producing the plays, but then found the task too awkward for society at the New Millennium.

In creating texts for *The Mysteries*, Kemp used the four extant cycles, the Cornish plays, and the miracle play *The Creation of the World*. But he also looked beyond the plays: obviously the gospels were one of the most important sources, but he also derived materials from the apocryphal gospels and the Koran. Of course, it is unlikely that the Koran influenced the original creators of the mystery plays. In addition, it is improbable that the Gnostic gospels could have affected the religious thought of local clerics in medieval Britain. Kemp and Mitchell in effect stripped away the medieval dramas and recreated a text based on the scriptures, and, as Sarah Beckwith pointed out, created Jesus as a Stanislavskian character.[8] In doing this Mitchell and Kemp extinguished any sense of theological ritual and fell into the trap recognised by Beckwith: 'Medieval Corpus Christi theatre never authorized itself from the historically derived text, or indeed the play text of performance, but as I have been arguing, understood scripture as intrinsically intertwined with the communities who performed it.'[9] In other words, the key to the plays is the relationship they formed with their producing authorities; the intertwining of theological, civic and guild influences. They were neither historical records of biblical time nor were they bound by the literary texts. In trying to historically locate the source material of the plays the Royal Shakespeare Company team ignored the connection between the material, its producers, and its sacramental function, which Beckwith sees as central.

The team began by approaching *The Passion*, which lent itself to their approach more easily than *The Creation*. Focusing on the teaching and life of Jesus gave Kemp a distinctive through-line, which was not initially to be found in *The Creation*. Gospel incidents were selected to fit with a quasi-Stanislavskian interpretation of Christ's life; others, particularly scenes which depicted Jesus's ministry, were created by Kemp.

Jack Miles's book *God: an Autobiography* provided the eventual key to unlocking *The Creation* by exploring the relationship between God and humanity. *The Creation* was thus seen as depicting the development of humanity to the point where Christ's intervention was needed. A through-line was established for God's actions, and the promise of the Oil of Mercy (derived from the Cornish plays) was interpreted as being fulfilled through Christ's appearance. In fact, the Tree of Mercy, shown on stage at various stages of its growth and finally with small rags tied on, reminiscent of so many European religious sites, provided not only a link between the two parts of the production, but helped consolidate the episodic scenes of *The Creation*.[10] The text, then, emphasised the through-line of God's relationship with a developing humanity, and interpreted Jesus as representing God-in-Man (or GIM, as he became known by the company in his humanised position). The 'humanisation' of Christ and God was further emphasised by casting the same actors to play their roles in both of the two parts of the production. But, as Paula Neuss has observed, there is a problem of modern-day revivals utilising one actor to play characters that would otherwise have been played by multiple actors in separate pageants. Contemporary actors try to find a homogeneity of characterisation which does not really exist.[11]

In amalgamating various cycle play texts and creating some of his own scenes, Kemp tried to keep the cadences of medieval language and utilised 'a slightly simplified version of the original Middle English.'[12] However, by returning to the source material of the Bible, and to the gospels in particular, many of the original cycle incidents and characters were omitted. There were no representations of

Hell, and consequently no demons; Satan became a worm-like persona who tempted Adam and Eve by throwing them a tangerine. The loss of the figurative figures such as the demons, and indeed any of the comic moments (which have usually been fully exploited by other modern-day producers), meant that Mitchell's production became very one-dimensional in tone.

The approach to acting style

Mitchell's approach to *The Mysteries* was heavily influenced by her emphasis on the interaction between actors forming the centre of the production. Her work during the two years prior to her direction of *The Mysteries* was to discover:

> how to make things occur between actors, genuinely, live, in front of an audience, and the total belief that if something live, like an electricity charge, is passed between two or three actors on stage, then a by-product of that would be an electricity charge which would go out to the audience. You don't need to pitch to the audience in that sense, but as long as you achieved that then something would be achieved in the audience.

The catalysts for Mitchell's journey were comments made to her by a teacher from the Gitis Theatre School in Moscow. On seeing Mitchell's *Ghosts* for the Royal Shakespeare Company at the Barbican in 1994, this teacher told her that, although she had a gift for staging, nothing was happening on stage between the actors. Although Mitchell had begun the process of 'stripping back' (eradicating false gestures and reactions) with *The Phoenician Women*, she 'couldn't really find her way through.' A turning point came through her encounter with the director Peter Brook:

> Last May I went to this extraordinary workshop which Peter Brook ran, and there were four British directors and about ten young French directors there. He just ran a three-day workshop, and the main agenda was: what do you do in order to prepare the actor? Of course we all came up with our statutory warm-up exercises and vocal exercises, but it became really clear that unless you find a way of preparing the actor, the actor isn't going to be able to act. So I became more and more interested in the actor and less certain about what my functional role should be as the director. By the time we walked into *The Mysteries* rehearsal room, we were faced with two incredibly complex agendas: one, reinventing the source material; and two, finding a way of rehearsing. I was convinced that if I could only find the right process, the right way of preparing, which would mean I would have to jettison so many habits and tricks of my own, and a new type of honesty in terms of how you communicate with actors, that we might move forward in terms of really bringing to life the space between two actors.

The working process was only made possible by a unique opportunity which allowed Mitchell to spend four and half months in the rehearsal room with her company of fifteen actors. This was possible because *The Mysteries* ran in two parts; Mitchell was in effect granted a double-length rehearsal period. The complexity of programming the two parts of *The Mysteries* with the main stage shows at Stratford-upon-Avon meant that few of her actors were involved in the repertory system, and consequently she had her own company for this period. Though the creation of what was for the most part a separate company runs against the repertory spirit of Stratford, for Mitchell the rehearsal period was a very positive experience:

> It's filled me with a lot of hope of what rehearsal rooms can be like, because by the end everyone took responsibility, which meant, say, in *Creation*, when we came to cut it, people taking phenomenal personal losses in terms of numbers of lines, and bit by bit all the ego and vanity and the mistrust and cynicism that actors inevitably have, all those things started to fall away.

It is evident that Mitchell's rehearsal process engendered the altruism which formed the core message that she and her team wished the spectators to experience when watching the production. This was demonstrated perhaps less convincingly by the ability of actors to accept their lines being cut, but more by the atmosphere that pervaded the company. The process of working together as a discrete company for that length of time gave way to a closeness and sense of trust amongst the actors which was evident in performance.

Mitchell's emphasis on the importance of the dynamics between the actors had a knock-on effect on other aspects of the production, and meant that the design was very sparse. Ideas for the design began by discussing the nature of the empty space of The Other Place and looking at how basic materials changed that space. Influenced by the work of environmental artists like Andy Goldsworthy, the use of elements became very important:

> We just had an empty model box and then bowls of different textures, and substances like sand or earth or whatever, and we talked about how you can just put a circle of earth in the room and that can change the perception of space in the audience – that can make the audience travel imaginatively.

Frequently the use of light and sound served as the setting for action. For example, after the Fall, Eden continued to be suggested as a physical presence from which Adam and Eve were now excluded by blue lighting and exotic sounds which spilled out from behind the closed gates upstage; the sound of the sea set the scene for Jesus's ministry throughout *The Passion*. Props were similarly sparse – the rule being, 'If the situation or narrative can be told without anything, then tell it without anything, but if for example you have to wash feet, is it going to be naff if you mime it? Probably "yes", so let's get a bowl of water.' Costuming consisted of plain natural cotton oatmeal robes with a Middle Eastern feel (see Plate 19).

Using the space

Together, the actors and their simple staging created a style that was 'sometimes more like an act of religious meditation than conventional drama.'[13] Watching them perform was like sitting in a rehearsal room observing genuine and authentic interaction (see Plate 20). At times the action unfolded slowly, with an emotional intensity rarely seen on stage. The use of the actors in a compositional form within the space gave a three-dimensional feel to the production. The acting was holistic, in that gesture was grounded in the physicality of the character and connected to the whole body of the performer; it never seemed to be imposed upon or adopted by an actor, as is the case with many performances.

The performance utilised thrust staging, whereby the audience were seated on three sides around the action. Action evolved fluidly from each stage entrance; particularly effective were entrances made in between the backs of the audience. A thrust stage is not an easy space in which to produce the mystery plays, because a formality and rigidity is often perceived. The Bryden production concealed the thrust stage of the Cottesloe Theatre by having the audience promenade and the action unfold amongst the spectators, or on raised platforms within the space. In this way something like the atmosphere and informality of the original staging was evoked. In contrast, Mitchell's production set up a formal relationship between the actors and spectators:

> What's been really interesting has been analysing the space between the actors and the audience. Because normally that space is actually quite narrow, and it's filled because the actor is very conscious of filling and giving to the audience and responding to the subtle changes in the audience. Here the fourth wall is down a lot, in fact it's down totally in *The Passion*. So it does require the audience having to come towards the actor, to take a few steps towards them. Physically you often see people start to lean forward.

Mitchell's approach to staging the text was to humanise the characters. The actors worked to find the Stanislavskian motivations which formed the impulses for their actions, but they were given latitude in how these were to be realised on stage:

> The parameters set for the performing of *The Mysteries* are that the intentions or objectives ... whatever you want to call them, are the scaffolding, but *how* they play them is their choice. So, for example, they can change the physical shape the so-called 'blocking'.

For example, *Noli me tangere*, the moment when the risen Christ appears to Magdalene and questions her relationship with Christ before commanding her to 'touch me not', was given a clear acting motivation in the production: 'We're playing that very literally, that the poor chap was on the Cross for a very long time, he's come out of the tomb, he's very sore.' In some ways, though, the literalness of the interpretation and the psychological approach to the moment reduced the impact of the occasion for the audience. The theological essence of *Noli me tangere* is that Christ's body is no longer a physical presence, and that his crucified body is awaiting ascension.

While the use of motivational acting techniques enabled the performers to produce playing of emotional intensity, it did lead to some problems. As John Peter noted: 'The style of acting and presentation are plain to the point of being minimalist: a far, far cry from a medieval performance which was boisterous and colourful.'[14] Though Peter's point about the style of medieval performance is misleading, it does highlight the issue that Mitchell's production chose a style of performing that reduced all the characters to human entities. So, for example, even God became a human being, and the actor interpreted his character by following psychological motivations and creating a through-line. Mitchell argued that:

> We decided that God in order to make 'man' – which was a historical generic term for human beings – in his likeness, if he made what we recognise as a male and female, then God had to be male and female, otherwise he couldn't have made the likeness.

Her literal reading of 'in his likeness' led to the humanisation of God's portrayal. In order to attempt to show God as both female and male the character was played by a genial elderly actor whose gentle tone was presumably chosen to show his feminised state. However, as Charles Spencer noted of God: 'He creates the world like a model-railway enthusiast happily pottering about with a new lay-out, and when he describes the Flood he puts one irresistibly in mind of a Michael Fish weather forecast.'[15] Again, it is clear that the company's decision to humanise all characters and incidents lessened the scope of the production.

Gender representation

Besides the texts and acting style, the representation of the female characters was another difficulty which the company faced. The extant texts contained a number of problems: limited women's roles, a plethora of sinful women (Eve, Mrs Noah, Gill, Pilate's wife, the Woman Taken in Adultery, and Mary Magdalene), and misogynistic moments such as Thomas's diatribe against Mary Magdalene.[16] For a modern audience (and for the actors) such portrayals are difficult. Of course this is a problem not limited to medieval drama, and directors of Shakespeare are often faced with the same dilemma:

> As a female director I was nervous with engaging with the sexism of the period, but normally when I was looking at something like Thomas Heywood's *A Woman Killed With Kindness* I think ultimately the best way of approaching it is to put the woman in the historical context, be as true to that as is possible, even if it is offensive, because sometimes in portraying the women as the victims they are textually, it can actually awaken people to more sense of the need for equality. A lot of times you see directors, and indeed actors, take the female roles in Shakespeare plays and try to manipulate them forward in time and actually it destroys, like a bit of knitting that unravels, and you lose the sense of who the woman is as you try to straddle those awful Shakespearean contexts in 1997.

In returning to the biblical versions of the pageants, Mitchell and her team discovered the discrepancies between the source material and the medieval versions of the texts. For example, in the biblical creation myth Adam is present when Eve bites the apple just after the serpent has tempted her: 'She took the fruit thereof, and did eat, and gave also unto her husband with her; and he did eat.'[17] By the Middle Ages, however, Eve remained alone during her temptation – perhaps a useful cautionary embodiment of the dangers of allowing women public freedom. Mitchell used this biblical moment to represent the portrayals of Adam and Eve. For Mitchell the Bible showed that Eve was the person who spoke to the tempter and engaged with the questions, while Adam stood by the tree saying absolutely nothing. In other words, Eve was an active presence while Adam was passive. In *The Mysteries* this point was stressed by Eve's repentance and remorse after the Fall, set against Adam's silence.

Mitchell's production also reconstructed the usual images of the Virgin and the Magdalene. By having a black actress, Josette Bushell-Mingo, play both Eve and the Virgin, fixed ideas about the status and ethnicity of those icons were disrupted. The Magdalene was also separated from her typology as a whore, since a different woman character was shown anointing Christ's feet and drying them with her hair. The concentration, instead, was on Magdalene's faith and her position as the first key witness to Christ's resurrection. In drawing on biblical and apocryphal material, though, Mitchell was selective and much of the misogyny of these sources was omitted. This, together, with the re-Judaising of the texts and omission of demons, led critics to accuse the production of political correctness.[18]

In other ways the production disrupted ideas of the fixed nature of sex and gender roles. Frequently characters kissed actors of the same sex, as happened when the female Angel Gabriel 'impregnated' the Virgin, and later when Christ greeted the disciples. Mitchell's traced the absence of fixed gender roles back to God:

> Historically it's very much that Adam was made in God's likeness, and the woman's a sort of rib by-product, which is the second Creation story, actually much later than the first one where he manifests two elements of himself as male and female. In that sense he is gender-blind, but of course in his anger, when he throws them out of Eden, he does give the childbirth punishment, he creates the tension between the sexes.

It is unclear what Mitchell was referring to in the existence of a second creation myth. The King James version of the Bible makes clear that Eve was created out of a rib, while the New International Version indicates that man and woman are made from his own image. Perhaps this led to Mitchell's confusion. However, her questioning of gender roles did lead to some interesting decisions in the production. One of the most startling moments of this 'gender-blind' production was Christ's birth. His appearance as a naked adult man in the lap of the Virgin at once disrupted assumptions about Christ, the Virgin, and their sexuality.

Whereas the modernisation of many of the ideas of gender and sexuality shattered preconceptions of the material, at other times Mitchell was careful to set the women in a medieval context. In many of the scenes with the disciples the women were kept on the periphery of the action, since placing them too close to Christ appeared too modern.

> We talked a lot about how the relationship between the male disciples absorbing the female ones would have been. In AD 26, or whenever it happened, it would have been very hard for them to be gender-blind, which is what Christ asks them to be. So we worked very hard on how the group of men, which comprises four fisherman, one intellectual, and eventually a tax collector, how they were going to deal with having women there supposedly on a level.

Without a doubt, Mitchell's approach to staging *The Mysteries* contained some forward-thinking interpretations of its women characters. Resisting the stereotypes of virgin and whore, she showed instead a world where gender was more flexible and less static than is all too often assumed of the medieval period.

Politics and personal faith

In returning to the source material of the mystery cycles, Mitchell's team avoided the problem of staging the politics of the plays. The extant texts sometimes highlight the lives of the citizens and are occasionally told from their point of view. For example, the Towneley Second Shepherds' pageant shows shepherds grumbling about poll tax and poverty; the Crucifixion is partly told through the soldiers; Joseph and Mary are depicted as ordinary citizens through the focus on Joseph's cuckoldry and Mary's poor donkey riding. However, Mitchell's interpretation of the plays overlooked the fact that they make such representations. She held that the mystery cycles above all were a tool utilised by the Church to assert its authority over the population:

> You know they still do mystery plays in Poland, at a place called Kalwaria Zebryzdowska, and I went to see them about four years ago. People would walk on huge pilgrimages to go there, and the local community spent the whole year preparing it. They spent all night in the church praying, and at five o'clock in the morning you wake up and you go in the snow and mud, you go from station to station in this huge, big park, and at the end of it the bishop or the archbishop, I don't know, preaches a sermon about, 'putting up with whatever life throws at you' to incredibly poor people, and you think, that's actually not good enough! It's a difference between faith and the Church – I think the mystery plays are what the Church wants people to put up with, and then there's a sense of personal faith as well ...

Mitchell's parallel between the pilgrimage in Poland and the English mystery plays is faulty. The park in Kalwaria Zebrzydowska, now a UNESCO World Heritage Site, was marked out as a place of worship for the Passion of Christ and the Virgin Mary in the late seventeenth century, and comprises a series of outdoor stations and chapels where homage can be made. Mitchell reads this as being Catholic propaganda, but the historical origins and methods of production of the mystery plays discussed in Chapter 1 show that the mystery plays are not merely the mouthpiece of the Church. Perhaps as a result of this reaction, Mitchell determined that the relevance of the plays for an audience today lay in personal beliefs, not in any wider sense of Christian faith.

Mitchell's production of the mystery plays, which stripped out any religiosity and replaced it with simple interactions between the actors, created a strong atmosphere of belief – but it was a belief in simple values rather than a production which drew on any Christian underpinning. Mitchell produced a version which was stark and moving – 'an almost Beckettian enquiry into man and his relation to God'.[19] Perhaps the sense of Beckettian enquiry was created by the lack of any context for the production in the same manner that *Waiting for Godot* or *Endgame* exist in an undetermined place. For Mitchell's production there was no political, religious or social framework, instead an emphasis on personal values. Mitchell fully realised the implications of her choice, and argued that the political versions which Harrison and Bryden had produced over ten years ago were no longer suitable for contemporary Britain:

> I think that Tony Harrison did it superbly, and he did it at a time when we could do it culturally. I don't think the audience would hear that any longer, I think that we're so politically cynical that I don't know that that production would speak – I think that you can do a production, which is what we've sort of done, about personal faith, God within you, and a sense of responsibility locally, to just one other person, that's enough, just love Zaccheus the tax collector, that's enough, or love another disciple, or forgive someone, just one person. It's a much more personal spirituality, because we can hear that now, but I wonder whether the politics of Tony Harrison's production would speak now.

Mitchell's decision to humanise and depoliticise her version of the mystery plays contrasted with another production of the mysteries on tour at the same time. Oxford Stage Company's version of Dario Fo's *Mistero buffo*, translated as *The Comic Mysteries*, directed by John Retallack, took an alternative approach. Producing Dario Fo's versions complicated the equation, as Robert Hanks noted:

> With any production of the mysteries, the audience is confronted with the question: in Britain, in the 'nineties, what possible relevance can there be in a medieval retelling of the Bible? Dario Fo's *Mistero Buffo* poses an even harder question: in Britain in the 'nineties, what possible relevance can there be in a medieval retelling of the Bible dressed up as a piece of 'sixties Italian Marxist agitprop?[20]

Fo, rather predictably, retold the mysteries from the point of view of the proletariat, and found every opportunity to lampoon the Roman Catholic Church and undermine the authorities. John Retallack saw Fo's version as creating 'a dialectic between the gospels and how the people understood them',[21] an idea which may be closer to the medieval mystery plays than Mitchell's production. He worked with Ed Emery to produce a new version of Fo's texts for the tour, and discovered that so much had to be adjusted: 'Terms like "the bosses" sounded so crass.'

The production found ways of incorporating satirical remarks on the approaching General Election, and the use of the song 'The World Turned Upside Down' at Crewe Lyceum the day after the Labour Party victory had a new resonance. Even so, there was a sense that the production was flawed by 'a problem inherent in Fo: his ironies rely on a straightforward moral and political message, an easy dichotomy of rulers and ruled, which seem unconvincing in post-industrial Britain.'[22] This is not to say that contemporary relevance cannot be found in the text. In a workshop held by Retallack on Fo's text, a Bosnian actress read the Madonna's speech from *The Slaughter of the Innocents* in a way that 'wasn't imaginable – it had a modern meaning.'

Mitchell's production of *The Mysteries* served as a vehicle to release her directorial vision, in that it allowed the development of an ensemble company, facilitated the exploration of acting techniques and addressed a sense of faith through concentrating on personal values and responsibility towards others. The production never became patronising or glib: instead, through focusing on the intensity of the interaction between the actors, the audience witnessed a moving interpretation of the gospels. In successfully bringing *The Mysteries* to life, Mitchell convincingly overcame many problems inherent in staging the texts today: issues of religious faith, the representation of women, and the playability of the roles by modern actors.

Mitchell's production, in working within the conventions of twentieth-century mainstream theatre, humanised and naturalised much of the action. As John Elliott suggests, part of the appeal of the plays has to do with the 'aesthetic appeal' of a style which differs from conventional theatre.[23] But Mitchell's production was never to discover this aesthetic appeal; instead she attempted to create a new aesthetic, one based on genuine human interaction.

The Barbican 1998

The story of Mitchell's mysteries does not end at Stratford-upon-Avon. The production was scheduled to transfer in 1998 to the Barbican, then the London home of the Royal Shakespeare Company. Mitchell and Kemp took the opportunity to dramatically reconsider the material before its transfer to London. They declared that the production (in particular *The Passion*) only properly reached its audience every few shows, and that *The Mysteries* was fragile and not suitable for actors performing in repertoire. In truth, few of Mitchell's actors performed in the repertoire of other plays; perhaps a more genuine reason for the radical reworking of the show was that Mitchell and Kemp were still frustrated by the material and wanted to penetrate/grapple with it further. Writing in the *New*

Statesman, Kemp declared: 'It was clear that if we were to get to the heart of the issues which had attracted us, we needed to do it in the voice of our age.'[24]

In the Barbican production *Creation* was set in the 1930/40s, and *Passion* in a present-day city – there were references to London, but it was a war-torn landscape with reminiscences of Bosnia. Christ was a down-and-out living on Matthew's Kensington doorstep. Matthew was a city broker and unreliable journalist of Christ's life. The production was more Sarah Kane than mystery play. The Old Testament tales of brutality were woven together: Judith was a nurse who hacked off the head of General Holofernes; David practically raped Bathsheba; Mary gave birth in a derelict building as a single mother swearing and cursing her child and blaspheming God. The nihilistic, brutal and violent world shown had, as one reviewer put it, 'lashings of Quentin Tarantino' – machine guns, helicopter gunships, and the F-word.[25] After Christ's death an irreconcilable Peter blew his brains out with a semi-automatic pistol.

The problem with the Barbican production was that in updating the material further the substance and structure of the mystery cycles was entirely removed. Instead Kemp created a pastiche of texts, drawing on moments of Dostoyevsky, Bulgakov and Rilke. In trying to find a modern allegory the team lost sight of the foundations of their material; as one reviewer put it all that remained was 'something like a Heath Robinson machine.'[26] Critics rightly pointed out that the title of the production, *The Mysteries*, was a misnomer. There was by this point a large disparity between the production team's objectives and the audience's expectations. It is baffling as to why the production, which had received a favourable reception at Stratford the previous year, should unravel to this degree. The case illustrates the point that complete reinterpretations of the plays lose their reason for being; without the central elements of the plays' organisation and content, they merely fall apart. Mitchell's production serves as a cautionary tale.

CHAPTER 8

The Coventry *Millennium Mysteries*

This section has already examined why two professional productions of the mystery plays were produced and has evaluated their success in fulfilling their directors' aims. The production at Coventry, held to mark the Millennium, was important in that it sought to bring the plays alive for an audience today by creating a programme of professional and community work which ostensibly examined the issue of multi-culturalism. The production accomplished this by having two distinct parts to the performance: the first part was enacted by community members and drew on a number of pre-existing diverse groups (such as the Fountain Theatre Company). The second part of the Coventry *Millennium Mysteries* was produced by professional groups and included collaboration with an international street theatre company, which as well as adding to the sense of globalisation, revealed how theatrical spectacle can enhance a production of the mystery plays. This chapter suggests, though, that the production was also important in generating a further meaning. The subtextual implications of the performance of the plays focused on the war-torn cathedral remains at Coventry. Underlying the celebratory nature of the production was a grim reminder of the devastation of the Second World War. This chapter looks at how the superficial themes of multi-culturalism and globalisation hid the darker subtext of the production, and how the popularity of the production owed as much to this as it did the former aspects.

The Coventry *Millennium Mysteries* performed in the summer of 2000 was a co-production between the Belgrade Theatre and the Polish street theatre company Teatr Biuro Podróży. The Belgrade, historically associated with one of the most important Theatre-in-Education programmes in England, used the opportunity to fuse professional and community experiences. The Old Testament stories were presented using a hundred community members who were divided into three different companies. The three companies performed versions of stories from Creation to Cain and Abel, The Flood and the Exodus. The second half, entitled 'Life and Death of Jesus Christ',[1] essentially covered the New Testament and was performed by six members of Teatr Biuro Podróży and eight British actors, most of whom had previously worked for the Belgrade. This production drew on a sense of the importance of the past, and specifically of the heritage of the site and its inhabitants.

Heritage

Margaret Rogerson, writing about the Millennium productions at York and Coventry, has noted the way in which the occasion of the Millennium allowed local communities to use a form of heritage theatre to express their identity.[2] She observed that these productions were 'not based on a belief that they are recreating an authentic replica from the Middle Ages; rather it grows from an understanding that they are taking something from the past and reworking it within a continuing modern heritage'.[3] However, there is considerable scope for the way in which a community might work with the notion of heritage. An investigation into heritage theatre has been undertaken by Anthony Jackson, whose work is useful in assessing the effectiveness of dramatising aspects of the past. Jackson analysed projects undertaken at museums and such sites in order to assess their efficacy. He concluded that while some heritage theatre was concerned only with the 'enlivening of the past', other projects made a real impact on how the participants felt about the past.[4] Certainly the production at Coventry drew on a number of continuing heritages: those of modern-day productions of the mystery plays at Coventry, a long history of commitment to community arts, an ongoing relationship with Teatr Biuro Podróży, and most importantly, the heritage of performance within the ruins of the cathedral. I will begin by questioning the validity of some of these heritages.

All that remains of the medieval Coventry play texts are two fragments, *The Shearman and Tailors play* and the *Weaver's Pageant*, although these were almost certainly part of a longer cycle of plays akin to those at Chester or York. Given the fragmentary state of the Coventry texts there has been no heritage of playing them; rather, a heritage of the performance of modernised amalgamations of mystery plays in the Coventry Cathedral ruins has been established. Twentieth-century versions have been played sporadically since Carina Robins's production of the fragments in the ruins in 1951, and include E. Martin Browne's version of the N-Town plays in 1962 at the consecration of the new cathedral.[5] Contemporary versions of the plays were initiated in 1978, when the Belgrade Theatre, in co-operation with the cathedral, reinstated the plays in a version written by Keith Miles. Miles used the extant Coventry pageants alongside material from York, Chester and Towneley to create the *Coventry Mysteries*, which were played regularly between 1978 and 1990, until they proved too expensive to maintain.[6] Productions were reprised in 1997 and have since been repeated on a triennial basis by the Belgrade Theatre.

The productions, always outside in the ruins of the cathedral, have been noted by reviewers for their interesting use of space, and for the way in which the building intersects with the dramas. For example, the 1970s productions used the central nave for much of the action, with three small platforms to the sides on which important action could be staged. This configuration mirrored that of the place-and-scaffold staging used originally in the production of some medieval drama (most likely parts of the N-Town plays). Some central action played on the raised stages which acted as a *locus*, a fixed platform that could be used to represent a specific location, while other action was played amongst the audience as they promenaded within the nave, which served as a *platea*, a public, open space. As John Velz noted of the 1978 production:

> The small but delighted audience was encouraged to mill about in the platea, brushed one moment by mothers of the Innocents singing the Coventry Carol, at another by the Torturers of Christ: the Jews shouting for Christ's blood were among us – perhaps were us. As the audience moved across the nave to follow the action from Herod's palace to Bethlehem and back and on into Egypt, we were physically engaged in the moral pilgrimage of the action.[7]

This commentary reveals the relationship that the outdoor performance engendered in the audience. At times the spectators were amongst the action, at others mirroring the action and exemplifying the message of the plays. It shows how the properties of the space were developed to create a specific relationship with the audience.

The importance of the cathedral site and the connection with the past was observed by the director of the 1979 production. In the programme notes for the production Ed Thomason recognised the importance of the notion of heritage in the setting and the action:

> What better setting than the old Cathedral ruins? An arena vibrant with the shades of a history and a past scarcely less beautiful and dramatic than the story of the plays ... we're not dealing with a museum piece, fossilised, dry, antique. The Mystery Plays are vital, immediate; the writing is alive and well and bursting to be spoken, acted out. Across six centuries the plays speak directly and meaningfully to the contemporary actor and his audience.[8]

Thomason's comments show that the significance of the cathedral ruins as home to the plays is not just archaeological; it is also about finding a contemporary resonance within the ruins. It is, as Rogerson suggested, that at Coventry something is taken from the past and reworked to form the continuing heritage.

The potential of the site for generating a close actor/audience relationship had been recognised by Browne in the 1960s. He noted that the production 'came nearest of any yet seen to that shared experience of the whole community which the original Corpus Christi performances must have given to the packed city crowd.'[9] In other words, the site itself was able to provide a connection between the past and the present and unlock the experience of the latter for the former. The heritage of productions of the mystery plays is something which influenced the Millennium production at Coventry, and it is a heritage of which director Bob Eaton was well aware. He revealed that 'When I became Director of the Belgrade ... I was determined to find a way in which we could take the tradition [of the production of the mystery plays] forward.'[10] But this was not his only inheritance from the Belgrade.

Opened in 1958, the Belgrade Theatre was the first repertory theatre to be built in over twenty years, and coincided with the Arts Council's investment in regional arts. From the outset the Belgrade was committed to a programme which emphasised community and education links. In 1965 it set up the first Theatre-in-Education company, a participatory form of drama education which was initially led by a team of actors, workshop leaders, teachers and social workers. The Coventry model inspired the establishment of TIE across the country, and the Belgrade company was renowned until changes in both funding and education policy in 1996 saw its closure. However, the theatre retains some outreach interest through both their Young People's programmes and Arts Alive, a community programme. It is through the Arts Alive programme that another part of the heritage of the *Millennium Mysteries* can be traced.

Arts Alive is a programme conceived in 1993 to bring greater diversity of theatre and performance to Coventry. Each summer Arts Alive runs a six-week festival which acts as an umbrella for visiting international companies, small-scale experimental work, youth and community events and city carnival celebrations. The programme is supported by Coventry City Council, who are eager that local work is developed from within the city so that a unique identity can be grown – and, as Jane Hytch, Belgrade Theatre producer, pointed out, it is important that this identity is grown from 'within.'[11] The desire to develop a distinct identity is spawned by the individual composition of the city, which has a large multi-ethnic population. The importance of promoting the identity of Coventry is embedded in the mission statement of the Belgrade Theatre – '[to] bring the world to Coventry and take Coventry to the world.'[12] The Coventry *Millennium Mysteries* were presented under the banner of Arts Alive. It was also Arts Alive that established the first connections with Teatr Biuro Podróży, which performed in the cathedral ruins in 1997, and returned to Coventry the subsequent two years with smaller indoor productions. Jane Hytch remarked in the programme for the *Millennium Mysteries* that it had been 'our ambition to co-produce a new piece of theatre with them ever since.'[13] It is clear, then, that the collaboration between the Belgrade and the Polish company was another aspect of this production that had a considerable heritage.

Teatr Biuro Podrózy was founded in 1988 by Pawel Szkotak. The work of the company, though influenced by Polish practitioners such as Jerzy Grotowski, Gardzienice and Theatre of the Eighth Day, belongs to the second generation of Polish theatre artists who are concerned with metaphysical expression. The company's name literally translates as 'Travel Agency', and suggests escapism, fulfilment of dreams and mythical journeys. In the early 1990s the group started to perform outdoors, and subsequently became renowned for this work. Their use of acrobatics, stilt-walking and fire has formed a vocabulary which, as Roman Pawloski reflected, is inspired by the mystery and morality plays.[14] By this he seems to mean that the largeness of the themes and abstract nature of the characterisations of medieval drama pervaded this work. For example, *Carmen Funebre* (Funeral Song), produced in 1993, depicted the horrors of a society under war. Giant search dogs, soldiers, and abstract figures of death paraded on stilts.

It is evident that the production of the Coventry *Millennium Mysteries* was steeped in its own heritage. The associations of previous modern productions of the mysteries at Coventry and the link between Coventry and Teatr Biuro Podrózy enhanced the sense that they were, in Rogerson's words, 'taking something from the past and reworking it within a continuing modern heritage'. However, an 'expression of local identity' was also to be found through the performances of the Old Testament by community members.

Community expression

In her discussion of the York mystery plays Sarah Beckwith observed that:

> One of the conflicts acted out in the revival of the Corpus Christi plays is between the plays as a theatre local and participatory – in short, a community theatre staged by and for its participants – and the plays as both an artistic spectacle and a tourist enticement.[15]

It is interesting to read the Coventry project with this comment in mind since the producers at the Belgrade Theatre deliberately decided to address this duality of modern-day revivals by splitting the production into two halves. The Old Testament stories were played by community members, and the New Testament by professional companies who offered artistic spectacle and provided a guaranteed tourist attraction and national newspaper coverage. This is not to say that the community versions did not provide artistic spectacle. (The close collaboration with the designer, Izabela Kolka, who was responsible for both productions, ensured this was not the case.) The community players chosen for the *Mysteries* were new to the Belgrade, and echoed the culturally diverse composition of the city. The Belgrade's strong outreach policy meant that the participants were viewed not just as a crowd for the plays but as creators and makers. The rehearsal period started in November 1999 so that time could be spent developing their skills and creating the work.

The use of spectacular design was present from the outset. The community players who performed the Creation, Adam and Eve and Cain and Abel pageants focused on telling the stories without words and thus relied strongly upon visual image. For example, in Creation angels with long feathers and devils with padded and quilted costumes with codpieces were central. Large structures, somewhat like the Eiffel Tower, formed Eden; these were scaled to show the hierarchy between heaven and earth; later they supported children's swings on which an elderly Adam and Eve swung. These images were created, it seemed, not just to communicate a sense of the narrative, but to question the assumption that lay behind many interpretations of the biblical myth. Multi-cultural representations were deliberately used so that the performance included Indian dancing and a large range of cultural mix amongst the performers, for example a black Noah summoned a multi-ethnic family aboard the ark. These devices shed new light on standard interpretations of the mysteries and biblical events; in doing so the production sought to create a rereading of the plays which encompassed a broader sense of multi-ethnicity.

Margaret Rogerson has reported on the various devices that were used to integrate the two halves of the production. The community directors were involved with the audition process for the professional production, and the Polish company taught stilt-walking to the community participants.[16] Jane Hytch also described how the directors from each of the community productions were in dialogue with Pawel Szkotak throughout the preparation process.[17] On the surface this production did much to engender the sense that they were, in Rogerson's words, 'taking something from the past and reworking it within a continuing modern heritage'.

The community involvement with the performance of the *Millennium Mysteries* was only part of the outreach work undertaken by the Belgrade to accompany the production. Education Officer Matthew Pegg revealed that at the outset of the project there was an ambitious programme of education work.[18] This included an education resource pack on the website, an artists-in-schools project, a medieval theatre project for the theatre's youth group, and a newly commissioned play by Neil Duffield to explore the context of the medieval world.[19] In actuality, versions of the first three projects accompanied the *Mysteries* but funding shortfalls postponed the third project. The eventual projects undertaken increasingly came to articulate the relationship between drama and the city. For example, the residency programme in schools culminated in a street theatre procession, and the Belgrade's youth group performed outdoors for the first time in its history with a version of Robin Hood.

Multi-cultural spectacle

Before the project commenced the Coventry production team set a clear objective to use the mystery plays as a vehicle for multi-cultural expression. Belgrade Theatre producer Jane Hytch hoped that the event would be 'a magnet to which people are drawn from all over the world to see new and extraordinary cultural events that build on the cultural identity and heritage of the city.'[20] Multi-culturalism is important for Coventry, since the composition of its inhabitants is so diverse. Writing about the ethnic make-up of the city in 1991, David Owen concluded:

> Minority ethnic groups (that is, ethnic groups other than white) form a much larger percentage of the population of the city of Coventry than they do of the British population as a whole. Nearly an eighth of Coventry's 294 thousand residents are from a minority ethnic group, compared to 5.5 per cent of the population of Great Britain.[21]

This evidence was matched by the results of the Census 2001, which recorded 16 per cent of the population of the city as non-white, compared to an average of 8 per cent over the whole of the country.[22] Aware of the unique composition of the city, Coventry is actively trying to foster a spirit of multi-culturalism by promoting the individuality of the city through projects like the 2006 Coventry Partnership whereby multi-ethnic projects with target groups can be supported, and through Coventry Inspires, a branding exercise for the city which seeks to encourage businesses to create a distinct identity for Coventry.

This sense of multi-culturalism was evident at the rehearsals for the Coventry *Millennium Mysteries*. At the initial rehearsal the director Pawel Szkotak declared that the focus of the production was on multi-culturalism and global identity, 'We want to create a performance which will be a meeting of cultures.'[23] The meeting of cultures is not necessarily the same thing as multi-culturalism – in fact it might be just the opposite; one a celebration of similarity, the other of difference. Indeed, Sheila Croucher identifies two contrasting sociological views held on multi-culturalism. The first relates to the notion of the melting pot, in which the input of many cultures is mixed together to form a single identity which shares common ideals. Set against this is the notion of ethnic diversity, in which the identity of individual sub-groups is strengthened.[24] Indeed, this contrasting dynamic of difference pervaded much of the rehearsal period. At the first rehearsal – what in the tradition of English theatre would have been a read-through of the text – Szkotak– in a very European fashion – presented his vision of the dramaturgy. He gave out copies of the scant textual script and described in detail what each scene would look like. During subsequent rehearsals while the English actors were often concerned with the clarity of the text, the Polish performers pursued the technical skills needed for their performances – stilt-walking, stick-fighting, fire-blowing – in order to create the 'big theatre event' that Szkotak desired.

Multi-culturalism was, however, signalled through the use of a variety of actors and cultural mediums chosen to express the Passion. Half the group of professional performers were members of Teatr Biuro Podrózy, and therefore Polish. The other half of the group were professional English actors, the majority had worked for the Belgrade Theatre before, and were local to the area; they included Indian and Black members and had an even gender balance.

Multi-cultural modes of representation were used during the plays. An angel with a white flowing dress on tall stilts released the huge globe (see Plate 21). The Kings appeared riding exotic stilt animals such as a bird, a tortoise, an elephant; the fourth King represented death and was masked (see Plate 22).[25] These images conjured up the atmosphere of a Latin American carnival. Later in the 'Life and Death of Jesus Christ' various entertainment acts were presented to Pilate;[26] these included artistic parades of exotic dancing (Indian), stick fights, and dancing on petal-strewn scented streets (which reflected many Spanish Corpus Christi traditions). Other techniques reflected Eastern theatre. A shadow play depicted Mary and Joseph's exile; at the end of the scene their escape was represented by a small model balloon which rose up from behind the screen to soar into the Coventry sky. The shepherds seem to have strayed from Chinese Opera; they wore long fur coats and used mime, dance and movement to create their responses. These depictions resonated with cultural eclecticism; each provided a snippet of various multi-global traditions. As Margaret Rogerson noted: 'While the production was located in the English city, its sentiments were projected beyond it.'[27]

Fusing digital technology with live performance increased the feeling of globalism. The Passion was performed with Christ (a silent wooden effigy) in a huge steel cage, and included the use of a giant screen onto which a *vox pop* was projected. Pilate queried who Christ was, and in answer to this question interviews with people on the Coventry streets were played on the screen. Although the interviews promoted local identity by reflecting a diversity of participants, the global technology that allowed such a moment further signalled one of the preoccupations of the staging through framing the moment with technology that is boundless and international.

Imagined communities

On the surface the production of the Coventry *Millennium Mysteries* provided an expression of communal and global unity. But in the production there were many aspects which counteracted this image. The first of these was the relationship between the audience and the act. Outdoor performance traditionally creates a close actor/audience relationship, and the remnants of the cathedral, now open to the sky, provided an ideal opportunity for this contract. As street performer Bim Mason noted, with outside performances 'the dramatic enactment is as much for the participants as it is for the spectators. Indeed there will be a less clearly defined separation between the two.'[28] This was ostensibly the case in the *Millennium Mysteries*; the spectators mingled around an unofficial traverse stage which was delineated by the paving stones which ran down either side of the cathedral space. This use of space gave way to a sense of creating a pseudo city street. The action moved from location to location within this open 'street' space and the audience promenaded to follow the scenes. But the contract was not entirely as it seemed: marshals often herded the spectators in the right direction to ensure that specific spaces would be free for the performers to set up the next scene. The genuine dialogue between actors and audience was somewhat manufactured by the intrusion of these marshals, and thus the 'immediacy and intimacy' that Bim Mason advocated as part of street theatre was not always present.

The contract between the actors and audience was a somewhat unfocused one. Playing the length of the ruins created a runway for the playing area, and thus thwarted the audience's instincts to be drawn into the event and crowd in a circle around the 'stage'. The production also played with the metaphorical distance between the actors and the audience, but in a manner which was not entirely consistent. At times the audience was invited to participate in the show, for example, the Bethlehem census comprised spectators being counted under common Christian names; soldiers imposing taxation handed out candles to spectators; and the Mothers of the Innocents' game with girls throwing watermelons to one another almost invited a participatory response as it drew the spectators into the game. But the closure of this ludic moment was harshly signalled when the melons were smashed to the ground in a symbolic massacre. At other times the audience were distanced from the events: the Passion was performed with Christ in a huge steel cage and, as previously discussed, included the use of a big screen onto which the *vox pop* was projected. The use of the previously mentioned eclectic techniques from Eastern theatre, a shadow play depicting Mary and Joseph's exile, and the Chinese Opera shepherds, added to many of the audience members' sense of separation from the event.

1 The York Plays at Leeds, 1975: *The death of Christ*

2 The York Plays at Toronto, 1998: *Crucifixion in an open space*

3 The York Plays at Toronto, 1998: *Crucifixion against a building*

4 York Guilds Plays, 2006: *Crucifixion*

5 York *Millennium Mysteries*: *Noah's Ark*

6 York *Millennium Mysteries: Crucifixion*

7 Chester Mystery Plays, 1951: *Noah's Ark*

8 Chester Mystery Plays, 2003: *Platea in front of the cathedral*

9 Chester Mystery Plays, 2003: *Water*

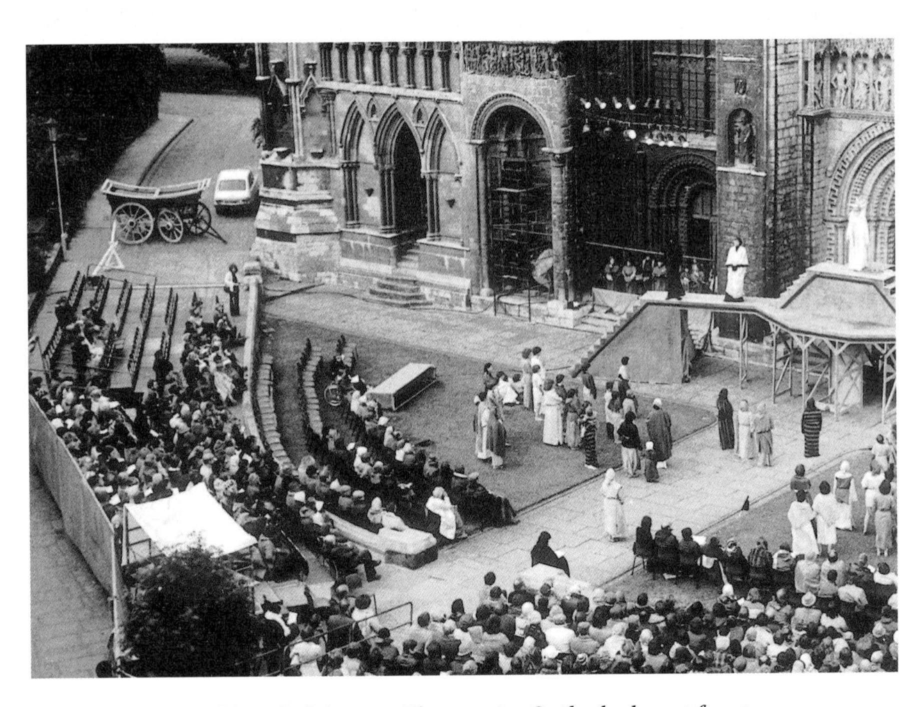

10 Lincoln Mystery Plays, 1981: *Cathedral west front*

11 Lincoln Mystery Plays, 2000: *The Kings*

12 Lincoln Mystery Plays, 2000: *Crucifixion*

13 Lichfield Mystery Plays, 2003: *Market Square*

14 Lichfield Mystery Plays, 2003: *Recreation field*

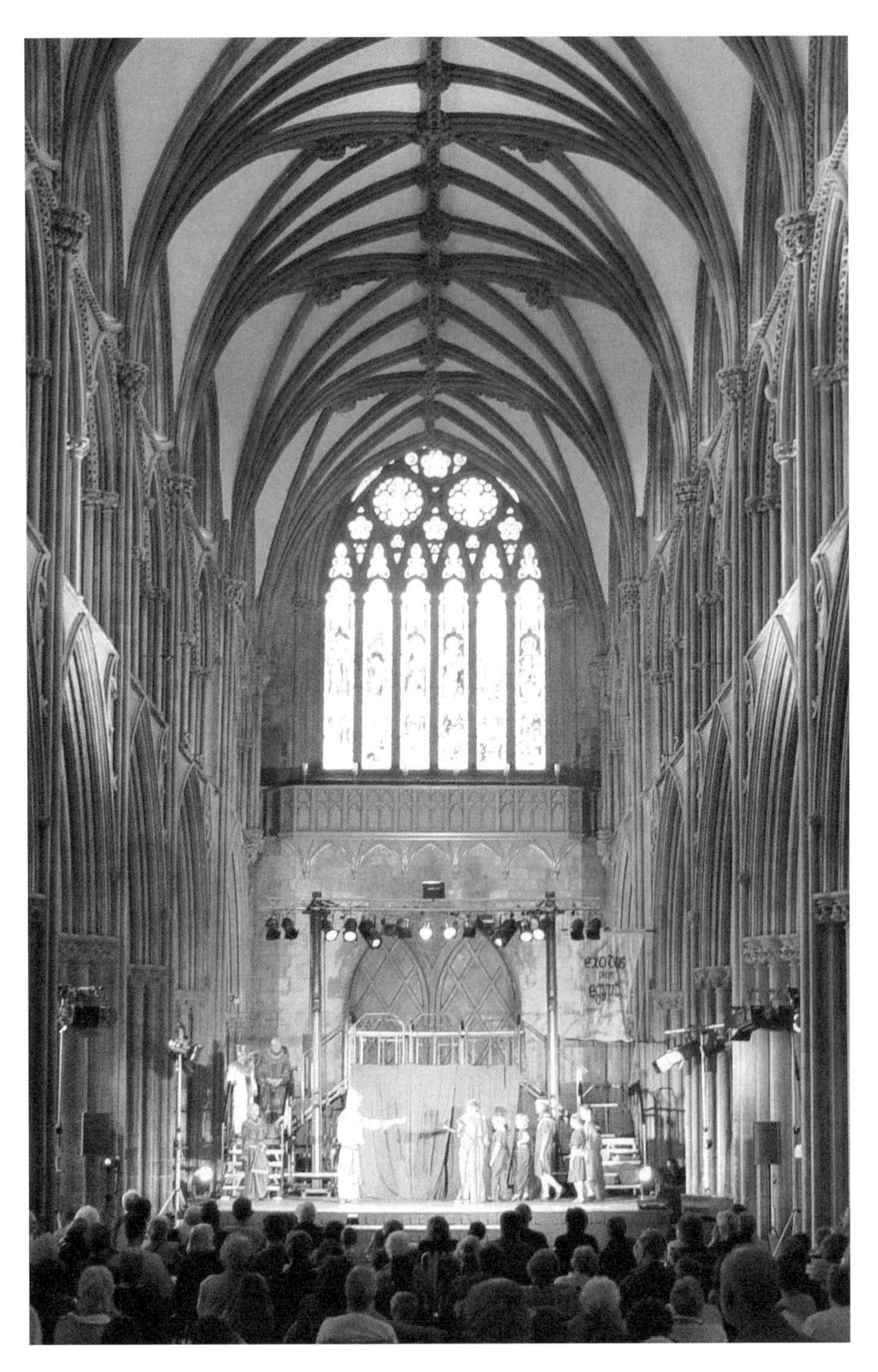

15 Lichfield Mystery Plays, 2003: *Inside Lichfield Cathedral*

16 National Theatre, *The Mysteries*: *Nativity*

17 National Theatre, *The Mysteries*: *Doomsday*

18 National Theatre, *The Mysteries*: *Doomsday globe*

19 Royal Shakespeare Company, 1997, *The Mysteries*: *Procession*

20 Royal Shakespeare Company, 1997, *The Mysteries*: *Christ's torture*

21 Coventry *Millennium Mysteries*: *The Globe*

22 Coventry *Millennium Mysteries*: *The Kings*

23 Worsbrough Mystery Plays, 1995: *Maypole dance*

24 Worsbrough Mystery Plays, 1998: *Crucifixion in front of St Mary's Church*

Additionally, in *The Life and Death of Christ* the use of narrators representing an angel and a devil, high on platforms above the audience, formed a type of Brechtian alienation, in which 'The audience identifies itself with the actor as being an observer, and accordingly develops his attitude of observing or looking on.'[29] From their detached vantage point the narrators described, translated and commented on events and thus made the audience aware of the presentation of the act. One of the most 'alienated' of scenes was Joseph's Trouble with Mary, where the scene was spoken in Polish and translated by the narrators. This had the effect of making the audience 'stand back' so that they watched the action, but listened to the voice-over translation. The examples that I have described demonstrate the ways in which the production created a strange toing and froing in terms of the relationship it held with the spectators; one moment contracting the audience to participate (as implicit crowds in some scenes) and the next commanding them to stand back and watch huge puppets, grand angels in white, elaborate animals in procession. In setting up this relationship it prevented the audience from developing a sense of '*communitas*' either with one another or with the performers. Instead a more complex relationship was created, in which Brechtian notions of alienation were used to make the audience see ideas in a new light.

There were other aspects where issues surrounding the production demonstrated ideologies that were at odds with the supposed values of the production. Jane Hytch revealed how a benevolent form of censorship was executed by the provost of the cathedral.[30] The content of the scenes was discussed with him and had to meet his approval. While the production was in the planning stages there was concern over using the smashed watermelons to represent the Slaughter of the Innocents, and whether the grotesque game was too disrespectful of the loss of life. So while the production was superficially a product of the local community and the collaboration between the Polish and English companies, it was in fact lightly controlled by the Coventry diocese.

The notion that the event was aimed at a unified community of spectators was further undermined by the publicity for the project. Two differing posters were produced for the *Millennium Mysteries*: one that would appeal to the audience that supported religious events, and a separate one targeted at those who enjoyed street theatre. While this is clearly evidence of clever and precise marketing, it does reveal that there was not a single, shared audience for the plays, nor a recognisable community, but rather a collective of smaller communities who watched the event. It is perhaps as Helen Nicholson has remarked:

> Concepts of community have been rethought as a result of new cultural, political and economic realities in which generations of men and women have found themselves with a sense of belonging to more than one place, or feel kinship to people with whom they share styles of living or political solidarity.[31]

It is perhaps more apt not to think of the way in which a performance can create a sense of shared community, but instead recognise that there are a multiplicity of imagined, intersecting communities that comprise the identity of the audience and performers. Benedict Anderson's notion of the 'imagined community' was outlined in Chapter 2. He suggested that shared cultural practices create the sense of a community in the participants, even though they may not actually constitute a real community. Applied to a reading of the Coventry *Millennium Mysteries*, this notion supposes that the shared activity of watching the plays created an imagined community (or, to apply Nicholson's notion, a number of imagined communities which are contained in a larger imagined community). But the communality of the spectators and some of the participants at Coventry may have been due to an underlying factor, that of the experience of post-war suffering and subsequent regeneration, which, although not overt, certainly formed part of the structure of the production of the mysteries.

War-torn Coventry

This chapter began by stating that the production of the Coventry *Millennium Mysteries* ostensibly set out to depict issues of multi-culturalism through spectacular theatrical techniques. However, the subtextual connotations of the production concerned the portrayal of post-War suffering and regeneration. The site of the Coventry plays, like the ruins of St Mary's Abbey at York, is very significant. Both are previous sacred sites that bear the marks of the crumbling architecture and resonate with past and present. Sarah Beckwith's research into the revivals of the plays at York investigated the importance of the ruined site to the atmosphere of the plays there. She drew on the work of Peter Cramer to examine the impact of ruins:

> They encourage us to think two things at once. Abandoned and broken, they confirm our suspicion that the past is not recoverable, but equally, being still there, they have survived – they stimulate in us a reflection of this past which can only be done in the present. Together these two operations – one of losing, the other of re-possessing – give to time its familiar density: the knowledge that it consists neither in contingent

events which peter out, nor in ideas living only in the mind, but in both.[32]

Beckwith noted that: 'In this sense, ruins are ideal; they are a way of seeing and engage our feelings at the deepest affective level of where we see ourselves in history.'[33] The ruins at Coventry are particularly effective, for they evoke the feelings of the past and a sense of repossessing the future. The cathedral that originally occupied the site was destroyed during an air raid on 14 November 1940. The remains, including a charred Cross made from scorched roof timbers and an altar of broken stones, speak of the atrocities of the Second World War. But the site has also become a place of the future and is an international site for reconciliation. Symbolically, when the Berlin Wall came down in 1989, Pastor Werner Kratschell of East Berlin spoke on national television from the ruins of Coventry Cathedral. It was at this moment that the site fulfilled a sense of Cramer's idea of repossessing the future.

The production of the Coventry *Millennium Mysteries* drew on the historic ruins in a significant way. Although I have outlined how the production performed a sense of community spirit and multi-culturalism, these aspects paved the way for an allegorical use of the war-torn cathedral ruins.

This production was also about celebrating survival and acknowledging shared horror. Skotak's dramaturgy began with Adam and Eve rolling a huge model of the globe – their task was interrupted by the sound of sirens, like a bomb warning signal. His direction then presented actors who had escaped from the war bringing on a cart in order to present the story of Christ's life. This framing device revealed one of the allegorical uses of the play: the similarity of the world war experiences of Poland and Coventry. Other aspects of the production invoked memories of the Second World War. The procession of patriotic acts in front of a leader, in this case Pilate, was mindful of Nazi parades. As Rogerson noted, Herod, Pilate and the Roman soldiers were all dressed in twentieth-century military uniforms; this further increased the theme of war.[34] Throughout the piece an undercurrent of military activity brewed: soldiers spilled out to shoot at the models of the escaping Mary and Joseph in their miniature helium balloon; the appearance of Pilate's police armed with knives (in a moment that is perhaps mindful of Hitler's Night of the Long Knives); and the off-stage gunshot of Judas's suicide, succeeded by the image of his yellow jacket (signifying cowardice) flapping in the wind from the top of the St Michael's Tower.

The performance of the *Mysteries* in the war-torn cathedral was a poignant one for the Polish theatre company. Poland suffered horrifically in the war. The invasion of the country by Germany meant that its scientific, cultural and educational life was suppressed. Its geographical power was further compromised when vast areas were annexed to Germany and 10 million Poles were redefined as living in Germany. Many Poles were deported to Labour camps in Germany, or subjected to hard labour in their own country. Nearly 3 million Poles were killed outright – almost a tenth of the population. Given this history, the significance of the performance amongst the bombed ruins could not go unfelt.

Overriding this image of destruction is that of regeneration. This is marked not only by the status of the site as an international symbol of reconciliation, but also through the city of Coventry's relationship with the mystery plays. The Belgrade has made a commitment to produce the plays every three years on the site of the ruins. Consequently the plays were performed in 2003 and again in 2006 in a spectacular version created by playwright Ron Hutchinson. Hutchinson updated the text to create an ironic version of Christ's passion that asked the question 'What if it happened right now?' and the site of the ruins was filled with a large water feature. This ability to continually let the ruins of the site refer to contemporary Coventry has regenerated the mystery play performance in the city. Although the Millennium productions aimed to foreground multi-culturalism, they rest more easily when interpreted against the image of regeneration that is represented by the site. The Coventry mysteries demonstrated that although a production may be undertaken for one set of values, it is often popular for another series of reasons.

SECTION III

The Mysteries in the Community

SECTION IV ~ The Mysteries in the Community

Although this section examines two contemporary productions of the mystery plays in which the texts were chosen to be staged for the values they offered to the producing community, the discussion of community has never been far from the surface. This is hardly surprising, since as Sheila Lindenbaum remarked of the medieval York plays, 'The play had as much to do with York's sense of its own identity and continuity as a community as with the desire to ensure the spiritual salvation of its individual citizens.'[1] The productions chosen for this section develop the notion of group identity and the sense of the continuity of a community.

So far the book has set out two definitions of community. First, it has discussed how, according to Helen Nicholson, community theatre 'is characterised by the participation of community members in creating a piece of theatre which has special resonance for that community.'[2] I have already argued that this definition does not strictly fit the manner in which the mystery plays operate in a community today, for the plays are not necessarily created by the community but rather they are often adapted by communities to reflect their local identity through reference to place names or other minor colloquialisms. The second aspect of community identity raised in earlier chapters is the interpretation of Benedict Anderson, who questions the existence of set communities of people, and instead proposes that communities are created through shared experiences, and can be equally valid whether they are 'imagined' or 'real' communities.

The productions that have been examined so far raise some questions about how community identity can be engendered in modern productions of the mystery plays. If Robert Bellah's definition of community is followed, one might argue that the production of any piece of drama forms a community:

> A community is a group of people who are socially interdependent, who participate together in discussion and decision making, and who share certain practices that both define the community and are nurtured by it.[3]

The act of creating drama results in the formation of a tightly knit group, and modern-day emphasis on the importance of the rehearsal process means that members of the production team spend long periods together. Many of the productions described in this book had a two year lead-up to the performance, so that community members, who often held full-time jobs, could have sufficient preparation time. Beyond the sharing of a formal rehearsal period, there are other ways in which the production of a play can engender feelings of communality. This was evident in the preparation for the York *Millennium Mysteries*. The rehearsals extended beyond mere practices of the pageants and instead a fringe of other support activities developed. For example, at one rehearsal director Greg Doran announced that a company member was looking for accommodation in the city as the commute to rehearsals was too challenging, and that another person was seeking work opportunities. One of the community actors in the piece, who played a soldier at the Cross, commented that being in the production was 'like a big family' – evidence that participating in such a project did create a communal feeling.[4]

There is, though, a large difference between the notion of community that prevails in productions like those of Katie Mitchell or Bill Bryden, in which professional actors were deployed to provoke a sense of community amongst the spectators. Indeed, what has become evident throughout this book is that the concept of community when applied to modern productions of the mystery plays has much to do with location. The productions at York, Chester, Lichfield and Lincoln celebrated the importance of locality, and in doing so raise the issue of the 'insider' and the 'outsider'. If productions are produced by communities for themselves, then a degree of protectivism is in operation; in a sense boundaries are being maintained and identity is established by excluding any threat. Many of the examples that are included in this book contain the figure of the 'outsider' who is often to be found in the form of the director. For many of these productions the director is a professional figure who enters the local area in order to stage the plays, but is in actual fact an outsider. Many of the directors who were interviewed for this book spoke of their awareness that they were outsiders and that they held a powerful, and potentially oligarchic role in entering communities in order to direct local versions of the mystery plays. Jane Oakshott was aware of this role in the plays she staged at Wakefield and York, and it is the desire to overcome this that drove her to establish the York guild plays, which made modern-day guilds responsible for the production of their own plays. It would be incorrect to suggest, however, that these external directors were not accepted by the companies (nor, indeed, the professional actors who played alongside the community players at York), for none of them iterated this point. Perhaps some light on the role of the outsider is shed by Ray Stevenson, the only professional actor in the York *Millennium Mysteries* company, who stated that 'I'm an outsider within.'[5] This phrase shows how a visiting professional actor was adopted by the community players.

This final section of *Modern Mysteries* examines productions for the communal values that they offer. The first concerns performances by Chichester Youth Theatre of Adrian Henri's adaptation of *The Wakefield Mysteries*, while the second looks at a south Yorkshire community that has produced its own amalgamation of the plays for the last twenty-five years. In both cases the experience of the participants was foregrounded and emphasis placed on the creation of local identity. This section analyses the extent to which the mystery plays offer a tool through which to provide community experience, asks what sort of experience the participants drew from their performances, and examines how the notion of local community identity can survive in the New Millennium. Given that this period is marked by increasing technology and the consequent globalisation that this brings, how can communities still bind themselves to the importance of location? As Helen Nicholson remarked, the New Millennium has been characterised by a 'paradigm shift from communities of locality to communities of identity, where the ideal of community has been de-territorialised and allied to mobility rather than stability, to the possibilities of multiple identities rather than those simply inscribed through geographic location.'[6] This section will finally ask how modern productions of the plays can survive given this shift in the nature of community.

CHAPTER 9

Chichester Youth Theatre and *The Mysteries*

A junior school gymnasium is bursting with around eighty young people. Many of the younger ones sit on the floor looking at magazines or games; others lean on gym benches and attempt to complete their homework. Occasionally the sound of a Gameboy is heard above the constant whisper of voices and rustling of sweet wrappers. The noise takes on an almost orchestrated rhythm. The mêlée of sounds slowly builds until they interrupt the rehearsal of *The Mysteries*. Co-director Andy Brereton curbs the noise, sometimes confiscates toys, and returns to directing the *Creation of Adam and Eve*. This pattern is repeated several times during the course of the evening.

As the rehearsals shift to explore Satan's temptation of Eve, there is a change. The scene is being directed to emphasise Satan's seduction of Eve. The older members of Chichester Youth Theatre, who play these two characters, develop the sexuality of the temptation, and as Satan runs his hand over Eve's breast she succumbs and resolves to eat the fruit. The rhythm of the ten-year olds waiting their turn changes. They continue to eat their food, read magazines, copy homework, play and chat, but at some point during the rehearsal of this scene most of the children look up momentarily and observe Satan touching Eve's breast. There is no acknowledgement of the moment, no embarrassed giggling, instead a new action, that of observing, is incorporated into their rehearsal ritual. And at nine o'clock, at the end of the rehearsal, it is not clear whether the young animals in Noah's ark have learned or remembered much about the staging of their Christmas play, but in a matter-of-fact way they have perhaps experienced and learned a little more about life.

Anthony Jackson has explored the use of 'living history' projects at museum and heritage sites to ask whether they 'contribute to an understanding of the past.'[1] He suggested that it is important when looking at such work to distinguish between educationally and theatrically valid work and 'mere heritage industry entertainment.' Theatre, he argued, can make a distinct contribution to how we think about the past, but it is important to discern between mere enlivening of the past, and the degree to which a genuine understanding might be gained.[2] Although Jackson analysed the educational value of drama at museum and heritage sites, some similar problems are encountered when groups perform drama from the historical past.

The production of Adrian Henri's *The Wakefield Mysteries* by Chichester Youth Theatre (December 1999 – January 2000), which formed a type of 'living history' just like those at heritage sites in Coventry and York, raises many such issues, and forces an exploration of the fundamental relationship between theatre and society. Staging a medieval text raises inevitable comparisons between the position of youth, theatre and society in the Middle Ages and today. As outlined in the first chapters of this book, a historical text poses many challenges for modern producers. These include decisions about how far a text should be modernised, problems of unfamiliar terminology, the difficulties of performing verse, and the varied expectations of performers and spectators in the second Millennium.

The cultural and social differences between medieval and contemporary England are vast. Medieval drama utilised a now unfamiliar style of representation; one that often jars with modern taste. As has been explored throughout this book, most present-day audiences and actors are more used to naturalism, and an acting style that is based on psychological realism; the mysteries do not provide this. I am interested here in asking why Chichester Youth Theatre chose to perform medieval drama, and what the group gained from approaching the challenge of these plays.

Chichester Youth Theatre

By the turn of the Millennium Chichester Youth Theatre was a large and vibrant organisation attached to Chichester Festival Theatre and run by the Education Department. It is not surprising that the Youth Theatre was very popular, given the prestige of the theatre and the affluence of the southern coastal region of England. At the time of producing *The Mysteries* the group had a membership of over 200 young people aged between ten and twenty-two. The directors at that time, Andy Brereton and Dale Rooks, ensured that the ensemble encountered a wide range of performance material. The Youth Theatre had previously presented a variety of enterprises such as street theatre, promenade summer shows, site-specific pieces and Christmas shows. The company was dedicated to training its membership in all areas of theatre production. For example, members were responsible for the stage management, lighting and sound design of *The Mysteries*. The acting ensemble was also encouraged to develop specific skills; in order to achieve this the group often travelled to specialist centres in the UK and abroad to receive training; for instance, they undertook an exchange to France to study physical theatre.

Andy Brereton and Dale Rooks chose *The Mysteries* as the group's Christmas show for several reasons. The 1999/2000 production was to be performed in the Festival Theatre's studio, The Minerva. Although Chichester Festival Theatre's artistic director, Andrew Walsh, had decided the theatre should not host a special

Millennium celebration, it was felt that performances of *The Mysteries* would at least acknowledge the event. The two parts of the production, *From Creation to Nativity* and *The Passion* were programmed to maximise their relationship with the festive period. *Creation*, which included the Nativity, was staged on Christmas Eve, while *The Passion and the Judgement*, which included the resurrection, the signal of a new beginning, was performed on New Year's Eve.

The Mysteries was also chosen for several reasons that were specific to the demands of Chichester Youth Theatre. The Youth Theatre had a large number of members; because of the episodic nature of the texts, the mystery plays provided many casting opportunities. Adrian Henri's version of the Towneley plays grouped the individual pageants into two parts. In doing this Henri achieved a greater through-line and continuity of character than was present in the original medieval staging. In his script the character of God was played by the same actor for the whole of the *Creation*. At Chichester a decision was taken to unify the production further by having some actors play the same characters in both *Creation* and *Passion*. For example, God (a female performer), Angel Gabriel, and Satan were played by the same actors throughout both parts, as were a chorus of good and bad souls who accompanied Gabriel and Satan respectively. Despite this dual casting, the production still offered an opportunity for a large number of performers from the youth theatre to be involved.

Brereton and Rooks had other grounds for selecting *The Mysteries*. As well as providing roles for 130 members, it was felt that the material offered opportunities for the development of skills of a particular sector of the group, the fourteen to sixteen year olds. Recent productions had relied on older members, and the directors were now keen to foster the skills of younger actors. Since Henri's text (and the original plays) required a large number of small parts and a few larger roles, this seemed like an appropriate context in which to nurture the younger teenagers. In addition, the Youth Theatre had recently recruited many young and inexperienced actors. Scenes such as the procession of the animals onto the ark allowed a substantial herd of ten and eleven year olds to gain some performance experience in the safety of a self-contained episode of the play.

Finally, *The Mysteries* was selected because the production offered many opportunities for the youth theatre to develop theatre skills. The original producers of the mystery plays understood the power of theatrical spectacle, and the pageants incorporate many lavish details. Records of Early English Drama reveal that it is possible the York Mercers used a system of pulleys to rotate scenic pieces in their production of the Doomsday pageant.[3] The Youth Theatre was able to use such moments of theatrical spectacle to develop specific skills. Basic puppetry skills were utilised during God's creation of the world. For example, the creation of fish and fowl was shown through the younger members of the group processing with stick puppets. Spectacle pervaded other aspects of the plays; the resurrection of Lazarus was movingly portrayed by the bringing to life of a bunraku-style puppet.

More specialist skills were employed in the production as a result of the dramatic realisation of heaven and earth. The set for the production resembled a giant fixed pageant waggon with its timber frame occupying two levels. The skeletal structure looked like a giant ark or ship, or a modern-day oil-rig platform, and it cleverly reflected the hexagonal shape of the auditorium. The two-tiered space provided an opportunity for the display of performance skills. Ropes and pulleys connected the spaces of heaven and earth, and enabled Gabriel and his chorus of good angels to perform rope and trapeze movements. In order to develop these skills the young actors in these roles attended specialist classes at Circomedia in Bristol and Circus Space in Hoxton, London.

Henri's text, adapted from the Towneley plays, included a large amount of music and song, and so a musical director oversaw the teaching and rehearsal of the musical numbers to the entire cast. Original plans for the production included further music through incorporating large-scale percussion accompaniment, but this idea proved over-ambitious, and the restraints of time meant that the plans were curtailed though vestiges remained; at points in the production actors crossed into the auditorium to use drums and cymbals to accompany scenes.

The theatricality of the plays meant that opportunities were available for members of the youth theatre to gain useful experience in many production aspects. Adrian Whitaker, a resident member of the Festival Theatre production staff, designed the set and costumes. The abstract nature of the concepts which are central to the plays, that of heaven and earth, provided scope for imaginative lighting design, which was undertaken by a member of the youth theatre. Similarly the demands of the text meant that the members responsible for properties had to acquire and make a diverse range of objects.[4]

Additionally, the directors used the parade of the animals onto Noah's ark as an opportunity for further theatre outreach. A competition was launched through the Festival Theatre for children too young to join the youth theatre to design costumes for the animals. The resultant costumes were marvellously elaborate and colourful. In fact, the spectacle of twenty pairs of children with painted faces wearing large padded brightly coloured costumes to represent their animals was one of the highlights of the production. The scale of the display was to be marvelled at.

It is not clear to what extent the directors of *The Mysteries* were aware of the problems that are faced when staging medieval drama. My observations of the rehearsal period certainly demonstrated that many of the challenges of the piece were in evidence long before the production opened. The difficulties that surrounded the play were mainly linked to the content and style of the dramas, but some local factors connected to the youth theatre created further challenges.

It was perhaps predictable that the religious nature of the plays would generate several difficulties, and it might be expected that members of the youth theatre raised in a secular society would have problems in responding to, or identifying with, the religious material.[5] However, there was not much evidence in rehearsals that the subject of the dramas provided problems for the cast. Their engagement with *The Mysteries* was on two levels: first, that of story-telling and second, concern with finding stage action for the text. Indeed, the actor playing Satan seemed surprised that in an interview a local newspaper reporter had enquired about his religious beliefs. Rehearsals paid no specific attention to the spiritual nature of the dramas. This led to a production that was successful in imaginatively unlocking the theatricality of *The Mysteries*, but one that fought shy of exploring the more difficult and deeper aspects of the piece.

Though the members of the youth theatre were in effect able to ignore the rather alien subject matter, it was the religious nature of the material that provoked comment amongst the community. The publicity material, a leaflet that folded to make a cube with each side adorned with a contemporary image, was dispatched to the printer only to be returned; the company refused to print the religious material. When the flyers were eventually printed and distributed the theatre received a complaint from a local vicar. He objected to the use of a logo of lips (somewhat reminiscent of The Rolling Stones) to represent *The Passion*. In addition, despite the large cast (each with attendant parents and grandparents), the production sold fewer advance seats than usual, and it was felt this was due to the lack of appeal of religious material.[6]

Other more localised problems affected the production. The co-directors felt that if each of them was responsible for one part of the production this might foster a sense of competition. Consequently, an alternate director led each rehearsal. Having observed some rehearsals, it was clear to me that at times there was a lack of continuity. Furthermore, differences of artistic opinion were in evidence in the final rehearsals, particularly the technical rehearsals. The decision not to split the company into two distinct parts is understandable; however, in maintaining the sense of an ensemble and frequently calling full-company rehearsals, the directors compounded the problem of undertaking a production with a very large and often inexperienced cast.

One of the most challenging problems that Chichester Youth Theatre faced was the actual performance style that the piece required. Presenting a piece from the theatrical past often means that young actors encounter a use of language that is very different to their own. There were two potential problems for the Chichester Youth Theatre actors: first, the texts were adapted from medieval verse drama; and second, the plays that Henri used as a source possibly originated from Wakefield. Henri's text maintained the verse structure of the Towneley plays but employed lively, contemporary language. He admitted, 'This is no way an academic transcription, but an attempt to preserve the spirit of the medieval texts in an actable modern version.'[7] This approach succeeded in making the texts more accessible for young actors. Although Henri's text, by his own admission, did not utilise a particularly northern sound, he felt it was 'important to keep the feeling that these were workers, artisans, farmers from one community playing the biblical parts'; a somewhat romanticised and inaccurate view of the original playing of the plays.[8] As a result of Henri's text Brereton spent a lot of time in rehearsals emphasising the importance of diction and rhythm, but it was difficult for the performers to capture a sense of the regional dialects needed by the characters. In revisiting the past, the young performers inadvertently highlighted geographical and social divides that exist in Britain today. The young southern middle-class actors struggled to represent northern farmers, and failed to portray any sense of the social hierarchy apparent in Henri's adaptation.

The other challenge that the actors faced was how to find an appropriate playing style. The plays are not realistic; instead 'The characters describe their feelings and situations rather than enact them naturalistically.'[9] For a modern-day actor this means embracing a greater use of rhetoric than is usually required. Indeed, non-naturalistic performance is demanding for the majority of contemporary professional actors raised on a drama school fare of Chekhov and post-war British drama. Director Andy Brereton identified the necessary playing style for the Chichester production as heightened realism. Rehearsals attempted to help actors achieve this state by focusing on the rhetoric and formality of the language. Diction and rhythm were emphasised in order to make the speaking less conversational and to adhere to the demands of the verse. However, the use of Stanislavskian exercises, such as constructing an outline and back story for their character, or creating an image of their persona through studying biblical costumes engendered a purely naturalistic response. I shall return to look at other aspects of the performance style later in this chapter as it is crucial to the youth theatre's experience of playing medieval drama.

Adrian Henri's The Mysteries

In discussing the problems that Chichester Youth Theatre encountered when staging the mystery plays I am aware that I am questioning their decision to tackle the material. However, Henri's text seemed extremely appropriate for a youth theatre cast. *The Mysteries* was first performed in 1988 by a community cast as a promenade piece in the open air of Pontefract Castle to mark the Wakefield 100 Festival. Henri, a Liverpudlian poet and playwright, was commissioned to reduce the original texts to two parts of approximately one-and-a-half hours each. His adaptation of *The Mysteries* focused on issues that are central to parent/child relationships.

Leah Sinanoghou has noted that the image of the Christ-child and his later resurrection form the primary dynamic of the mystery plays.[10] The narrative scheme of the plays follows the journey from Christ's birth, through his passage to the ministry, and on to his eventual Crucifixion and re-embodiment through the resurrection. In other words, the plays can be seen to chart a journey of growing up. Although the early pageants draw on the Old Testament, incidents are used to prefigure those that are later important to salvation history and the life of Christ. For example, the sacrifice by Abraham of his son, Isaac reflects God's Crucifixion of Christ. In adapting the plays for contemporary performance, Henri chose to foreground moments of the father/child relationship.

Henri revealed in the introduction to the plays that his text placed an emphasis on three key episodes of father/son betrayal. He saw Abraham's sacrifice of Isaac, Judas's betrayal of Christ (endorsed by God), and Jesus on the Cross as central to the plays. Henri marked these moments by the accompaniment of the song 'Father, Father.'[11] In this way he demonstrated God's culpability in the demise of Christ and thereby emphasised the complexity of the father/son relationship.

The production of *The Mysteries* at Chichester demonstrated the effectiveness of Henri's text for youth theatre performance. The enactment of the sacrifice of Isaac by children performing in front of an audience composed of their parents and grandparents was deeply affecting. There was an absolute hush in the auditorium at the moment when on stage a parent prepared to sacrifice their child. Similarly movingly was the *Slaughter of the Innocents*. The chorus of Mothers of the Innocents were dressed in t-shirts and skirts and carried bundles – blue blankets – which represented their children. After the soldiers killed their children the blankets were thrown open to reveal red linings that represented the blood of the Innocents. The mothers' vocal lament that followed the barbaric act further increased the emotional impact of the moment.

The second issue which Henri identified as important to his adaptation was that of morality. He admitted: 'What the plays are about, for me, is above all man and woman's struggle to choose between dark and light, envy and humility, pride and compassion.'[12] This sense of moral engagement was clearly encouraged in the rehearsal process. In rehearsals Brereton carefully emphasised the moral dilemma that each character faced, and he attempted to get the actor to focus on elucidating that matter. This didactic element of the plays was further enhanced in performance by having characters on stage watch the action. As I noted earlier, this principle extended to the rehearsal room itself: frequently younger children watched their elders rehearse. This issue of learning morality through the performance of the plays is something that I will investigate below, for it is central to the experience that members of the Youth Theatre had when performing the mystery plays.

Adrian Henri's adaptation of *The Mysteries* seemed fitting for youth theatre productions. He focused on issues that helped to make the plays accessible for younger players and spectators. In fact, the strength of the 'new, popular poetry, catching natural speech rhythms, dialect, song and rhyme' and the 'earthy and celebratory' subject matter led Norma Cohen to suggest that 'its text should be grabbed by all enlightened drama teachers'.[13]

Youth and the mystery plays

As stated at the outset, I am interested in asking what the Youth Theatre members gained through staging a mystery play. I have already suggested that the challenges predominantly lay in the performance style. However, there are other aspects of the plays that provided opportunities for the youth group. What is fascinating is that the decision for a youth theatre to stage medieval drama is vindicated by examining the original performance contexts of the drama themselves. In other words, by revisiting the past it is clear that the mystery plays have much to offer young people.

There is little academic research into the involvement of children and youths with the mystery plays in medieval England. However, evidence that children did perform in medieval drama does exist. The series Records of Early English Drama has collected and edited cases of early performances; these entries include child performance. For example, at Coventry the Weavers' records from 1551 show an 'Item payd to the Angelles and the womon for the child'.[14] This was presumably a baby for the purification. At Chester the Coopers' 1576 records show a piece of costuming being provided for a child who was a mascot for the Midsummer show: 'a perre of gloves to the chylde yat caryede the arres and a quarte of wyne to hys mother and for the makynge of hys cloke xid'.[15] There are other opportunities in the mystery plays texts for child performance. These include The Brome Isaac, Christ in *Christ and the Doctors*, who is portrayed as an archetypal wise child, and a child Mary in the N. Town *Mary Play*. Civic and household records show that children undertook a wide range of performance activities. Numerous records show children dancing at civic events, and a 'young maide' tumbler performed for the Stafford family in Gloucester. But these performances were unlikely to have improved the moral education of the participants.[16]

More extensive records of child performance in medieval drama exist from France. Lynette Muir has detailed performances of the Passion play at Valenciennes in 1547 that included fourteen boys and four girls. Evidence suggests that a boy and a girl played the Virgin.[17] It is clear that speaking roles were assigned to children at Mons, where the young Mary was first played by a seven-year-old girl who had eight lines, and then by a fourteen-year-old who held over 300 lines.[18] It is difficult to know why children are documented as having speaking roles in France, but not in England. It is possible that more extensive records were maintained in a continuing Catholic country, but that these were destroyed in England.

There is some evidence that suggests young adults or youths participated in the mystery plays. Records of dramatic performances show that young men possibly played women's roles. It is clear that 'Ryngolds man Thomas' played the role of Pilate's wife at Coventry in 1496.[19] But this evidence is far from conclusive. This male performer could be a young apprentice, but he might be a journeyman. Moreover, if apprentices played female parts then they were not the boy actors of the Elizabethan theatre; Richard Rastall has pointed out that it is likely that these male apprentices were probably seventeen or eighteen years of age.[20]

In one of the few articles dedicated to exploring the role that children held in the mystery plays, D. Thomas Hanks Jr revealed the central importance of the mystery plays to medieval youth. He argued that children inevitably watched the plays since they were performed on holy days. Hanks suggested that children enjoyed their spectatorship and specifically watched the moments when other children and youths performed. But he argued there were particular aspects of the plays that were attractive to child audiences. Most importantly he believed that the plays offered a child: 'A great deal of instruction in the values of their culture: specifically, they learned a philosophical and theological concept of history implicit in cycle structure, they learned the devotional stories central to their Christian tradition.'[21]

Hanks suggested that one of the central functions of the mystery plays was to instruct medieval youth in matters related to culture and society, as well as Christianity. I would like to spend some time looking at this issue, because it seems critical to an analysis of Chichester Youth Theatre's involvement with the plays.

Morality and the mysteries

Research by medieval historians suggests that at the very point of production of the mystery plays the issue of the education and instruction of youths was of paramount importance. For example, the work undertaken by Barbara Hanawalt has proposed that between the fourteenth and the sixteenth centuries there was a growing concern with the moral education of youth. The plethora of child-rearing manuals, such as the advice collected in the *Babee's Book* (*c.* 1475) and the didactic narratives, 'The Childe of Bristowe' and 'The Goodwife taught Her

Daughter' (both dating from between 1350 and 1500) are a testimony to such a hypothesis.

Hanawalt argued that although no specific youth culture existed, as it does today, there is evidence that the Middle Ages recognised 'stages of life that corresponded to childhood and adolescence'.[22] Moreover, she believed that during the fifteenth century there was evidence of a growing concern for the need for moral education. A low birth-rate led to a shortage of apprentices, who increasingly came to be selected from the lower classes and needed greater polishing, or were older and more difficult to control.[23] Since only 50 per cent of the lay male population could read, Hanawalt deduced that 'The strongest teacher of morals, then, was the opinion of others', and that, 'Above all, youth was to accept the conservative, Christian values of the society and to give the impression of stability.'[24] Hanawalt's evidence suggests that during medieval times there was a concern to instruct youth. It is reasonable to presume that for this sector of the audience the didactic function of the plays was extremely important.

I wish now to consider how a production of the plays today can engender a moral response for both their audience and the participants. In a debate about ethical education, Brian Edmiston has raised issues about the way in which children, through the use of drama, develop moral understanding. He identified two approaches in the acquisition of ethical values. First, 'Through their analysis of stories, and use of drama to do so, children learn to be more virtuous in the social roles they are born into or acquire.'[25] Second, Edmiston has utilised a Bakhtinian framework to argue that, 'Values are not acquired from outside us, but rather, they are forged in dialogue.'[26] He continues, 'Learning to be ethical requires that we use imagination to consider past, present and future events from other people's positions.'[27]

In contrast, Joe Winston's analysis of dramatic dialogues suggested a different reading of the mechanics through which ethical understanding is achieved: dramatic exchanges allow for the exploration of moral ambiguity; drama often emphasises a pattern of cause and effect; and lastly emotional engagement with the dramatic situation enables moral development.[28] Edmiston's approach, in contrast, stressed that morality is learned dialogically.

In order to apply Edmiston and Winston's differing theses to the mystery plays, I shall draw on the work of Meg Twycross. In an article aptly entitled 'Books for the Unlearned', she has examined the didactic function of the mystery plays.[29] It is worth comparing how Twycross's analysis fits with the ideas of an ethical education. She has pointed out that 'As with any drama written within a framework of values of right and wrong, so the action provokes us implicitly or explicitly to make judgements, and having made them, to relate them to our own behaviour.'[30] This would seem to be in keeping with the notion of an ethical education as postulated by Edmiston. Since the technique requires that we evaluate the dramatic action in relation to our own values, this established a type of dialogic relationship. In contrast to Winston's hypothesis, Twycross has suggested that our emotional identification with characters is often through surrogates such as Peter and Mary Magdalene, since that of Christ is beyond identification. She has argued that some of the cycles used the device of an outside voice, a type of narrator or commentator such as the Chester Expositor, who addressed the audience directly, in order to reinforce the didactic message.[31]

Twycross's analysis embraced the notion of 'dialogic' discourse. She observed that characters sometimes speak as moral guides by acting in a non-naturalistic 'third-person style' that is defined as 'a character telling the audience what he is doing at the same time as he is doing it.'[32] In other words, an actor can both embody a character and present a character at the same time.[33] It is through this system that actors of the mysteries engage with a moral dimension. In order to assess its effectiveness on the Chichester Youth Theatre actors I would like to revisit the issue of the difficulty of the acting style of the plays.

Twycross's analysis identified a way in which the mystery plays became dialogic rather than overtly didactic. They followed a pattern more akin to that of Edmiston than Winston. In Twycross's words, the plays presented 'a type of dramatic illusion which is radically different from the type with which we have been brought up, where characters are only supposed to say the kind of things they would say if they were really in that situation.'[34] It is this style that the youth theatre had difficulty with; a style that is not about emotional identification with a character, but that of representation of a type. As I suggested earlier, some of the rehearsals attempted to explore a non-naturalistic style by focusing on the rhetoric of the language. However, the heightened realism that director Andy Brereton rightly called for remained beyond the reaches of the youthful participants.

It was difficult for the young actors at Chichester to achieve the necessary dialogic relationship with the mystery plays. In order for them to achieve this it was necessary for the actors to be able to show and tell simultaneously. This third-person style is a necessary requirement for actors of the mysteries in order that the full impact of the plays be realised for the actors and spectators. I am suggesting that the challenge of staging the mysteries in this case was not to be found in the remote content or alien language and verse, but in the acting style itself. The complexity of a pre-naturalistic drama style unsettled the performers.

I began by asking whether the mystery plays are appropriate material for a youth theatre to encounter, given that they are a form of heritage drama and consequently provide a challenge on a number of counts. The plays provided the

Chichester participants with some understanding of the past, but unfortunately the complexity of the acting style prevented them from forming a useful dialogic relationship with the material. However, it is worth pointing out that medieval drama offers an opportunity for young actors to train in a different mode of theatrical presentation; one that is very alien from today's largely naturalistic diet. Ironically, by revisiting the past in staging the mystery plays, youth theatres are offered a living lesson in diverse performance styles.

CHAPTER 10

Community Theatre at Worsbrough

The use of drama in the community, as Helen Nicholson has pointed out, raises the issue of what 'community' may mean, and is 'not so much a matter of recovering or rediscovering the lost narratives of a homogenous past, but of making a contribution to redefining their actual and symbolic boundaries in the present and for the future'.[1] This emphasis on reclaiming the present and future is akin to the observations made by Margaret Rogerson when she suggested that modern-day mystery play production 'grows from an understanding that they are taking something from the past and reworking it within a continuing modern heritage'.[2] Many productions of the plays around the Millennium occurred in places which have spurious links to the past production of the cycles. In performing the dramas, the producing communities are not rediscovering a lost narrative but creating a bond on which to build a present and future relationship. This is particularly true of the Worsbrough plays, which were initially appropriated in 1977 by Chris Evans, the head of drama at Worsbrough High School, through inspiration taken from a school visit to the plays at nearby York. Though the intention was to create a one-off celebration to mark Queen Elizabeth II's Silver Jubilee in 1977, local support for the plays has meant they have played triennially for the last twenty-five years. This chapter will ask how Worsbrough has successfully maintained popularity for the productions of the plays, and whether the mysteries will continue to serve the community in the future.

Perhaps one reason for the success of the plays here is that they have grown out of local enthusiasm. Chris Evans's original intention was to develop them as a school play, but a local working party saw the potential for the mystery plays to be adopted more widely. After much searching, the churchyard of St Mary's Church in Worsbrough village was chosen as the setting for the plays. In some years this meant that, with the permission of the vicar, gravestones had to be temporarily removed so that a large, flat playing area could be created. With a cast of 400 (many of them schoolchildren), the initial production of the plays was financially supported by regional bodies and local traders: Yorkshire Arts, South Yorkshire County Council, Barnsley Metropolitan Borough Council and the Barnsley Chronicle Newspaper Group gave financial support, while much in-kind aid was given by local tradespeople; a situation akin to the production of the original dramas. Margaret Ottley noted how:

> A hotelier set aside one of his rooms for the make-up and storage of costumes, which were sewn by a small array of volunteers, some from fabrics given by Barnsley market traders, some from materials found by ransacking Worsbrough and Birdwell lumber rooms and attics. A working man's club held a fund-raising evening to help financially.[3]

This grassroots support for the plays led to a strong sense of ownership of the plays, and is part of the reason why the plays have survived so well in modern-day Yorkshire. As Julia Smith noted, the plays are 'a truly community event with everyone pulling together, working as a team'.[4] This sense of the team is one which embraced both the performers and the audience (who mainly comprise the local community – although international visitors are not unknown). For example, the staging in 2001 emphasised the close proximity between the actors and audience since much stage action was played on the ground in front of the semi-circle of audience seating.[5] Julian Wroe, Chair of the Mystery Plays Board, commented that in the 2001 production of the Worsbrough plays the audience could almost touch the action, and this observation aptly serves as a metaphor for the sense of shared community which occurred between the actors and spectators at Worsbrough.[6]

One of the reasons that the plays have been successful is because the community on which they are built is not the 'imagined community' of Benedict Anderson, but a real one. Worsbrough and Birdwell (the neighbouring village which co-supports the plays) are located within thirty minutes of Barnsley, Doncaster, Sheffield, Wakefield, Bradford and Leeds. While the location of the plays is close to many metropolitan areas, the producing area comprises two small villages which suffered economic depression during the twentieth century following the decline of the mills and mines. Location is significant here for two reasons, first because the producing community was originally so small that a large proportion of the local population had to be involved, and second, given the economic depression of the region, the local area was in need of events which celebrated achievement. Writing on the 1983 production, Ottley noted that:

> The Worsbrough venture could not have been better timed. With Barnsley seeking to promote itself as a centre for touring holidays, and Worsbrough village a short drive from the M1 motorway, the Worsbrough mystery plays may soon become a 'must' for every culture-conscious tourist.[7]

These remarks are pertinent, for they recognise the attempt by the surrounding locale to launch itself as a tourist destination. But Ottley's comments also raise an issue about who is the intended audience for these plays? Is it, as she suggested, the culture-conscious tourist, or is it the local community itself? Although the passing tourist may very well reap benefit from the production, many of the production decisions reflected greater concern with the production of an artefact which primarily represented and belonged to the community.

From the original seeds of 'Cycle 77', as it was known, came further productions in 1980 and 1983, all directed by Chris Evans. His appointment to a new job meant that the 1986 cycles were directed by John Kelly, and were sponsored by Yorkshire TV and McLean Homes. As Julian Wroe remarked:

> Many of the teenagers who appeared in major roles in 1986 had been the infant school children who first boarded Noah's Ark in 1977. The teenagers of 1977 were now the colliers, schoolteachers, nurses, unemployed and the mums and dads of 1986 ... The family of Worsbrough had become an extended family with actors and helpers from Leeds, Sheffield, Doncaster, Rotherham and Wakefield becoming increasingly involved.[8]

It has been the ability of Worsbrough to both develop local references and select from external practices that has made them so successful. So for example, in 1989 Worsbrough used a promenade adaptation of Tony Harrison's *The Mysteries* and a ten-piece live folk band. (The influence of this remained strong in the 2001 production of the plays, where pre-recorded folk rock music was used and some songs from the Harrison version adopted.) However, the 1989 cycle production is known locally as 'the disaster' because the promenade system was unpopular with the elderly, and was felt be an imported production.[9]

Other incidents demonstrate how the plays work on a system of local accretion. The Worsbrough plays often utilise a character called Old Wyrc as a narrator and link-person.[10] In 1992 the actor Derek Haughton's car broke down on the M1 motorway on the way to a performance. He ran to the nearest house, which turned out to be that of Arthur Scargill, at that time leader of the National Union of Miners, who drove him to the plays. Since then the character of Wyrc has always worn a miner's lamp on his belt as a tribute to Scargill.[11]

Since 1995 Worsbrough has staged a version of the text written by John Kelly, and derived from the York, Chester and Towneley cycles, which are copyrighted as 'The Worsbrough Mystery Plays'. As Julia Smith noted, this script draws together 'local material and personalised pieces that have crept into previous performances'.[12] Indeed, these local amendments continue with each performance, so that the play texts are fluid and changeable. In Julian Wroe's words, the script has 'adapted itself'; these adaptations include incorporating references to local pubs and churches to reflect the Yorkshire idiom. This adaptability is partly to do with the fact that the plays are community driven and controlled. The control of the production, in effect, resides with the director, and Worsbrough has always found them from within the community. Bill Fisher, who directed the plays in 1995, 1998 and 2001, is the latest in the lineage.

Another interesting feature of play production at Worsbrough is that the event is self-contained. Though the organising board initially tried to instigate social events in the intervening years between the productions, these were not popular; it became apparent that the investment was with the plays themselves and not linked to events. Participants did not feel the necessity to be part of an identifiable group in the intervening years, and were dedicated only to the plays themselves. Similarly, the group has received many offers to perform the plays in other locations, but this has always been turned down, with the exception of performing a few pageants at nearby Barnsley to celebrate the Millennium; however the participants found the experience there was very different from that at Worsbrough.[13]

Though a number of staging devices celebrate the specificity of the location, the Worsbrough plays have also utilised a process of accretion to collect ideas from other national productions and incorporate them into their plays, as Bill Fisher commented they 'plagiarised anything they could'.[14] In 2001 some of the staging devices were borrowed from the Coventry *Millennium Mysteries*, such as the census count in which common names were chalked onto a door. The Worsbrough version adapted this to suit their own locality, and marked off the names in 'ickeys', a Northern term used in counting games. Another staging feature taken from Coventry was the Slaughter of the Innocents, which was staged through having girls play with watermelons which soldiers later shattered onto the ground to symbolise the infanticide. As mentioned earlier, other parts of the 2001 production still showed the vestiges of the Tony Harrison production staged in Worsbrough in 1989. The use of a rock sound track and many songs, including the hymn 'Look up, Look up', the folk dance used at the start, the slapsticks used for the Noahs' fight, and the blue sheets for the Baptism were all derived from the Harrison version. However, some staging features are original to Worsbrough, and have become identifiable local features; these include the use of assorted coloured helium balloons released to represent the rainbow, fireworks at the end of the performance, a maypole dance (see Plate 23), a local Yorkshire dale song sung by the Shepherds, and the spotlit Crucifixion against the darkness of the church (which is lit from inside through the stained glass window).

Kristina Simeonova has analysed how two cultural modes can be traced in the mystery plays: the high culture of the biblical texts, and the low culture of the carnivalesque; together these two worlds 'are neither static nor isolated: they parallel, comment, connote one another'.[15] She suggested that there are a number of ways in which these two modes undertake a dialogic interaction in the Towneley Second Shepherds' play. Her model is interesting because it stands up as an example of how an artefact may be altered by carnival structures. It can be used as a metaphor to demonstrate the relationship between the mystery plays and the adaptations made at Worsbrough. Simeonova suggested there are three ways in which low carnival culture impinges upon the high text of the plays: these are through parenthetic accretion, peripheral merging and the carnivalisation of central structures. The relationship between the culture of the Worsbrough plays and those of the mystery play texts acts in accordance with many of these ideas. For example, many Worsbrough inventions are incorporated into their own play text through a process of accretion, such as the use of the narrator figure, Wyrc, which is particular to the place of Worsbrough. At other times there is peripheral merging whereby practices taken from productions outside Worsbrough are merged back into the plays. Evidence of this can be seen through the Bryden/Harrison influences which remain eleven years after the production was first played at Worsbrough. Lastly, the Worsbrough stamp is placed on some of the central structures. The Crucifixion of Christ against the silhouette of St Mary's Church is one such example of this mode (see Plate 24). Here some of the central moments of the drama are challenged, so that rather than the Crucifixion alone having central importance, the icon of Christ over the stained glass windows of the church takes central focus; consequently the place of Worsbrough is foregrounded. It is this imprinting of the local identity onto an imported text that has meant that the plays at Worsbrough have endured the passage of time so well, and have found a place in local cultural expression.

Worsbrough community

The success of the Worsbrough community in sustaining the mystery plays is not an isolated incident. The local Yorkshire community has demonstrated other ways in which it can generate its own sustainability. Since the decline of the coal industry in the late 1980s the region has placed an emphasis on tourism, and by the Millennium nearby Barnsley had received 2 million visitors each year and generated £63 million of investment. The key to this success was not through the efficiency of external agencies, but rather by the development of a tourist forum comprising over 100 local businesses and only three local government representatives. Ann Untisz, principal development and promotions manager with Barnsley Metropolitan Borough Council noted, 'The local business community needed to be spearheading the campaign with our administrative and financial back-up and that's the secret of its success.'[16] This view is supported by the chair of the group, the local hotelier John Wigfield: 'We all came together and discovered what each of us had to offer. With the local authority we promoted the positive side of coming to Barnsley and we marketed it both here and abroad. It has been a phenomenal success.'[17] The ability to act as an effective community is shown through examples of both the mystery plays and tourism; it is perhaps not surprising that the community is able to draw together so well since it is a very homogenous society. According to the 2001 census 99 per cent of the Barnsley population are white British, and 81 per cent of the population are Christian.[18]

In a study of another mining community, that of Ashington, some 140 miles north of Barnsley, Dawson has examined clubs for the elderly and assessed how these might articulate a notion of living within the community. Dawson noted that while some of the clubs are organised by social services, they are more often run by elderly volunteers 'in-line with the co-operative movement which is firmly established in the area.'[19] Dawson saw in these clubs the continuation of the welfare associations set up in the early twentieth century by mining groups in which 'Much is made of the uniqueness of locality, and, in particular, of its people's language and dialect, their drinking habits, and their association with the dirt of the coal-mining industry.'[20] He also noted how the clubs create a distinctive identity by setting their members apart from others (usually those that they considered to be different and outside of the community). In the case of Northern clubs, this sense of the outsider was usually represented by the South.

The community of Worsbrough mirrors many of Dawson's findings. It is an area surrounded by former collieries, such as that of Barrow at Worsbrough, Thorncliffe at Birdwell and Cortonwood, Darfield, and Mitchell at Wombwell. The protection of their shared locality and antipathy to the outsider, which Dawson found at Ashington, is also to be seen in the sense of competition that Worsbrough mystery plays holds with nearby York. Julian Wroe was keen to point out that the York mystery plays attracted considerable funding and media attention, yet, during the years that productions of the plays at York and Worsbrough had coincided, spectators claimed to prefer the Worsbrough experience. Wroe was very critical of the poor levels of funding received by Worsbrough for the mystery plays, and indeed the low degree of public funding that reached Barnsley in general – an issue which he claimed the local Member of Parliament had raised in the House of Commons.[21] In articulating these views, Wroe aligned himself with a facet of the Ashington community noted by Dawson, 'In celebrating community, participants within the clubs offer an image of the mutuality of the oppressed.'[22] But, as Dawson argued, part of the reason why the sense of community is regarded as a prevalent feature of Northern life is because of the adversity suffered by those regions and the subsequent necessity of binding together.

The community involved in producing the plays at Worsbrough, though, is not a fixed or exclusive one. Indeed, part of the success of the plays is that they have expanded to allow new members to join. Initially the plays were to be performed by the High School, but this was widened to include members of Worsbrough and Birdwell villages, and in the subsequent years those from Barnsley, Sheffield, Leeds, Doncaster, Rotherham and Wakefield.[23] Similarly, although the initial group was defined by those participating in the plays, the congregation from St Mary's Church have also been included. After the final dress rehearsal on Sunday a service of dedication is held where the full congregation come to the stage set and the plays are blessed. In 2001 this service was conducted by the Bishop of Sheffield, a mark of the recognition of the importance of the plays.

Other community models

The importance of community in the mystery plays is evident in many productions. Phil Butterworth observed that one of the outcomes of the 1958 production of the Wakefield plays at Bretton Hall was to generate a sense of belonging: 'Communication of the strong sense of community purpose was felt and referred to by witnesses and correspondents.'[24] Butterworth noted that director Martial Rose still relished the achievements that had been made from finding a cohesive communal approach to the dramas forty years after the experience: 'the most shaking realisation was that individually we were nothing out of the ordinary as teachers and students, but as a community we achieved something far above the level of our individual competence.'[25] The power of participating in the mystery plays has left their mark on many people. Eileen Skaife, a participant in York plays from the original 1951 production until 1980, recollected that at the end of each production: 'You feel very sad because a way of life was going to end, you see, and all the companionship as well as the great satisfaction in playing something like that.'[26]

Two models of community drama that have been dealt with in this book so far include those at Lichfield and York. They are revisited here in order to assess the success of their community playing and to offer a contrast to the experience of Worsbrough. At Lichfield the plays were developed in 1994 by community arts worker Glen Buglass in order to develop community values in the city; he saw in the plays the potential to build a more cohesive community. This was a quality perceived by others too. The Royal Mail, one of the sponsors of the plays, observed: 'Like all community projects, its success will rely heavily on all those involved pulling together as a team.'[27] A sense of the way in which a local identity might be built through the plays was also recognised by Patricia Tarrant-Brown, the costume mistress, who described how she begged people in the streets to take part and that she believed anyone and everyone could participate. Furthermore, she noted the importance of embedding the plays in local culture, which meant that they would need to evolve and develop so that they belonged to the city.[28] However, Tarrant-Brown's enthusiasm was not always felt by the whole of Lichfield. For example, Councillor Margaret Stanhope remarked that:

'These people seem to set great stall in dressing up, playing around and prancing round the city centre but I just cannot see the worth of it.'[29]

Director Robert Leach commented that in setting up the Lichfield plays it was often difficult, as an outsider, to get recognition from community groups, and that he was frequently regarded with suspicion.[30] In truth, the 1994 production did not succeed in establishing a community of players, but instead drew on multiple smaller communities for each pageant. As Leach revealed, the plays were eventually performed by 'discrete groups which have an autonomous existence beyond the Mysteries – youth theatres, folk groups, local churches, schoolteachers, council workers, or just groups of friends'.[31] In expressing a sense of community, the Lichfield plays showed how an 'imagined community' might be constructed by establishing a superficial shared culture that was layered over the participating pre-existing groups.

Another model of community participation can be found in the York mystery plays. As Eileen Skaife acknowledged above, participating in the plays created a sense of community for those involved. Since York has had such a long history of mystery play production, the sense of the plays providing a community is more developed there than anywhere else. As Margaret Rogerson nostalgically observed of the Millennium production: 'When the stage lights went down for the last time in the Minster, these revival regulars and other who were newcomers to the mysteries were looking forward to meeting with old and new friends for the next revival.'[32] Rogerson located how a sense of community identity was created at York through campaigns conducted by the local paper. For example, she tracked how press coverage of the Millennium production sought to include those not directly participating in the plays by giving a sense of the organisation and preparation of the event.[33] But the history of the mystery play production at York belies the notion that community can be clearly achieved. Many of the participants of the Museum Garden plays, as noted in Chapter 7, are alienated by the indoor versions of the plays. The establishment of the guild plays in 1994 has formed another dynamic in the battle for the York plays. While some participants are happy to cross between the productions, others fight for the importance of their own versions. So the vision of the director for the 2002 York guild plays, Mike Tyler, of genuine 'community integration' was something of a utopian hope.[34]

Mysteries' end

The Worsbrough plays emerged, in many ways, as an exemplary example of how community versions of the mystery plays can operate. While other productions suffered from accusations of imported directors, struggling membership or exploiting the heritage industry, the plays at Worsbrough were a vibrant example of community practice that was hard to fault. However, at the beginning of the new Millennium something happened at Worsbrough, and the plays, seemingly so embedded into local culture, collapsed. The plays were produced again in 2004, but this time under limited conditions. A free performance of a few eclectic pageants linked together by the narrator Old Wyrc were staged in a corner of the churchyard. Bill Fisher, the last person to stage a full-length version of the plays, noted that the community spirit had dwindled because the objectives for producing the plays had been met or were exhausted, or priorities had changed.[35] Fisher pointed to a number of reasons that jeopardised the productions of the plays. First, the costings attached to the productions and methods of securing sponsorship grew increasingly complicated; a pressure known all too well at York. Second, the notion of community had dwindled for several reasons, most notably because of the decrease in population in the area; Fisher felt the lack of roots put down by participants in the intervening years between the plays demonstrated the instability of the community commitment. Third, the decline in rural church stability; St Mary's Church, which formed part of the mystery play audience, now shares its vicar with other rural churches, and is only open one in every three weeks. Lastly, many of the amateur actors who were participants have grown increasingly involved in launching and sustaining new local indoor theatres in Barnsley. The energy of many participants has been redirected into establishing the Lamp Room at Barnsley, a community and amateur dramatics venue. The amateur groups have left behind the outdoor texts of the mystery plays in favour of plays by known writers.

Though Worsbrough may have reached its 'Mysteries End', in many ways it has stayed true to its community objectives. New priorities have been put in place and indoor playing is seen to fulfil these more adequately. True to medieval times, the modern productions of mystery plays only survive for as long as they serve a purpose, and in 'redefining their actual and symbolic boundaries in the present and for the future',[36] the mystery plays have possibly disappeared from Worsbrough.

SECTION V

Conclusion

CHAPTER 11

Mysteries End?

In 1970 Peter Brook directed what was considered to be a seminal production of Shakespeare's *A Midsummer Night's Dream*. The Stratford-upon-Avon stage of the Royal Shakespeare Company was not filled with the then usual neo-Romantic trees painted onto a backdrop, and actors were not adorned with Elizabethan-style costumes; instead, all that was present was a white box. Within this white box fairies appeared as circus figures and swung on trapeze equipment, climbed ladders, and lazed on suspended leaves. The production encouraged the audience to utilise their imaginations and emphasised the importance of theatre as play as well as the spoken word. Brook's production illustrates how any historical text can be taken and reinterpreted from a radical angle. In fact, productions of *A Midsummer Night's Dream* since the 1970s have demonstrated how it can be staged utilising a number of different angles and concepts. In this sense the mystery plays are no different from other historical dramas: they are open to various interpretations and, as the productions described in this book suggest, they can become all things to all people.

Though some of the participants in these productions maintain that the success of the mystery plays is their ability to provide a platform for any type of interpretation, I do not believe this is why they have found favour at the turn of the Millennium. Although the mystery plays are often chosen because they seem to represent all things to all people, the truth of their success is just the opposite. They seem to work best when they are produced for very specific occasions and conditions. Although on the surface they are as malleable as *A Midsummer Night's Dream*, in practice they thrive when undertaken for specific celebratory reasons or to fulfil the needs of a particular expression of local identity.

The plethora of productions around the turn of the Millennium had much to do with the spirit of that time. It provided an opportunity for reflection and new goal setting. The United Nations, for example, established a programme of eight Millennium Development Goals aimed at eradicating world poverty, ill-health and increasing education and equality to be achieved by 2015.[1] This new spirit of reflection at the turn of the Millennium invited people to contemplate a time-scale and think of the past, future and present. For many, the celebration of 1,000 years was allied to the birth of Christ, and the mystery plays offered an opportunity to explore this dimension of the New Millennium. In the same manner in which the Festival of Britain sparked the modern-day reproduction of the mystery plays, the New Millennium offered a symbolic celebration of their rejuvenation.

It is notable that many of the productions discussed above are specific to an occasion (be it the Millennium, or another one). For example, the Leeds production of the York cycle in 1975 was fashioned to celebrate the university's centenary, and the original Worsbrough plays commemorated the Queen's Silver Jubilee in 1977. Other productions were undertaken to observe the Millennium: the York *Millennium Mysteries* in the Minster, the Chichester Youth Theatre production, and the Coventry *Millennium Mysteries*. There is a notable difference as to whether these commemorative productions were played solely to mark a specific occasion, or whether they indicate the establishment of a new tradition of mystery play performance that will be maintained in the future. At both Coventry and Worsbrough the occasional performance of their inauguration led to the establishment or revitalisation of the mysteries. In both these cases the plays offered their communities an opportunity to express their local identities, and thus enthusiasm for their continued playing developed.

Despite the collapse of the plays at some venues, the survival of the plays in the twenty-first century still looks to be strong. There are particularly well-established traditions at Chester, Lichfield and Coventry, while at Lincoln the passing of the plays from one director to another has occurred smoothly and the series seem likely to continue. At York, though the large-scale versions seem to have collapsed, the guild productions on waggons on the streets is growing in strength, and since 2002 the event has spread to encompass two weekends.

It is interesting to see why modern-day playing has survived in some locations, while elsewhere it has perished. There are some similarities between the circumstances that surround the surviving plays. The strongest surviving traditions come from the Midlands and North West (the cities of Coventry, Lichfield and Chester); for many, the plays are associated with Yorkshire, so this is a significant change.[2] Another striking similarity between these productions is that each of them is associated with its cathedral. At Chester they are performed on the cathedral green, at Coventry in the remains of the bombed cathedral, and at Lichfield the third and final playing station is the cathedral. Despite this link with a building, all three versions also manage to maintain outdoor playing traditions. These factors appear to have helped the traditions to continue.[3]

It is apparent that modern-day producers of the mystery plays do not necessarily choose the plays for their subject matter. (In fact the professional productions in this book show an awareness that plays associated with religion tend to sell fewer tickets.)[4] The mystery plays are chosen rather for their epic scale, decorum and the wealth of their story-telling potential. Frequently the productions described in this book have sought to divert the religious focus of the plays into a contemporary parallel, as with those of the Royal Shakespeare Company and Royal National Theatre. Other productions have chosen to emphasise the spectacular nature of the plays, and have displaced the plays' religiosity into impressive theatrical idioms, such as giant stilt-walking, elaborate costumes, make-up and masks. It cannot be argued that the majority of plays are chosen because of the opportunity to explore contemporary devotion, though this may be the case for some smaller productions by church groups, the larger community-based versions were instead selected for the wealth of opportunities they offered.

It is clear from the examples investigated in this book that the playing of the mystery plays provides the supporting communities with an opportunity to explore their identity. It is perhaps for this reason that modern productions of plays that are still being played, such as those at Lichfield, Chester, Coventry and amongst the guilds at York. At Lichfield the mystery plays make up a small part of a festive calendar which includes Shrovetide fairs, mock courts, mayoral processions, and folk festivals. This commitment to public celebration is one way in which the city, dwarfed by nearby Birmingham, can carve out its own sense of history and identity. It is perhaps for this reason that the plays, set up through the interests of lecturer Robert Leach, have survived despite having no clear affiliation to a specific commemorative event. The association with local identity is also a factor for the play production at Coventry, where the plays met with great support and were rejuvenated through the Millennium production. In this city the community objectives of the play production are matched by local investment in projects which enhance the development of a city identity. Similarly it is the expression of local identity that enables the continuation of the York guild productions. Richard Rastall observed that in producing the plays, 'All the guilds concerned found that they had, and were proud of, a sense of ownership of their plays.'[5] The case of Worsbrough demonstrates how productions of the plays survive while there is still a need for them. Once local energy was dissipated by establishing a local indoor amateur theatre in Barnsley, the mystery plays became less fundamental to the expression of identity.

Playing the medieval stage

The staging of medieval drama today has offered a series of opportunities which extend beyond issues of community values, religious expression or local identity, but are about coming to terms with the demands of a tradition of playing which is alien to the dominant forms of dramatic representation to be found within contemporary society. The challenge of playing the mystery plays raises questions about how to engage with the spatial relationship between the stage and action, how to present non-human characters and epic events, and how to discover a playing style that will communicate the texts to a modern audience.

The experiments with spatial configurations and playing spaces have been one of the most successful dimensions of modern-day productions. The productions that have merely emulated indoor proscenium arch arrangements have often been the most awkward in terms of the dynamic set up between the audience and the actors. Amongst these productions are the indoor versions of the pageant waggon experiments at Toronto in 1977, Katie Mitchell's production for the Royal Shakespeare Company, Greg Doran's York *Millennium Mysteries* in the Minster, and the Theatre Royal productions of the York Mystery Plays in 1992 and 1996. These productions have all grappled with the formality of indoor spaces and of fixed divides between the actors and spectators which are too rigid and formal for the mystery plays. Two indoor productions overcame potential problems by displacing the formal contract between actors and audience. Bill Bryden's production at the Royal National Theatre stripped the theatre bare and recreated the sense of an open town square within the promenade staging, while at Chichester the design for the plays incorporated trapeze equipment, and the evocation of a circus allegory broke conventional models of spectatorship.

It is not the case that outdoor versions of the plays automatically find a fluid and dynamic relationship with the audience. The criticism levelled by John Elliott against the York Mystery Plays in the Museum Gardens attacked the inappropriate rigidity of the ruins of the abbey walls and the formality of the fixed audience seats. Similarly, some of the stagings of the Chester plays on the cathedral green have in effect created unyielding actor/audience relationships in which there is a formal divide between fixed, ranks of covered seating and the stage arena.

The productions which have discovered the most dynamic relationships between the actors and audience are those that have promenaded in the streets, such as at Lichfield, the York guild plays and the academic experiments at Leeds and Toronto.[6] Other dynamic practices have been established through the Lincoln 2000 plays, which played with the diversity of the cathedral space, and Worsbrough, which has reconfigured it relationship with its audience for each production and in particular emphasised a close proximity between the actors and the audience.

Another success of modern-day productions is the manner in which the epic nature of the mystery play texts has allowed a diversity of theatrical techniques to be utilised to great effect. For example, in the Coventry *Millennium Mysteries* giant stilt-walkers and street theatre devices created a spectacular production. At Worsbrough the use of helium balloons and fireworks also took advantage of the outdoor staging. The demands of the plays to stage deities, angels and Satan and to create a host of environments such as an ark, a Crucifixion scene, and doomsday have allowed productions to create fantastical set and costumes. The York *Millennium Mysteries* utilised the scale of the gothic Minster to create elaborate stagings with beautiful puppets for the Creation scene, a whole miniature ship for the ark, and Satan's excessively long tail. The glory of the building was also reflected in the ornate music and choral singing and the lighting of the nave with a rainbow of colour. Often, as in this production, the epic demands of the mystery plays have enabled producers to bring together the text, building and theatrical effects to create a spectacular result.

One aspect of modern-day stagings of the plays that has proved more difficult is that of the acting style. The difficulties of approaching the stylisation required was most acutely felt by the young actors in the Chichester Youth Theatre version, and apparent even in the Bill Bryden production for the Royal National Theatre. Attempts to find an appropriate style include those initiated by Browne, who outlined some of the rules that he found for playing medieval drama. The more useful amongst these are: 'Gesture must come from the body, and its weight must follow the arm in a big gesture' and 'Find a reason for dropping a gesture as well as for making it; and give the gesture time to make its effect on the audience before you drop it.'[7] Other modern-day experiments that have merit are those by Phil Butterworth, who observed that there are a number of different modes that an actor can use in medieval drama: 'It is possible, for example, for an actor to speak "to," "at," "with," or "through" an audience.'[8] He further noted that: 'These differences can be real in the actor/audience relationship depending on intention and context.'[9] So while it is clear that medieval drama can offer a range of registers for a modern-day audience (and a range larger than that of most contemporary plays), there have been no experiments with acting style so far that have produced convincing results.

In dealing with the mystery plays participants do not enter into a type of archaeological investigation in which they unearth primitive remains of drama; rather the complexity of the mode of production and presentation offers a rich canvas against which to practice theatre today. Surprisingly, the complexity of medieval drama is such that it can provide contemporary society with opportunities to rethink and challenge the models of drama that are prevalent today.

If we are still unclear about many aspects of medieval drama production, it does little to affect the popularity of these plays today. Though this book, for ease of analysis, has often identified patterns within productions, it is their disparity that is most remarkable. What is clearly successful is the individuality that they offer a community. From the mid-twentieth century onwards there has been a fascination with the plays which led William Tydeman to note in the 1990s that: 'Today there is probably greater awareness of the existence, nature and appeal of fourteenth- and fifteenth-century English drama than at any time since its creation.'[10] Although this fascination was most acutely felt at the turn of the Millennium, it shows little likelihood of receding.

Notes

Preface

1 Peter Brook, *The Empty Space* (Harmondsworth: Penguin Books, 1972), p. 18.

2 Edith Hall, 'Introduction', *Dionysus since 69: Greek Tragedy at the Dawn of the Third Millennium*, ed. Edith Hall, Fiona Macintosh and Amanda Wrigley (Oxford: Oxford University Press, 2004), pp. 5–6.

3 John Elliott, *Playing God: Medieval Mysteries on the Modern Stage* (Toronto: University of Toronto Press, 1989), p. viii.

4 The *platea* is an open, general space, and is contrasted by the *locus*, or specific location, often built from platforming.

5 Julia Smith, 'The rival mystery plays', *Dalesman* 57.4 (July 1995), p. 40.

Section I ~ Introduction

1 For a further discussion on this, see the introduction to Carolyn Dinshaw, *Getting Medieval: Sexualities and Communities, Pre- and Postmodern* (Durham, HN: Duke University Press, 1999).

2 Ibid., p. 43.

3 Ibid., p. 206.

1 Playing the Drama: Mystery Plays in Medieval England

1 The York REED entry shows pageant waggons being stored, which indicates performances may have been undertaken by this point, however, the record may be a later addition and does not provide concrete evidence of mystery play performance at this point.

2 Derek Brewer estimates that by 1500 about half the population could read: see Derek Brewer, 'The social context of medieval English literature', *The New Pelican Guide to English Literature*, vol. 1: *Medieval Literature*, ed. Boris Ford (London: Penguin, 1991), p. 23.

3 To take just one example, at Hoxne Church in Suffolk there are wall paintings aimed at doctrinal instruction, such as representations of the Seven Deadly Sins, the Seven Works of Mercy and the Seven Ages of Man. Derek Pearsall, 'The visual world of the Middle Ages', *The New Pelican Guide to English Literature*, vol. 1: *Medieval Literature*, ed. Boris Ford (London: Penguin, 1991), p. 315.

4 Documents from medieval York suggest that the plays were important for the instruction and moral improvement they offered, and were played to honour God and the city of York.

5 I will adopt the convention of referring to the individual episodes as pageants, and the whole series of pageants as the plays.

6 It is unclear whether the Towneley plays are linked to Wakefield. Their name comes from the family with whom the manuscript resided, but scholars increasingly suggest that this link is tenuous.

7 It is thought that sometime between 1465 and 1476 the York plays displaced the Corpus Christi ecclesiastical procession to the following day: see Richard Beadle, 'The York cycle', *The Cambridge Companion to Medieval English Theatre*, ed. Richard Beadle (Cambridge: Cambridge University Press), p. 90.

8 The work by Meg Twycross, reported at the *Medieval English Theatre* conference in 2005, utilising ultra-violet and x-ray techniques to re-examine the York *Ordo paginarum* may throw many of these ideas into dispute. The reconsideration of documentary evidence suggests the 4.30 a.m. start was a later addition, and dates from between 1509 and 1517.

9 See Garrett P. J. Epp, 'The Towneley plays, or, the hazards of cycling', *RORD* 32 (1993), pp. 121–50, and Barbara Palmer, 'Recycling "The Wakefield Cycle": the records', *RORD* 41 (2002), pp. 88–130.

10 Richard Schechner, *Performance Studies* (London: Routledge, 2002), p. 45.

11 Ibid., p. 49. All subsequent quotations are taken from this page.

12 See E. K. Chambers, *The Mediaeval Stage*, 2 vols. (Oxford: Oxford University Press, 1903); V. A. Kolve, *The Play Called Corpus Christi* (Stanford: Stanford University Press, 1966); Mervyn James, 'Ritual, drama and social body in the late medieval English town', *Past and Present* 98 (1983), pp. 3–29; Charles Phythian-Adams, 'Ceremony and the citizen: the communal year at Coventry, 1450–1550', *Crisis and Order in English Towns*, ed. Peter Clark and Paul Slack (London: Routledge & Kegan Paul, 1989, pp. 57–85); Miri Rubin, *Corpus Christi: The Eucharist in Late Medieval Culture* (Cambridge: Cambridge University Press, 1991); Sarah Beckwith, *Signifying God* (London and Chicago: University of Chicago Press, 2001; Claire Sponsler, 'The culture of the spectator: conformity and resistance to medieval performances', *Theatre Journal* 44 (1992), pp. 15–29.

13 Phythian-Adams, 'Ceremony and the citizen', pp. 57–85.

14 James, 'Ritual, drama and social body', p. 4.

15 Rubin, *Corpus Christi*, p. 272.

16 Sarah Beckwith, *Signifying God: Social Relation and Symbolic Act in the York Corpus Christi Plays* (Chicago: University of Chicago Press, 2001), p. 47.

17 Claire Sponsler, *Drama and Resistance: Bodies, Goods, and Theatricality in Late Medieval England* (Minneapolis: University of Minnesota Press, 1997), p. 160.

18 Alan Nelson, *The Medieval English Stage: Corpus Christi Pageants and Plays* (Chicago: University of Chicago Press, 1974), p. 14.

19 In terms of both the composition of actors within the frame of the waggon and the proxemics between the actors on the stage.

20 I am indebted to the debates held at the *METh* conference at Southampton 2005 which covered this issue.

21 Henri Lefebvre, *The Production of Space*, trans. D. Nicholson-Smith (Oxford: Blackwell, 1991), pp. 93–4.

22 David Wiles, *A Short History of Western Performance Space* (Cambridge: Cambridge University Press, 2003), p. 21.

23 Ibid., p. 74.

24 *York: Records of Early English Drama*, ed. Alexandra F. Johnston and Margaret Rogerson, vol. 1 (Toronto: University of Toronto Press, 1979), pp. 55–6.

25 The Mercers' records show that damask painted cloth was used on the back of the waggon. *York: REED*, p. 56.

26 Meg Twycross, 'The theatricality of medieval English plays', *The Cambridge Companion to Medieval English Theatre*, ed. Richard Beadle (Cambridge: Cambridge University Press, 1994), p. 45.

27 With the exception of the Shepherds' and Nativity pageants, and possibly the two Magi pageants.

28 Bim Mason, *Street Theatre and Other Outdoor Performance* (London: Routledge, 1992), p. 16.

29 Susan Bennett, *Theatre Audiences: A Theory of Production and Reception* (London: Routledge, 1990), p. 93.

30 Observing the York Guild productions in 2006, it was evident that a hush went through the audience as the action began, and they remained respectfully quiet; however, a reasonable number of the audience came and went.

31 *Two Coventry Corpus Christi Plays*, ed. Hardin Craig, Early English Text Society, ES 87 (London: Oxford University Press, 1957), Coventry, Shearman and Taylors' Play, l. 783.

32 Indeed, Phil Butterworth directed an experiment in which the soldiers in the York *Crucifixion* played all their comments through direct address. See Philip Butterworth, 'The York *Crucifixion*: actor/audience relationship', *METh* 14 (1992), pp. 67–76.

33 Meg Twycross and Sarah Carpenter, *Masks and Masking in Medieval and Early Tudor England* (Aldershot: Ashgate, 2002), p. 10.

34 Colin Counsell, *Signs of Performance: An Introduction to Twentieth-Century Theatre* (London: Routledge, 1996), p. 86.

35 Donna Smith Vinter, 'Didactic characterisation – the Towneley *Abraham*', *Medieval English Drama*, ed. Peter Happé (London: Macmillan, 1984; reprint 1993), p. 87.

36 Ibid., p. 81.

37 Ibid., p. 85.

38 *York: REED*, pp. 24–5. The work by Meg Twycross on the *Ordo paginarum* has brought the reliability of this data into dispute: see Meg Twycross, 'Forget the 4.30 am start: recovering a palimpsest in the York *Ordo paginarum*', *METh* 25 (2003), pp. 98–152.

39 Meg Twycross, 'Transvestism in the mystery plays', *METh* 5.2 (Dec. 1983), p. 152.

40 Vinter, 'Didactic characterisation', p. 87.

41 Edmund Leach, *Rethinking Anthropology* (London: Athlone Press, 1961), p. 125.

42 Ibid., p. 126.

43 For further discussion of how typologies may work, see Kolve, *The Play Called Corpus Christi*.

44 C. Richardson and J. Johnston, *Medieval Drama* (London: Macmillan, 1984), p. 65.

45 This list is not exhaustive. There were other productions which are not covered in this book, such as those at Newport Pagnell. Long Crendon, in Oxfordshire, present a selection of mystery plays annually, and did so at the Millennium.

46 Janette Dillon noted that the use of time within *The Croxton Play of the Sacrament* falls into eleven different categories: see Janette Dillon, 'Performance time: suggestions for a methodology of analysis', *METh* 22 (2000), pp. 33–51.

47 Allan Kaprow, 'The Happenings are dead: long live the Happenings!', *Essays on the Blurring of Art and Life*, ed. Jeff Kelley (Berkeley: University of California Press, 1993), p. 63.

48 Ibid., p. 62.

49 Guy Claxton, *Hare Brain, Tortoise Mind* (London: Fourth Estate, 1997), p. 2.

50 Peter Meredith, 'The York cycle at Toronto: October 1 and 2, 1977', *RORD* 20 (1977), p. 112.

51 Betsy Taylor, 'The York cycle at Toronto', *Cahiers Élisabéthains* 55 (April 1999), p. 58. An eyewitness of the Lichfield 1994 plays suggested that the effect of them was like Wagner's *Ring* cycle: see letter held in Robert Leach's personal archive.

2 Playing the Plays Today: Staging, Concepts, Community

1 Elliott, *Playing God*, pp. 142–3.

2 Ibid., p. 142.

3 Hall, 'Introduction', p. 2.

4 Brook, *The Empty Space*, p. 11.

5 Ibid., p. 73.

6 Arthur Bartow, *The Director's Voice* (New York: Theatre Communications Group, 1988), p. 283.

7 Ibid., p. 313.

8 R. Mulryne and M. Shewring, eds., *The Cottesloe at the National: Infinite Riches in a Little Room* (Stratford-upon-Avon: Mulryne & Shewring, 1999), p. 82.

9 Raymond Williams, *Keywords* (London: Fontana, 1983), p. 76.

10 Kenneth Pickering, *Drama in the Cathedral*, 2nd edn (Malvern: Churchman Publishing, 2001), p. 35.

11 Ibid., p. 36.

12 Ibid. Ironically, Guthrie was later given a chance to direct the York mystery plays but refused on the grounds that the site of the abbey was too limiting.

13 The Medieval Players, which began life as the Cambridge Medieval Players in 1974 under the direction of Carl Heap, were interested in creating a theatrical style inspired by Guthrie. McCaw, one of the actors in the company, reminisces that director Carl Heap would often cite Tyrone Guthrie as an inspiration for the work of the Medieval Players. Guthrie's desire to work beyond illusionary theatre and to challenge the boundaries of form was key to the Medieval Players' ethos. While Guthrie broke the confines of the proscenium arch by having the audience on three sides with his production of *Ane Satyre of the Thrie Estiatis*, the Medieval Players worked with a transportable booth and trestle stage that could be set up anywhere.

McCaw observes how the company performed in village halls, gymnasiums, shopping precincts and football pitches. This style of performance allowed the company to develop a strong interplay between the actors and the audience. He notes of the company – in language that draws upon Brook's terminology – that 'Ours is the poor theatre of minimal technical paraphernalia, or direct audience address, which appeals to their imagination through suggestive gesture, a theatre of skill and spectacle': see Dick McCaw, 'Old theatre for new', *Leeds Studies in English* 32 (2001), p. 287.

14 Pickering, *Drama in the Cathedral*, pp. 101–2.

15 Ibid., p. 97.

16 In the event a local newspaper leaked the name of Joseph O'Connor, who played Christ.

17 See Beckwith, *Signifying God*, p. 8, and Elliott, *Playing God*, p. 77. Ossie Heppell recalls how Joseph O'Connor, who played Christ, was not allowed to be seen within the city pubs. Ossie Heppell, interviewed by Mike Tyler, York Mystery Plays, 8 September 1999.

18 Beckwith, *Signifying God*, p. 5.

19 Marshall, 'Modern productions of medieval English plays', *The Cambridge Companion to Medieval English Theatre*, ed. Richard Beadle (Cambridge: Cambridge University Press, 1994), p. 191.

20 Quoted in Beckwith, *Signifying God*, p. 7.

21 For details of Rose's 1958 production of the Wakefield cycle, see Philip Butterworth, 'Discipline, dignity and beauty: the Wakefield mystery plays, Bretton Hall, 1958', *Leeds Studies in English* 32 (2001), pp. 49–80.

22 In 1973 Butterworth also directed three Towneley pageants in the grounds of Bretton Hall, when playwright John Godber played God. I am grateful to him for supplying details of the Bretton performances.

23 For a discussion on the issues raised by reading the REED collections, see Theresa Coletti, 'Reading REED: history and the records of early English drama', *Literary Practice and Social Change in Britain, 1380–1530*, ed. Lee Patterson (Berkeley: University of California Press, 1993), pp. 248–84, and the special edition of *Medieval English Theatre* 17 (1995).

24 Helen Nicholson, *Applied Drama: The Gift of Theatre* (Basingstoke: Palgrave, 2005), p. 10.

25 Catherine Itzin, *Stages in the Revolution* (London: Eyre Methuen, 1980), p. xii.

26 Jellicoe had also used this format earlier to write *The Rising Generation* in 1967 for the Girl Guides Association, but this was not performed by them.

27 Itzin, *Stages in the Revolution*, p. xii.

28 Marshall, 'Modern productions of medieval English plays', p. 296.

29 http://www.statistics.gov.uk/cci/nugget.asp?id=293 (accessed 14 September 2006).

30 According to statistics on the Church of England website: see http://www.cofe.anglican.org/info/statistics/ (accessed 3 September 2006).

31 Marshall, 'Modern productions of medieval English plays', p. 297.

32 Paula Neuss, 'God and embarrassment', *Themes in Drama*, vol. 5: *Drama and Religion*, ed. James Redmond (Cambridge: Cambridge University Press, 1983), p. 244.

33 Marshall, 'Modern productions of medieval English plays', p. 304.

34 http://www.millennium.gov.uk/index.html (accessed 6 October 2006). The commission was established to distribute monies raised by the National Lottery.

35 See Jen Harvie, *Staging the UK* (Manchester: Manchester University Press, 2005), p. 1.

36 Ibid., p. 30.

37 Ibid., p. 12.

Section II ~ Playing Spaces

1 Meg Twycross, '"Places to hear the play": pageant stations at York, 1398–1572', *REED Newsletter* 2 (1978), pp. 10–33.

2 For further discussion of this, see Katie Normington, *Gender and Medieval Drama* (Cambridge: D. S. Brewer, 2004), pp. 79–81.

3 Teresa Heitor *et al.*, 'Breaking of the medieval space: the emergence of a new city of enlightenment'. Proceedings of Space Syntax, Second International Symposium, Brazil, 1999, vol. 2: http://www.spacesyntax.net /symposia/SSS2/sss2_proceedings.htm (accessed 2 October 2006).

4 Wiles, *A Short History of Western Performance Space*, p. 10.

5 Ibid., p. 11.

3 Pageant Staging: Experiments with the York Cycle

1 See the remark made in Marshall, 'Modern productions of medieval English plays', p. 302. See also Nelson, *The Medieval English Stage*, p. 14.

2 Peter Meredith, 'The two Yorks: playing Toronto and York', *Early Theatre* 1 (1998), p. 160.

3 E. Martin Browne gave his support to the Leeds project: 'I am indeed very much interested by your York Mystery Play project. It sounds incredibly ambitious! But worth the huge effort.' See letter from E. Martin Browne, 15 January 1975, Leeds University Archives.

4 Jane Oakshott and Richard Rastall, 'Town with gown: the York cycle of mystery plays at Leeds', *Towards the Community University*, ed. David C. B. Teather (London: Kogan Page, 1982), p. 215.

5 Ibid.

6 *University of Leeds Reporter* 71 (29 May 1975), p. 1.

7 Hilda Purvis, the surviving sister of the Reverend Purvis, was delighted by the performances at Leeds, and the rights of the text were donated to the University: 'Personally I am very grateful that my brother's work has found such a secure home, and will be of benefit to your students in the future.' See letter from Hilda Purvis, 25 May, 1975, held in University of Leeds Archives.

8 Oakshott and Rastall, 'Town with gown', p. 222.

9 Ibid., p. 225.

10 Evidence from the 1988 and 1992 productions of a selected number of the York plays by Meg Twycross showed that this was contrary to her experience. See David Mills, 'The York mystery plays at York', *METh* 10:1 (1988), pp. 69–70.

11 The photographs are held by Peter Meredith; some slides are deposited in the University of Leeds Archive.

12 Meredith, 'The York cycle at Toronto', p. 113.

13 Ibid., p. 114.

14 From notes by Oakshott held in her personal archive.

15 Glynne Wickham, *Early English Stages, 1300–1600*, vol. 1 (London: Routledge & Kegan Paul, 1959–81), pp. 169–73.

16 Oakshott and Rastall, 'Town with gown', p. 225; Meredith, 'The York cycle at Toronto', p. 112; see also Marshall, 'Modern productions of medieval English plays', p. 303. Oakshott had anticipated that each waggon would take six to eight people to move it: see letter from Jane Oakshott to organising directors, 20 March 1975; held within her personal archives.

17 Comment from Oakshott's own notes on the production held in her personal archives.

18 Ibid., p. 224.

19 Marshall, 'Modern productions of medieval English plays', p. 303.

20 Oakshott and Rastall, 'Town and gown', p. 225.

21 Ibid.

22 Held in Oakshott's personal archives.

23 Meredith, 'The York cycle at Toronto', p. 113.

24 Personal interview with Jane Oakshott, May 2002.

25 David Parry, 'The York mystery cycle at Toronto, 1977', *METh* (1979), p. 19, and Meredith, 'The York cycle at Toronto', p. 112.

26 This group began as Professor Leyerle's seminar group (thus PLS) in 1964, when he began teaching at Toronto University.

27 Sheila Lindenbaum has criticised the monotony and incomprehensibility of this text, and believes that its use prevented an exploration of the composition of the whole York cycle. See Sheila Lindenbaum, 'The York cycle at Toronto: staging and performance style', *Medieval English Drama*, ed. Peter Happé (London: Macmillan, 1984), p. 208.

28 Sheila Lindenbaum disputed this and believed the larger pageants did seem rather cramped: see Lindenbaum, 'The York cycle at Toronto', p. 203. David Bevington asserted that only eight disciples could fit the stage: see Bevington, 'The York cycle at Toronto: October 1 and 2, 1977', *RORD* 20 (1977), p. 109. However, Peter Meredith suggested that the use of two stair blocks at either side of the waggon beautifully accommodated the full complement of disciples: see Meredith, 'The York cycle at Toronto', p. 113.

29 As Parry pointed out, the prologue could not begin before the waggon was in position, as the actor could not compete with the noise of the moving waggon, however, once it was in place and while it was still being set up the actor could take over: see Parry, 'The York mystery cycle at Toronto', p. 20.

30 Ibid.

31 Ibid., pp. 19–20.

32 Lindenbaum, 'The York cycle at Toronto', p. 205.

33 Fuller details of the waggon dimensions used can be found in Parry, 'The York mystery cycle at Toronto', pp. 19–31.

34 Of course, the modern-day waggons are often farm carts and are sprung; they are thus less stable than medieval purpose-made waggons would have been.

35 Parry, 'The York mystery cycle at Toronto', p. 28. Lindenbaum commented that in casting Parry as God, 'the analogy (and distinction) between the human and divine artificer was made by the smooth stage machinery carrying God to his heavens and the script that the overworked human actor consulted for some of his lines': see Lindenbaum, 'The York cycle at Toronto', p. 204.

36 Meredith, 'The York cycle at Toronto', p. 112.

37 Parry, 'The York mystery cycle at Toronto', p. 29.

38 David Bevington noted that 'Dramatically, the time spent indoors on Saturday was not as rewarding as that spent outdoors on Sunday': see Bevington, 'The York cycle at Toronto', p. 109.

39 Lindenbaum, 'The York cycle at Toronto', p. 202.

40 Ibid., p. 206.

41 Thomas Hahn, 'The York cycle at Toronto: October 1 and 2, 1977', *RORD* 20 (1977), p. 118.

42 Parry, 'The York mystery cycle at Toronto', p. 29.

43 Lindenbaum, 'The York cycle at Toronto', p. 203.

44 Gail McMurray Gibson, 'The York cycle at Toronto: October 1 and 2, 1977', *RORD* 20 (1977), p. 114.

45 See, amongst others, J. K. Bonnell, 'The serpent with the human head in art and mystery play', *American Journal of Archaeology* series 2, 21 (1917), pp. 255–91, and M. D. Anderson, *Drama and Imagery in English Medieval Churches* (Cambridge: Cambridge University Press, 1963).

46 Parry, 'The York mystery cycle at Toronto', pp. 26–7.

47 Lindenbaum, 'The York cycle at Toronto', p. 202.

48 Ibid., p. 209, and Kathleen Ashley, 'The York cycle at Toronto: October 1 and 2, 1977', *RORD* 20 (1977), p. 110.

49 Bulletin 6: 'Time, timing, and rehearsing', sent by the organisers to producing companies. As Joel Kaplan pointed out, it is in effect impossible to monitor the aims behind forty-seven different productions. Although the co-ordinating committee had one set of aims, participating groups had 'aims vastly different from one another': see Joel Kaplan, 'Afterwards', *Early Theatre* 3 (2000), p. 276.

50 Bulletin 6: 'Time, timing and rehearsing'. This point is disputed by Ralph Blasting, who argues that this practice 'rings false', and the set-up of the waggons was part of the enjoyment experienced by the audience: see Ralph Blasting, 'The Toronto York cycle: design and technical display', *Early English Theatre* 1 (1998), p. 154.

51 Alexandra Johnston, 'York cycle 1998: what we learned', *Early Theatre* 3 (2000), p. 199.

52 Ibid.

53 Eyewitness accounts of the production suggest that 'some voices were showing the strain even after two stations': see Taylor, 'The York cycle at Toronto', p. 56.

54 Johnston, 'York cycle 1998', p. 202. Contrary to this, the actors at Leeds in 1975 indicated that they liked the repeated performance opportunities, and were just getting into their stride after the three stations: see group questionnaires, Jane Oakshott, personal archives.

55 Johnston, 'York cycle 1998', p. 200. The playing at various different stations brought into question the appropriateness of some of the end-on staging. Joel Kaplan remarks that end-on staging may have worked in the restrictions of a York street, 'but to continue in the face of Toronto's station 2, a sunken pathway facing a vast grass lawn, seemed positively perverse': see Kaplan, 'Afterwards', p. 277. Kaplan's point suggests that some spaces are not suited to pageant playing. This point does highlight the difficulty in balancing the demands of academic experiments with practical performance considerations. As Garret Epp pointed out, 'questions of waggon orientation seemed merely academic relative to other performance issues': see Garret Epp, 'Playing in all directions: the York plays, Toronto', *Early Theatre* 1 (1998), p. 150.

56 David Bevington, 'Context and performance: the York plays at Toronto', *Early English Theatre* 1 (1998), p. 147.

57 Ibid., p. 148.

58 See Twycross, 'Places to hear the play', pp. 10–33.

59 Butterworth, 'The York *Crucifixion*', p. 74.

60 Johnston, 'York cycle 1998', p. 201, and Taylor, 'The York cycle at Toronto', p. 57. At the second station the audience retreated to the shade of the trees, leaving a vast space in front of the waggons. Johnston suggested that many groups ruined the 'in the street' effect by trying to fill the space and coming forward of their waggon (e-mail 21 August 2001).

61 Cited in Megan Lloyd, 'Reflections of a York survivor: the York cycle and its audience', *RORD* 39 (2000), p. 226.

62 Johnston, 'York cycle 1998', p. 200.

63 For full details, see *York: REED*, vol. 1, p. 55.

64 It is clear that at York the *Death of Mary*, *Assumption*, *Coronation*, *Doomsday*, and *Ascension* (which had lifting gear) all had roofs. Late sixteenth-century illustrations and the text of the play suggests that the *Nativity* also had one. At Chester there were several pageants that called for scenic effects which might suggest the necessity of a roof: *The Purification and Doctors* has a temple with a steeple, *The Harrowing of Hell* a dungeon, the *Baptism* some sort of structure for the Father to speak from and the dove to be lowered; *Temptation* needs Christ to be set on top of a temple; *The Creation and Fall of the Angels* needs levels.

65 Watching the outdoor performance of the Worsbrough plays in 2001 highlighted for me the relationship between the texts and time. Although the version played was a compressed compendium of plays, it became apparent that the last few pageants were aware of the falling darkness. The texts seemed to make far greater reference to issues of light than their earlier counterparts, although plays such as the *Nativity* and the *Magi* require a star (which, given that they would have been performed around late morning, may have been represented by scenic pieces rather than light).

Plays like the *Harrowing of Hell* would have been performed in daylight and possibly utilised pyrotechnics.

66 Bob Potter, 'The York plays: University of Toronto, 20 June 1998', *METh* 19 (1999), p. 122.

67 See Potter, 'The York plays', p. 122, and Blasting, 'The Toronto York cycle', p. 154.

68 Johnston, 'York cycle 1998', p. 199, and Blasting, 'The Toronto York cycle', p. 155, respectively.

69 Potter, 'The York plays', p. 122.

70 Blasting, 'The Toronto York cycle', p. 155.

71 Johnston, 'York cycle 1998', p. 202.

72 *Chester: Records of Early English Drama*, ed. L. M. Clopper, REED vol. 2 (Toronto: University of Toronto Press, 1979), pp. 80–1.

73 Johnston, 'York cycle 1998', p. 203.

74 There remains much work to be done on the issue of sight-lines and the pageant waggons, and modern-day waggons are rarely high enough for much action to be seen from the first-floor windows. The 1988 plays at York by Meg Twycross videoed the view of the plays seen from the Lady Mayoress's rooms in Petergate, where she is known to have watched the plays in 1527 and 1538.

75 In medieval times some actors played in more than one pageant. (This also occurred during the 'Leeds experiment'.)

76 David Bevington commented on the 1977 production at Toronto that 'it was refreshing to discover how natural it seems to have a succession of different Gods, Adams, and Eves, not only physically alike but strikingly different in style of interpretation: see Bevington, 'The York cycle at Toronto', p. 109.

77 Barbara Palmer, 'The York cycle in performance: Toronto and York', *Early Theatre* 1 (1998), p. 142.

78 Epp, 'Playing in all directions', p. 151. This view is supported by Betsy Taylor, who notes that the female Christ in this pageant was far superior to any others, although she admits that the accuracy of the male impersonation in this play showed up weaknesses within others: see Taylor, 'The York cycle at Toronto', pp. 57–8.

79 The records held by Poculi Ludique Societas show that the producers had difficulty in controlling various productions, most notably the *Last Judgement*. E-mails from David Klausner to the director Stephen Johnson (sent 11 May 1998) attempted to squash a contemporary interpretation of the pageant.

80 See *York: REED*, vol. 1, p. 25

81 Meg Twycross, 'Playing "The Resurrection"', *Medieval Studies for J. A. W. Bennett*, ed. P. L. Heyworth (Oxford: Clarendon, 1981), p. 277.

82 Elliott, *Playing God*, p. 131.

83 See Peter Happé, 'Acting the York mystery plays: a consideration of modes', *METh* 10.2 (1988), pp. 112–16.

84 As Joel Kaplan pointed out, 'attempts at performance reconstruction are effectively compromised by our inability to provide period spectators': see Kaplan, 'Afterwards', p. 276.

85 Potter, 'The York plays', pp. 121–2. David Parry makes a similar observation about a child sitting at the foot of Pilate's throne in the 1977 production (Parry, 'The York mystery cycle at Toronto', p. 26). See also the discussion of the relationship between children and the plays in Chapter 9.

86 Lloyd, 'Reflections of a York survivor', pp. 228–9.

87 Ibid., p. 231.

88 Ibid., p. 232.

89 Jane Oakshott, 'York guilds' mystery plays 1998: the rebuilding of a dramatic community', *Drama and the Community: People and Plays in Medieval Europe*, ed. Alan Hindley (Turnout: Brepols, 1999), p. 270.

90 Dorothy Chansky, *In Theatre* 40 (19 June 1998), pp. 32–3.

91 Meredith, 'The two Yorks', p. 161.

92 Ibid.

93 Richard Rastall, 'The mystery plays 25 years on', *The Reporter* 452 (22 May 2000).

94 Oakshott, 'York guilds' mystery plays 1998', p. 286.

95 Quoted in ibid., p. 287.

96 Mike Tyler, 'Review of York mystery plays 2002', *RORD* 42 (2003), p. 160.

97 Margaret Rogerson, 'Review of York mystery plays 2002', *RORD* 42 (2003), p. 167.

98 Julia Smith, '... To the mysterious', *Dalesman* (July 2000), pp. 32–3.

99 Twycross, 'The theatricality of medieval English plays', p. 47.

4 From Outside to Inside: Fifty Years of the Plays at York

1 Anthony Dawson and Paul Yachnin, *The Culture of Playgoing in Shakespeare's England: A Collaborative Debate* (Cambridge: Cambridge University Press, 2001), p. 102. This view fits with those of Benedict Anderson discussed in Chapter 2 in terms of creating an 'imagined community'.

2 Ibid. See the arguments put forward in the previous chapter by Megan Lloyd, who notes both the collective and individual experience of watching the Toronto 1998 plays.

3 Ruth Evans draws attention to the inappropriate laughter that is recorded as accompanying the missing York Fergus play. See Ruth Evans, 'When a body meets a Fergus: Fergus and Mary in the York cycle', *New Medieval Literatures*, ed. Wendy Scase, Rita Copeland and David Lawton (Oxford: Clarendon Press, 1997), pp. 193–212.

4 Sheila Lindenbaum, 'Ceremony and oligarchy: the London Midsummer watch', *City and Spectacle in Medieval Europe*, ed. Barbara Hanawalt and Kathryn Rogerson, Medieval Studies at Minnesota, vol. 6 (Minneapolis: University of Minnesota Press, 1994), p. 179.

5 *Non-Cycle Plays and Fragments*, ed. N. Davis, Early English Text Society SS 1 (Oxford: Oxford University Press, 1970), pp. 114–15.

6 John Elliott, 'Playing the Godspell', *RORD* 15–16 (1972–3), p. 126.

7 Margaret Rogerson, '"Everybody got their brown dress": mystery plays for the Millennium', *New Theatre Quarterly* 17.2 (May 2001), p. 129.

8 Marshall, 'Modern productions of medieval English plays', p. 291.

9 Browne admitted that the drawing by Hubert Cailleau influenced him most. See E. Martin Browne with Henzie Browne, *Two in One* (Cambridge: Cambridge University Press, 1981), p. 184.

10 Ibid., p. 184.

11 Interview with Ossie Heppell by Mike Tyler, 8 September 1999. http://www.yorkmysteryplays.org/index_highres.htm (accessed 15 April 2006).

12 A. L. Laishley, 'The York mystery plays', *Yorkshire Life Illustrated* (June 1954), p. 15.

13 Ibid.

14 Beckwith, *Signifying God*, p. 7.

15 Ibid., p. 9.

16 Kenneth M. Cameron, 'The Lincoln plays at Grantham', *RORD* 10 (1967), p. 142.

17 Elliott, 'Playing the Godspell', p. 125.

18 Ibid., p. 126.

19 John Elliott, 'Review of 1976 York mystery plays', *RORD* 20 (1977), p. 98.

20 Robin Thorber is cited in Elliott, 'Review of 1976 York mystery plays', p. 98.

21 See Peter Happé, 'Review of 1980 York mystery plays', *RORD* 13 (1980), pp. 81–3.

22 Charles Whitworth, 'Review of 1984 York plays', *Cahiers Élisabéthains* 26 (Oct 1984), p. 108.

23 John Elliott, 'Review of 1984 York mystery plays', *RORD* 17 (1984), p. 187.

24 Mills, 'The York mystery plays at York', pp. 69–70.

25 Ibid., p. 69.

26 Beckwith, *Signifying God*, p. 161.

27 Wiles, *A Short History of Western Performance Space*, p. 23.

28 Alderman Keith Wood, interviewed by Mike Tyler, 13 December 2001. http://www.yorkmysteryplays.org/index_highres.htm (accessed 15 April 2006).

29 These figures are from the *Yorkshire Evening Post*, 7 November 1991.

30 Review of York mystery plays, *The Independent*, 15 June 1992.

31 Review of York mystery plays, *The Guardian*, 16 June 1992.

32 Review of York mystery plays, *Northern Echo*, 1 July 1992.

33 Review of York mystery plays, *The Independent*, 15 June 1992.

34 Review of York mystery plays, *The Guardian*, 2 March 1996.

35 Review of York mystery plays, *Financial Times*, 12 June 1996.

36 Review of York mystery plays, *Daily Telegraph*, 2 June 1996.

37 Sarah Paul, 'The 1996 York cycle of mystery plays: mirrors of the community', *The Month*, Sep/Oct 1996, p. 395.

38 Alderman Keith Wood, 13 Dec, 2001.

39 Lynda Murdin, *Yorkshire Post*, 28 June 2000.

40 York Millennium Mystery Plays, Programme.

41 Kevin Berry, 'Review of *York Millennium Mystery Plays*', *The Stage*, June 2000.

42 Joshua Abrams, 'Review of *York Millennium Mystery Plays*', *Theatre Journal* 53.1 (2001), p. 151.

43 Michael Coveney, *Daily Mail*, 30 June 2000.

44 Review of York Millennium mystery plays, *Yorkshire Evening Post*, 22 June 2000.

45 Rogerson, 'Everybody got their brown dress', p. 134.

46 Review held in the clippings book at York Minster library.

47 Paul Taylor, 'Review of the York *Millennium Mysteries*', *The Independent*, 27 June 2000.

48 Robert Hewson, *Sunday Times*, 2 July 2000.

49 Paul Taylor, *The Independent*, 26 June 2000.

50 Smith, '... To the mysterious', p. 23.

51 Rogerson, 'Everybody got their brown dress', p. 134.

52 Reported by Ian Shuttleworth, *Financial Times*, 26 June 2000.

5 Spatial Practices: Chester, Lincoln and Lichfield

1 Lefebvre, *The Production of Space*, pp. 38–9.

2 Nugent Monck produced three pageants in Chester in 1906 as a try-out for a more elaborate full production in 1909, which was unfortunately not endorsed: see David Mills, 'Reviving the Chester plays', *METh* 13 (1991), pp. 39–51.

3 Margaret Rogerson has outlined the success of York at establishing itself on the tourist map: see Rogerson, 'Living history: the modern mystery plays in York', *RORD* 43 (2004), pp. 12–28.

4 In the early years the plays were performed more frequently. A selection of pageants were also performed in 1952.

5 Letter from Graham Webster to Director of Education, 20 December 1949, cited in David Mills, 'The 1951 and 1952 revivals of the Chester plays', *METh* 15 (1993), p. 112.

6 Most of the text was prepared by his wife Betty, though it was thought important that Revd McCulloch be credited too: see letter from Betty McCullogh to Mr Cottam (secretary of Cheshire Rural Council), 15 February 1951 (Chester City Archives DPU/7).

7 Mills, 'The 1951 and 1952 revivals of the Chester plays', p. 120.

8 Cited in ibid.

9 Review of Chester Mysteries, *Manchester Guardian*, 20 June 1951.

10 Letter from Burkinshaw to Chester Chronicle, 25 June 1952. Chester City Archives, DPU/12.

11 Letter from Christopher Ede to Burkinshaw, 23 August 1957. Chester City Archives, DPU/14.

12 Letter from Burkinshaw to Ede, 21 August 1957. Chester City Archives, DPU/14.

13 Note from Lawlor and Sisson, 9 May 1962. Checter City Archives, DPU/19.

14 Letter from Burkinshaw to Miss Natalie McCracken, 5 February 1963. Chester City Archives PUB 52 PAP/MEF.

15 Letter sent 29 June 1962. Chester City Archives, DPU/19.

16 Letter TC/MEF PUB: 52. Chester City Archives, DPU/19.

17 Letter from Burkinshaw to Christopher Ede, 6 December 1965. Chester City Archives, DPU/19.

18 Roose-Evans asserts that the convention of the Big Top was suggested by Alexander Schouvaloff, director of the North West Arts Association: see James Roose-Evans, *Inner Journey, Outer Journey: Finding a Spiritual Centre in Everyday life* (London: Rider & Co., 1987), p. 60.

19 Ibid., p. 56.

20 Stanley Kahrl, 'Medieval drama in England, 1973: Chester and Ely', *RORD* 15–16 (1972–3), p. 118.

21 Brook, *The Empty Space*, pp. 73, 74.

22 Kahrl, 'Medieval drama in England', p. 119.

23 Lefebvre, *The Production of Space*, p. 38.

24 Kahrl includes a quotation from the 1973 programme in which Roose-Evans stated that 'no clear picture of Christ's teaching emerged' from the original cycle: see Kahrl, 'Medieval drama in England', p. 120.

25 Ibid.

26 David Mills, *Recycling the Cycles: The City of Chester and its Whitsun Plays* (Toronto: University of Toronto Press, 1998), p. 218.

27 Ibid.

28 Edward Burns, 'Seeing is believing: the Chester Play of the Nativity at Chester Cathedral Summer 1987', *Cahiers Élisabéthains* 34 (Oct 1988), p. 2. For further information on WSI, see http://www.welfare-state.org/homepage.htm. The group disbanded in April 2006 and an archive is being established at Bristol University.

29 Burns, 'Seeing is believing', p. 3. The influence of the cathedral also occurred through invisible means. Burns reveals that the church authorities were initially doubtful about the use of *The Last Judgement*, but eventually sanctioned its use (ibid., p. 8).

30 Ibid.

31 Lefebvre, *The Production of Space*, p. 40.

32 Burns, 'Seeing is believing', p. 9.

33 Elizabeth Beroud and Angela Maguin, 'The Chester Mysteries 1992', *Cahiers Élisabéthains* 42 (October 1992), p. 66.

34 Quoted in David Mills, 'The Chester mysteries 1992', *METh* 12 (1992), p. 120.

35 Ibid.

36 In fact, it could be argued that in some ways the production had appropriated the cathedral. Bob Cheeseman was invited by the dean and chapter of the cathedral to deliver a sermon at a Sunday matins service, though the production also created tensions with the cathedral; one of the canons found the notion of the representation of God by three actors to be blasphemous. See Beroud and Maguin, 'Chester Mysteries 1992', pp. 67, 70.

37 In this light, the Chester 1992 plays can be seen to use the place-and-scaffold spaces in a manner similar to the *locus* and *platea*. For further readings of the functions of the *locus* and *platea*, see Robert Weimann, *Shakespeare and the Popular Tradition: Studies in the Social Dimension of Dramatic Form and Function* (Baltimore: Johns Hopkins University Press, 1978).

38 Beroud and Maguin, 'Chester Mysteries 1992', p. 71.

39 Personal interview with George Roman, 30 August 2000.

40 The production of the Lincoln plays was also presented at Southwell, Neustadt, Viterbo, Rome, Perpignan, Camerino and in Portland, USA. The focus here is on the relationship between the space and the performance and for that reason only the productions played at Lincoln are analysed.

41 Alan Fletcher, 'Lincoln mystery plays', *RORD* 18 (1985), p. 208.

42 Ibid.

43 *Lincoln Mystery Plays*, 2000, Programme.

44 Peter Happé, 'The Lincoln cycle of mystery plays', *RORD* 14 (1981), p. 198.

45 *Lincoln Mystery Plays*, 2000, Programme.

46 Pamela Brown, 'The Lincoln Cycle of mystery plays', *Shakespeare Bulletin* 13 (1995), pp. 21–2.

47 See 'Magnificent swansong', *Lincolnshire Chronicle*, 21 July 2000.

48 *Lincoln Mystery Plays*, 2000, Programme.

49 Robert Leach, *The Lichfield Mysteries* (Birmingham: Clydesdale, 1994), introduction.

50 For an account of how visual arts may affect a production see Theresa Coletti and Kathleen Ashley, 'The N-Town Passion at Toronto and late medieval passion iconography', *RORD* 14 (1981), pp. 181–7.

51 See http://lichfield-mysteries.freeserve.co.uk (accessed 21 June 2000).

52 *Lichfield Mysteries*, 1994, Programme.

53 Review of Lichfield Mysteries, *The Lichfield Mercury*, 5 May 1994.

54 The observations that follow are all taken from a personal interview with Robert Leach, 31 July 2001.

55 Martin Stevens, '"Processus Torontoniensis": a performance of the Wakefield Cycle', *RORD* 18 (1985), p. 192.

56 Ibid., 198.

57 Lefebvre, *The Production of Space*, p. 43.

Section III ~ Contemporary Concepts

1 Maria Delgardo and Paul Heritage, *In Contact with the Gods: Directors Talk Theatre* (Manchester: Manchester University Press, 1996), p. 1.

2 Beckwith, *Signifying God*, p. 182.

3 Ibid., p. 189.

6 Bryden/Harrison's *The Mysteries*, Royal National Theatre

1 For full details of the production history see Mulryne and Shewring, *The Cottesloe at the National*, p. 71.

2 Beckwith, *Signifying God*, p. 180.

3 Elliott, *Playing God*, p. viii.

4 Bill Bryden, 'Spectacular space for "The Passion"', *The Festival Scotsman*, 18 August 1980.

5 Mulryne and Shewring, *The Cottesloe at the National*, p. 81.

6 Tony Harrison quoted in John Walker, 'Promenade of "Passion" gets audience into act', *International Herald Tribune*, 23 August 1978.

7 Mulryne and Shewring, *The Cottesloe at the National*, p. 83.

8 Ibid.

9 Paul Hirst, 'Miracle or mirage?: The Thatcher years, 1979–1997', *From Blair to Blitz*, ed. Nick Tiratsoo (London: Phoenix, 1997), p. 193.

10 The 1970s saw the peak of trade union membership. It ran at 54 per cent of all workers in 1979, while by 1995 this had dipped to 33 per cent. See Duncan Gallie, 'The labour force', *Twentieth Century British Social Trends*, ed. A. H. Halsey with Josephine Webb (London and New York: Macmillan Press and St Martin's Press, 2000), p. 309.

11 Hirst, 'Miracle or mirage?', p. 194.

12 Benedict Nightingale, 'Theatre', *Harpers and Queen*, September 1977.

13 Karl Dallas, 'God spake in dialect', *The Morning Star*, 21 December 1985.

14 ME, 'Review of *The Mysteries*, National Theatre', *RORD* 21 (1978), p. 99.

15 Benedict Nightingale, *The Times*, 21 December 1999.

16 Michael Billington, *The Guardian*, 21 December 1999.

17 Hirst, 'Miracle or mirage?', p. 205.

18 John Gross, *Sunday Telegraph*, 26 December 1999.

19 Charles Spencer, *Daily Telegraph*, 20 December 1999.

20 This is not to assume that all members of the audience were attracted to the plays because of their religious content.

21 Peter Brierley, 'Religion', *Twentieth Century British Social Trends*, ed. A. H. Halsey with Josephine Webb (London and New York: Macmillan Press and St Martin's Press, 2000), p. 655.

22 Ibid., p. 656.

23 Church-going and Christianity are not necessarily the same thing. While a small proportion of the population attends Church, as these statistics show many more believe in God and can claim to be Christians.

24 Ibid., p. 663.

25 Christopher Grier, *Evening Standard*, 21 January 1985.

26 Charles Spencer, *Daily Telegraph*, 20 December 1999.

27 At other moments the design concepts had been expanded to include visual jokes: the wise men travelled on glorious dromedaries made from old Dunlop tyre stands, and wore traffic cones as head-dresses.

28 Carole Woodis, *City Limits*, 25 January 1985.

29 Harrison's amendments are clear. The revised text shows a greater use of Latin, which is used to counterpoint the Yorkshire idiom. At points the use of 'local' references and Yorkshire turns of phrase are incorporated. For example, Cain declares 'Farewell. When I am dead / Bury me in Wakefield by t' quarry head': see Tony Harrison, *The Mysteries* (London: Faber, 1985), p. 30. Noah emits the Yorkshire expletive 'oh heck' when he realises that God has approached him. (The Noah expletive is only contained within the prompt book and not the printed text.) Other significant changes made by Harrison for the 1985 production included the addition

of the Abraham and Isaac pageant, the reworking of the Three Kings speeches and their interaction with Herod and his son, and, most importantly, an alteration to the close of the piece. Jack Shepherd noted that the text which he helped create for the performance at Edinburgh in 1980 ended with a devised scene between God and the Devil: see Jack Shepherd, 'The "Scholar" me: an actor's view', *Tony Harrison*, ed. Neil Astley (Newcastle: Bloodaxe Books, 1991), p. 425. Harrison drew upon the Chester cycle and replaced this with a speech by Death.

30 See Martin Hoyle, *Financial Times*, 20 May 1985.

31 Shepherd, 'The "Scholar" me', p. 425.

32 Bill Bryden, *Kaleidoscope*, BBC Radio 4, December 1985: transcript in the Royal National Theatre archive.

33 Francis King, *Daily Telegraph*, 27 January 1985.

34 ME, 'Review of *The Mysteries*', p. 98.

35 David Staines, 'The English mystery cycles', *The Theatre of Medieval Europe*, ed. Eckehard Simon (Cambridge: Cambridge University Press, 1991), p. 93.

36 Ibid., p. 94.

7 Katie Mitchell's *The Mysteries*, Royal Shakespeare Company

1 Edward Kemp, *The Mysteries, Part One: The Creation* (London: Nick Hern Books, 1997), p. v.

2 Unless otherwise indicated, all Mitchell's statements are taken from a personal interview with the author at The Other Place, 15 March 1997.

3 Marshall, 'Modern productions of medieval English plays', p. 310.

4 David Tushingham, *Live One: Food for the Soul* (London: Methuen, 1994), p. 89.

5 According to Mitchell's view expressed in the interview.

6 Charles Spencer, 'Mystery stripped back to the basics', *Daily Telegraph*, 10 March 1997.

7 Kemp, *The Mysteries: Part One*, p. vi.

8 Beckwith, *Signifying God*, p. 187.

9 Ibid.

10 Kemp noted that the structure of the text owed more to episodic than linear plot development: 'In some strange marriage of Brecht and Beckett the story emerges not through any conventional unfolding of the plot, but through the coincidence of a series of highly charged episodes': see Kemp, *The Mysteries, Part One*, p. xi.

11 Neuss, 'God and embarrassment', p. 245.

12 Kemp, *The Mysteries: Part One*, p. xiv.

13 Spencer, 'Mystery stripped back to the basics'.

14 John Peter, 'Acting in the best faith', *Sunday Times*, 16 March 1997.

15 Spencer, 'Mystery stripped back to the basics'.

16 For a full reading of women's characters in the mystery plays, see Normington, *Gender and Medieval Drama*.

17 *Genesis* 3:6.

18 For comments on the political correctness of the production, see Peter, 'Acting in best faith,' and Nick Curtis, *Evening Standard*, 10 March 1997.
19 Michael Billington, 'God's in his heaven,' *The Guardian*, 10 March 1997.
20 Robert Hanks, 'Soft targets,' *The Independent*, 27 March 1997.
21 Personal interview with John Retallack, 14 May 1997. Subsequent statements by Retallack are from this source.
22 Hanks, 'Soft targets.'
23 Elliott, *Playing God*, p. 143.
24 Edward Kemp, 'Anti-Semitism, Islamophobia and sexism plague the mystery plays. How does a modern playwright junk the propaganda without losing the plot?,' *New Statesman* (23 Jan 1998), p. 39.
25 Bill Hagerty, *News of the World*, 25 January 1998.
26 James Kingston, *The Times*, 23 Jan 1998.

8 The Coventry *Millennium Mysteries*

1 In avoiding the term 'Passion' the production disassociated itself from Christian terminology and ideologies, and attempted to open itself up to wider appeal.
2 Rogerson, 'Everybody got their brown dress,' p. 123.
3 Ibid., 124.
4 Anthony Jackson, 'Inter-acting with the past – the uses of participatory theatre at museums and heritage sites,' *Research in Drama Education* 5.2 (2000), p. 209. The ideas outlined here are also discussed in Chapter 9 in relation to the Chichester Youth Theatre production of the mysteries.
5 John Elliott, 'A checklist of modern productions of the medieval mystery cycles in England,' *RORD* 13–14 (1970–71), p. 263. E. Martin Browne's use of the N-Town plays was probably based on a long-standing error of interpretation – the manuscript of what is now referred to as the N-Town plays was annotated 'Ludus Coventriae' in the seventeenth century. This probably meant no more than 'the kind of plays they used to do at Coventry,' but was then later taken to imply that they were the original Coventry Plays.
6 Pickering, *Drama in the Cathedral*, p. 297.
7 John Velz, 'The Coventry cycle of mystery plays, 1978,' *Cahiers Élisabéthains* 15 (April 1979), p. 126.
8 Ed Thomason, 'From the director's rehearsal notes,' *Coventry Mysteries*, 1979, Programme.
9 E. Martin Browne, 'The medieval play revival,' *Contemporary Review* 219 (1971), p. 135.
10 *Coventry Millennium Mysteries*, Programme.
11 Personal interview with Jane Hytch, 19 June 2000.
12 *Coventry Millennium Mysteries*, Programme.
13 Ibid.
14 Roman Pawlowski, 'Teatr Biuro Podrozy from Poland: mystery plays for the twenty-first century,' *TheatreForum* 10 (Winter/Spring 1997) p. 89.
15 Beckwith, *Signifying God*, p. 16.
16 Rogerson, 'Everybody got their brown dress,' p. 132.

17 Personal interview with Jane Hytch, 19 June 2000.

18 Personal interview with Matthew Pegg, 27 June 2000.

19 For further details, see Rogerson, 'Everybody got their brown dress', pp. 132–3.

20 *Coventry Millennium Mysteries*, Programme.

21 David Owen, 'The ethnic composition of Coventry in 1991', National Ethnic Minority Data Archive Information Paper 95/2, Centre for Research in Ethnic Relations, August 1995. See http://www.warwick.ac.uk/~errac/coventry.pdf (accessed 29 March 2006).

22 See Census online http://www.statistics.gov.uk/cci/nugget.asp?id=455 for results for country, and http://neighbourhood.statistics.gov.uk/dissemination/LeadTableView.do?a=3&b=276801&c=coventry&d=13&e=15&g=373870&i=1001x1003x1004&m=0&enc=1&dsFamilyId=47 for Coventry (accessed 24 October 2006).

23 R. Brown, 'Spiritual tourists', *Total Theatre* 12.2: (2000), p. 5.

24 Sheila Croucher, *Globalization and Belonging: The Politics of Identity in a Changing World* (Lanham, MD: Rowman & Littlefield, 2004), p. 192.

25 These Kings could also be interpreted as the Four Horseman; their eerie presence signifying death which was appropriate for the dramatic sequences dealing with Christ's death.

26 Pawel claimed that this image mirrored the parades set up by the 1990s Russian president, Yeltsin, who reinstated national holidays such as 12 June Independence Day. However, as will be discussed later, it was also reminiscent of the nationalistic parades held in Nazi Germany.

27 Rogerson, 'Everybody got their brown dress', p. 130.

28 Mason, *Street Theatre*, p. 16.

29 John Willett, *Brecht on Theatre* (London: Methuen, 1964), p. 93.

30 Personal interview with Jane Hytch, 19 June 2000.

31 Nicholson, *Applied Drama*, p. 94.

32 Peter Cramer, *Baptism and Change in the Early Middle Ages, c. 200–c. 1150* (Cambridge: Cambridge University Press, 1993), p. 247, cited in Beckwith, *Signifying God*, p. 15.

33 Ibid.

34 Rogerson, 'Everybody got their brown dress', p. 130.

Section IV ~ The Mysteries in the Community

1 Lindenbaum, 'The York cycle at Toronto', p. 209.

2 Nicholson, *Applied Drama*, p. 10.

3 Robert Bellah, *et al.*, *Habits of the Heart* (Berkeley: University of California Press, 1985), p. 333.

4 *Northern Echo*, 16 June 2000. At the rehearsal on 28 July 2000 a member of the cast stated that he had been in every production of the plays since 1957. The productions at York demonstrate the sense of belonging that can be achieved through such events.

5 *The Journal*, June/July 2000.

6 Nicholson, *Applied Drama*, p. 84.

9 Chichester Youth Theatre and *The Mysteries*

1 Jackson, 'Inter-acting with the past', p. 202.

2 Ibid., p. 209.

3 For full details see *York: REED*, p. 55.

4 Properties required included a golden apple tree with real apples which descended to represent Eden, and an abstract Red Sea (strings of large red plastic balls which could be parted to allow crossing).

5 Though arguably this was less so for residents of Chichester than elsewhere. The Census 2001 results show that in Chichester 77 per cent of its population were Christian, as opposed to 71 per cent nationally. See http://neighbourhood.statistics.gov.uk/dissemination/LeadTableView.do?a=3&b=277136&c=chichester&d=13&e=15&g=495899&i=1001x1003x1004&m=0&enc=1&dsFamilyId=17 (accessed 23 October 2006).

6 Personal interview with Andy Brereton, December 1999.

7 Adrian Henri, *The Wakefield Mysteries* (London: Methuen, 1991), p. vi.

8 Ibid., p. v.

9 Meg Twycross, 'Books for the unlearned', *Themes in Drama* 5: *Drama and Religion*, ed. J. Redmond (Cambridge, Cambridge University Press, 1983), p. 81.

10 Leah Sinanoglou, 'The Christ Child as sacrifice: a medieval tradition and the Corpus Christi plays', *Speculum* 48.3 (1973), p. 508.

11 Henri, *The Wakefield Mysteries*, p. v.

12 Ibid., p. vi.

13 Cohen's statement from *The Times Educational Supplement* is quoted in the blurb of Henri, *The Wakefield Mysteries*.

14 *Coventry: Records of Early English Drama*, ed. R. W. Ingram (Toronto: University of Toronto Press, 1981), p. 189. Coventry Weavers' AB 1551 f. 39. The carpenters' records from 1554 also show payments to a woman for a child.

15 *Chester: REED*, p. 96. Coopers' 1576 Record f.3r–v.

16 *Cumberland, Westmoreland, Gloucestershire: Records of Early English Drama*, ed. Audrey Douglas and Peter Greenfield (Toronto: University of Toronto Press, 1986), p. 12. Household Accounts of Edward Stafford, 1520–1.

17 Lynette Muir, 'Women on the medieval stage: the evidence from France', *METh* 7.2 (1985) p. 107.

18 Ibid., p. 108.

19 *Coventry: REED*, p. 86.

20 Richard Rastall, 'Female roles in all-male casts', *METh* 7.1 (1985), pp. 25–50. Rastall argued that puberty probably occurred later in medieval times than in modern times because of the affects of climate and nutrition, so that these players may still have been pre-pubescent.

21 D. T. Hanks Jr, '"Quicke Bookis' – the Corpus Christi drama and English children in the Middle Ages', *Popular Culture in the Middle Ages*, ed. J. Campbell (Bowling Green, Ohio: Bowling Green University Popular Press, 1986), pp. 211–12.

22 Barbara Hanawalt, *Growing up in Medieval London* (New York: Oxford University Press, 1993), p. 5. Hanawalt suggested that the passage from childhood to adulthood was marked by various factors. These include that at the age of twelve years a child was deemed to be responsible for a criminal act, that sexual availability signalled a significant change from child to woman, and that the taking up of an apprenticeship marked a rite of passage (ibid., pp. 112–13).

23 Barbara Hanawalt, '"The Childe of Bristowe" and the making of middle-class adolescence', *Bodies and Disciplines*, ed. Barbara Hanawalt and David Wallace (Minneapolis: University of Minnesota Press, 1996), p. 156.

24 Hanawalt, *Growing up in Medieval London*, p. 86.

25 Brian Edmiston, 'Drama as ethical education', *RIDE* 5.2 (2000), p. 64. Edmiston believed this was the approach taken in Joe Winston, *Drama, Narrative and Moral Education: Exploring Traditional Tales in the Primary Years* (London: Farmer, 1998).

26 Edmiston, 'Drama and ethical education', p. 64.

27 Ibid., p. 67. Edmiston attributed this comment to Michael Johnson, *Moral Imagination: Implications of Cognitive Science for Ethics* (Chicago: University of Chicago Press, 1993).

28 Winston, *Drama, Narrative and Moral Education*, p. 113.

29 Twycross compared the effect of the mystery plays with that of medieval spiritual literature, such as *Bonaventure*, Nicholas Love's 1410 translation of the *Meditationes vitae Christi*.

30 Twycross, 'Books for the unlearned', p. 79.

31 The Chichester production used the staging of God in this way. The actress playing him spoke directly to the audience in order to guide them or impart information. In contrast, he spoke to characters on stage through amplification, which gave God 'authorial' power, but had the effect of making him remote and inaccessible to stage characters.

32 Twycross, 'Books for the unlearned', p. 90. Twycross draws upon Peter Meredith's work at this point. See in particular Peter Meredith, '"Nolo Mortem" and the Ludus Coventriae play of *The Women Taken in Adultery*, *Medium Aevum* 38.1 (1969), pp. 38–54.

33 Twycross, 'Books for the unlearned', p. 91.

34 Ibid., p. 89

10 Community Theatre at Worsbrough

1 Nicholson, *Applied Drama*, p. 84.

2 Rogerson, 'Everybody got their brown dress', p. 123.

3 Margaret Ottley, 'Worsbrough's mystery plays', *Dalesman* 45.8 (Nov 1983), p. 662.

4 Julia Smith, 'The rival mystery plays', p. 38.

5 Bill Fisher noted that the setting of the 2001 plays was inspired by a visit to the Stephen Joseph Theatre at Scarborough, where action is set in the round. The use of the *mappa mundi* diagram on the stage also increased the sense of the shared experience of the plays; the actors and audience were as one within the world. Personal interview with Bill Fisher, 1 March 2006.

6 Personal interview with Julian Wroe, 2 July 2001.
7 Ottley, 'Worsbrough's mystery plays', p. 664.
8 Julian Wroe, 'The Worsbrough Mystery Plays: the first 21 years', *Worsbrough Mystery Plays*, 1998, Programme.
9 Personal interview with Julian Wroe, July 2001.
10 The name comes from Wyrc's burg, which was Worsbrough's original place name.
11 Ironically, the symbol of the miner's lamp connotes Harrison's plays in which Brian Glover as God wore a miner's lamp.
12 Smith, 'The rival mystery plays', p. 40.
13 Personal interview with Bill Fisher, 1 March 2006.
14 Ibid.
15 Kristina Simeonova, 'The aesthetic function of the carnivalesque in medieval English drama', *Bakhtin: Carnival and Other Subjects*, ed. David Shepherd (Amsterdam: Editions Rodopi, 1993), p. 74.
16 Paul Humphries, 'Tourists breathe new life into Barnsley', *The Guardian*, 9 March 2001.
17 Ibid.
18 http://neighbourhood.statistics.gov.uk/dissemination/LeadKeyFigures.do?a=3&b=5941350&c=worsbrough&d=14&e=15&g=362751&i=1001x1003x1004&m=0&enc=1 (accessed 6 November 2006).
19 Andrew Dawson, 'The mining community and the ageing body: towards a phenomenology of community', *Realizing Community*, ed. Vered Amit (London: Routledge, 2002), p. 22.
20 Ibid., p. 29.
21 Personal interview with Julian Wroe, 2 July 2001.
22 Dawson, 'The mining community', p. 30.
23 Given this expansion, it is even more surprising that the plays at Worsbrough have maintained such a clear sense of identity.
24 Butterworth, 'Discipline, dignity and beauty', p. 65.
25 Ibid.
26 Eileen Skaite, interviewed by Mike Tyler, 19 August 1999: see http://www.yorkmysteryplays.org/index_highres.htm (accessed 15 April 2006).
27 *Lichfield Mysteries*, 1994, Programme.
28 Ibid.
29 Unidentified newspaper article held in personal archives of Robert Leach.
30 Personal interview with Robert Leach, 31 July 2001.
31 *Lichfield Mysteries*, 1994, Programme.
32 Rogerson, 'Everybody got their brown dress', p. 126.
33 Ibid., pp. 126–7.
34 Tyler, 'York mystery plays 2002', pp. 158–61.
35 Personal interview with Bill Fisher, 1 March 2006.
36 Nicholson, *Applied Drama*, p. 84.

Section V ~ Conclusion

11 Mysteries End?

1 http://www.un.org/millenniumgoals/ (accessed 11 April 2006).

2 This association with Yorkshire stems from the fact that two of the four extant texts are thought to originate from there, that the strongest records of early civic performance come from York, and that the modern-day revivals of the plays in 1951 are most associated with York. One of the highest profiled modern-day productions, that of the National Theatre, aligned the plays with Yorkshire, through the use of the idiom of the regional accent.

3 It is impossible to suggest exactly why the association with cathedrals have had such an important impact on the productions. Perhaps one contributing factor is that it shows how keen local institutions are to support the mystery plays, and that the image of the plays sits more comfortably with participants and audiences if they are linked to the church. The use of the cathedral provides considerable prestige.

4 This was the experience of the productions by the Royal Shakespeare Company, Coventry and Chichester.

5 Rastall, 'The mystery plays 25 years on'.

6 Even within this use of space some stations were more suitable than others. Chapter 6, which covers the Toronto experiment, discusses how some of the four stations were more appropriate than others.

7 E. Martin Browne, *The Production of Religious Plays* (London: Philip Allan & Co., 1932), p. 38.

8 Philip Butterworth, 'Is there any further value to be gained from re-staging medieval theatre?', *RORD* 43 (2004), p. 5.

9 Ibid.

10 William Tydeman, 'An introduction to medieval English theatre', *The Cambridge Companion to Medieval English Theatre*, ed. Richard Beadle (Cambridge: Cambridge University Press, 1994), p. 1.

Bibliography

Abrams, Joshua. 'Review of York Millennium Mystery Plays'. *Theatre Journal* 53.1 (2001), pp. 149–51.

Anderson, Benedict. *Imagined Communities: Reflections on the Origin and Spread of Nationalism*. London: Verso, 1983; 2nd edn 1991.

Anderson, M. D. *Drama and Imagery in English Medieval Churches*. Cambridge: Cambridge University Press, 1963.

Ashley, Kathleen. 'The York Cycle at Toronto: October 1 and 2, 1977'. *RORD* 20 (1977), pp. 110–12.

Bartow, Arthur. *The Director's Voice*. New York: Theatre Communications Group, 1988.

Beadle, Richard. 'The York Cycle'. *The Cambridge Companion to Medieval English Theatre*. Ed. Richard Beadle. Cambridge: Cambridge University Press, 1994, pp. 85–108.

Beckwith, Sarah. 'Ritual, Theater, and Social Space in the York Corpus Christi Cycle'. *Bodies and Disciplines*. Ed. Barbara Hanawalt and David Wallace. Minneapolis: University of Minnesota Press, 1996, pp. 63–86.

—— *Signifying God: Social Relation and Symbolic Act in the York Corpus Christi Plays*. Chicago: University of Chicago Press, 2001.

Bellah, Robert, *et al. Habits of the Heart*. Berkeley: University of California Press, 1985.

Bennett, Susan. *Theatre Audiences*. London: Routledge, 1990.

Beroud, Elizabeth, and Angela Maguin. 'The Chester Mysteries 1992'. *Cahiers Élisabéthains* 42 (Oct 1992), pp. 65–71.

Berry, Kevin. 'Review of York *Millennium Mystery Plays*'. *The Stage*. Jun 2000.

Bevington, David. 'The York Cycle at Toronto: October 1 and 2, 1977'. *RORD* 20 (1977), pp. 107–10.

—— 'Context and Performance: The York Plays at Toronto'. *Early Theatre* 1 (1998), pp. 143–9.

Billington, Michael. 'God's in His Heaven'. *The Guardian*, 10 Mar 1997.

—— 'Review of the RNT *Mysteries*'. *The Guardian*, 21 Dec 1999.

Blasting, Ralph. 'The Toronto York Cycle: Design and Technical Display'. *Early Theatre* 1 (1998), pp. 152–6.

Bonnell, J. K. 'The Serpent with the Human Head in Art and Mystery Play', *American Journal of Archaeology* series 2, 21 (1917), pp. 255–91.

Brewer, Derek. 'The Social Context of Medieval English Literature'. *The New Pelican Guide to English Literature 1. Medieval Literature*. Ed. Boris Ford. London: Penguin, 1991. pp. 15–40.

Brierley, Peter. 'Religion'. *Twentieth Century British Social Trends*. Ed. A. H. Halsey with Josephine Webb. London and New York: Macmillan Press and St Martin's Press, 2000, pp. 650–74.

Brook, Peter. *The Empty Space*. Harmondsworth: Penguin Books, 1972.

Brown, Pamela. 'The Lincoln Cycle of Mystery Plays'. *Shakespeare Bulletin* 13 (1995), pp. 21–2.

Brown, R. 'Spiritual Tourists'. *Total Theatre* 12.2 (2000), pp. 4–5.

Browne, E. Martin. 'The Medieval Play Revival'. *Contemporary Review* 219 (1971), pp. 132–7.

—— *The Production of Religious Plays*. London: Philip Allan & Company, 1932.

—— with Henzie Browne. *Two in One*. Cambridge: Cambridge University Press, 1981.

Bryden, Bill. 'Spectacular Space for *The Passion*'. *The Festival Scotsman*, 18 Aug 1980.

—— *Kaleidoscope*. BBC Radio 4. Dec 1985.

Burns, Edward. 'Seeing is Believing: The Chester Play of the Nativity at Chester Cathedral, Summer 1987'. *Cahiers Élisabéthains* 34 (Oct 1988), pp. 1–9.

Butterworth, Phillip. 'The York *Crucifixion*: Actor/Audience Relationship'. *METh* 14 (1992), pp. 67–76.

—— 'Discipline, Dignity and Beauty: The Wakefield Mystery Plays, Bretton Hall, 1958'. *Leeds Studies in English* 32 (2001), pp. 49–80.

—— 'Is There any Further Value to be Gained from Re-Staging Medieval Theatre?' *RORD* 43 (2004), pp. 1–11.

Cameron, Kenneth M. 'The Lincoln Plays at Grantham'. *RORD* 10 (1967), pp. 141–51.

Chambers, E. K. *The Mediaeval Stage*. 2 vols. Oxford: Oxford University Press, 1903.

Chansky, Dorothy. *In Theatre* 40 (19 Jun 1998), pp. 32–3.

Chester Mysteries, review, *Manchester Guardian*, 20 Jun 1951.

Chester: Records of Early English Drama. Ed. L. M. Clopper. Toronto: University of Toronto Press, 1979.

Christopher, James. 'The Chester Mystery Plays'. *The Times*, 3 Jul 1997.

Claxton, Guy. *Hare Brain, Tortoise Mind*. London: Fourth Estate, 1997.

Coletti, Theresa. 'Reading REED: History and the Records of Early English Drama'. *Literary Practice and Social Change in Britain, 1380–1530*. Ed. Lee Patterson. Berkeley: University of California Press, 1990, pp. 248–84.

Coletti, Theresa, and Kathleen Ashley. 'The N-Town Passion at Toronto and Late Medieval Passion Iconography'. *RORD* 14 (1981), pp. 181–7.

Counsell, Colin. *Signs of Performance: an introduction to twentieth-century theatre*. London: Routledge, 1996.

Coveney, Michael. 'Review of York *Millennium Mysteries*'. *Daily Mail*, 30 Jun 2000.

Coventry *Millennium Mysteries*. Programme.

Coventry: Records of Early English Drama. Ed. R. W. Ingram. Toronto: University of Toronto Press, 1981.

Croucher, Sheila. *Globalization and Belonging: The Politics of Identity in a Changing World*. Lanham, Maryland and Oxford: Rowman & Littlefield Publishers, 2004.

Cumberland, Westmoreland, Gloucestershire: Records of Early English Drama. Ed. Audrey Douglas and Peter Greenfield. Toronto: University of Toronto Press, 1986.

Curtis, Nick. 'Review of RSC *The Mysteries*'. *Evening Standard*, 10 Mar 1997.

Dallas, Karl. 'God Spake in Dialect'. *The Morning Star*, 21 Dec 1985.

Dawson, Andrew. 'The Mining Community and the Ageing Body: Towards a Phenomenology of Community'. *Realizing Community*. Ed. Vered Amit. London: Routledge, 2002, pp. 21–37.

Dawson, Anthony, and Paul Yachnin. *The Culture of Playgoing in Shakespeare's England – A Collaborative Debate*. Cambridge: Cambridge University Press, 2001.

Delgardo, Maria, and Paul Heritage. *In Contact with the Gods: Directors Talk Theatre*. Manchester: Manchester University Press, 1996.

Dillon, Janette. 'Performance Time: Suggestions for a Methodology of Analysis'. *METh* 22 (2000), pp. 33–51.

Dinshaw, Carolyn. *Getting Medieval: Sexualities and Communities, Pre- and Postmodern*. Durham, NC: Duke University Press, 1999.

Edmiston, Brian. 'Drama as Ethical Education'. *RIDE* 5.2 (2000), pp. 63–84.

Elliott, John. 'A Checklist of Modern Productions of the Medieval Mystery Cycles in England'. *RORD* 13–14 (1970–71), pp. 259–66.

—— 'Playing the Godspell'. *RORD* 15–16 (1972–3), pp. 125–7.

—— 'Review of 1976 York Mystery Plays'. *RORD* 20 (1977), pp. 97–8.

—— 'Review of 1984 York Mystery Plays'. *RORD* 17 (1984), p. 187.

—— *Playing God: Medieval Mysteries on the Modern Stage*. Toronto: University of Toronto Press, 1989.

Epp, Garrett. 'The Towneley Plays, or, The Hazards of Cycling'. *RORD* 32 (1993), pp. 121–50.

—— 'Playing in All Directions: The York Plays, Toronto'. *Early Theatre* 1 (1998), pp. 149–52.

Evans, Ruth. 'When a Body meets a Fergus: Fergus and Mary in the York Cycle'. *New Medieval Literatures*. Volume 1. Ed. Wendy Scase, Rita Copeland and David Lawton. Oxford: Clarendon Press, 1997, pp. 193–212.

Fletcher, Alan. 'Lincoln Mystery Plays'. *RORD* 18 (1985), pp. 207–9.

Gallie, Duncan. 'The Labour Force'. *Twentieth Century British Social Trends*. Ed A. H. Halsey with Josephine Webb. London and New York: Macmillan Press and St Martin's Press, 2000, pp. 281–323.

Gardiner, H. C. *Mysteries End*. New Haven: Yale University Press, 1946.

Gibson, Gail McMurray. 'The York Cycle at Toronto: October 1 and 2, 1977'. *RORD* 20 (1977), pp. 114–17.

Greenfield, Peter. 'Review of RSC *The Mysteries*, 1997'. *RORD* 37 (1998), pp. 129–30.

Grier, Christopher. 'Review of RNT, *Mysteries*'. *Evening Standard*, 21 Jan 1985.

Gross, John. 'Review of the RNT Mysteries'. *Sunday Telegraph*, 26 Dec 1999.

Hagerty, Bill. 'Review of RSC, *The Mysteries*'. *News of the World*, 25 Jan 1998.

Hahn, Thomas. 'The York Cycle at Toronto: October 1 and 2, 1977'. *RORD* 20 (1977), pp. 117–21.

Hall, Edith. 'Towards a Theory of Performance Reception'. *Arion* 21.1 (Spring/Summer 2004), pp. 51–89.

—— 'Introduction'. *Dionysus since 69: Greek Tragedy at the Dawn of the Third Millennium*. Ed. Edith Hall, Fiona Macintosh and Amanda Wrigley. Oxford University Press, 2004, pp. 1–46.

Hanawalt, Barbara. *Growing up in Medieval London*. New York: Oxford University Press, 1993.

—— '"The Childe of Bristowe" and the Making of Middle-Class Adolescence'. *Bodies and Disciplines*. Ed. Barbara Hanawalt and David Wallace. Minneapolis: University of Minnesota Press, 1996. pp. 157–78.

Hanks, D. T., Jr '"Quicke Bookis" – The Corpus Christi Drama and English Children in the Middle Ages'. *Popular Culture in the Middle Ages*. Ed. J. Campbell. Bowling Green, Ohio: Bowling Green University Popular Press, 1986, pp. 118–27.

Hanks, Robert. 'Mystery Tour'. *The Independent*. Tabloid Section, 5 Mar 1997, pp. 4–5.

—— 'Soft Targets'. *The Independent*, 27 Mar 1997.

Happé, Peter. 'The Lincoln Cycle of Mystery Plays'. *RORD* 14 (1981), pp. 198–9.

—— 'Review of 1980 York Mystery Plays'. *RORD* 13 (1980), pp. 81–3.

—— 'Acting the York Mystery Plays: A Consideration of Modes'. *METh* 10.2 (1988), pp. 112–16.

—— *English Drama before Shakespeare*. Essex: Longman, 1999.

Harrison, Tony. *The Mysteries*. London: Faber, 1985.

Harvie, Jen. *Staging the UK*. Manchester: Manchester University Press, 2005.

Heitor, Teresa *et al.* 'Breaking of the Medieval Space: The Emergence of a New City of Enlightenment'. Proceedings of Space Syntax, Second International Symposium, Braziol, 1999. Volume 2. Accessed http://www.spacesyntax.net/symposia/SSS2/sss2_proceedings.htm. Accessed 2 Oct 2006.

Henri, Adrian. *The Wakefield Mysteries*. London: Methuen, 1991.

Hewson, Robert. 'Review of York *Millennium Mysteries*'. *Sunday Times*, 2 Jul 2000.

Hirst, Paul. 'Miracle or Mirage?: The Thatcher Years, 1979–1997'. *From Blair to Blitz*. Ed. Nick Tiratsoo. London: Phoenix, 1997, pp. 191–217.

Hoyle, Martin. 'Review of RNT, *Mysteries*'. *Financial Times*, 20 May 1985.

Humphries, Paul. 'Tourists Breathe New Life into Barnsley'. *The Guardian*, 9 Mar 2001.

Itzin, Catherine. *Stages in the Revolution*. London: Eyre Methuen, 1980.

Jackson, Adrian. 'Inter-acting with the Past – The Uses of Participatory Theatre at Museums and Heritage Sites'. *RIDE* 5.2 (2000), pp.199–215.

James, Mervyn. 'Ritual Drama and Social Body in the Late Medieval Town'. *Past and Present* 98 (1983), pp. 3–29.

Johnston, Alexandra. 'York Cycle 1998: What We Learned'. *Early Theatre* 3 (2000), pp. 199–203.

The Journal, Jun/Jul 2000.

Kahrl, Stanley. 'Medieval Drama in England, 1973: Chester and Ely'. *RORD* 15–16 (1972–3), pp. 117–23.

Kaplan, Joel. 'Staging the York: *Creation* and *Hortularus* Toronto 1998'. *METh* 19 (1997), pp. 129–43.

—— 'Afterwards'. *Early Theatre* 3 (2000), pp. 275–8.

Kaprow, Alan. 'The Happenings are Dead: Long Live the Happenings!' *Essays on the Blurring of Art and Life*. Ed Jeff Kelley. Berkeley: University of California Press, 1993.

Kemp, Edward. *The Mysteries, Part One: The Creation*. London: Nick Hern Books, 1997.

—— *The Mysteries, Part Two: The Passion*. London: Nick Hern Books, 1997.

—— 'Anti-Semitism, Islamophobia and sexism plague the mystery plays. How does a modern playwright junk the propaganda without losing the plot?'. *New Statesman*, 23 Jan 1998, pp. 38–9.

King, Francis. 'Review of RNT, *Mysteries*'. *Daily Telegraph*. 27 Jan 1985.

Kingston, James. 'Review of RSC *The Mysteries*'. *The Times*, 23 Jan 1998.

Kolve, V. A. *The Play Called Corpus Christi*. Stanford: Stanford University Press, 1946.

Laishley, A. L. 'The York Mystery Plays'. *Yorkshire Life Illustrated*, Jun 1954, pp. 14–21.

Leach, Edmund. *Rethinking Anthropology*. London: Athlone Press, 1961.

Leach, Robert. *The Lichfield Mysteries*. Birmingham: Clydesdale, 1994.

Lefebvre, Henri. *The Production of Space*. Trans. D. Nicholson-Smith. Oxford: Blackwell, 1991.

Lichfield Mysteries 1994. Programme.

Lichfield Mysteries, review, *The Lichfield Mercury*, 5 May 1994.

Lincoln Mystery Plays 2000. Programme.

Lindenbaum, Sheila. 'The York Cycle at Toronto: Staging and Performance Style'. *Medieval English Drama*. Ed. Peter Happé. London: Macmillan, 1984, pp. 199–211.

—— 'Ceremony and Oligarchy: The London Midsummer Watch'. *City and Spectacle in Medieval Europe*. Medieval Studies at Minnesota. Vol. 6. Ed. Barbara Hanawalt and Kathryn Rogerson. Minneapolis: University of Minnesota Press, 1994, pp.171–88.

—— 'Rituals of Exclusion: Feasts and Plays of the English Religious Fraternities'. *Festive Drama*. Ed. Meg Twycross. Cambridge: D. S. Brewer, 1996, pp. 54–65.

Lloyd, Megan. 'Reflections of a York Survivor: The York Cycle and Its Audience'. *RORD* 39 (2000), pp. 223–35.

McCaw, Dick. 'Old Theatre for New'. *Leeds Studies in English* 32 (2001), pp. 275–87.

'Magnificent Swansong'. *Lincolnshire Chronicle*, 21 Jul 2000.

Marshall, John. 'Modern Productions of Medieval English Plays'. *The Cambridge Companion to Medieval English Theatre*. Ed. Richard Beadle. Cambridge: Cambridge University Press, 1994, pp. 290–311.

Mason, Bim. *Street Theatre and Other Outdoor Performance*. London: Routledge, 1992.

ME. 'Review of *The Mysteries*, National Theatre'. *RORD* 21 (1978), p. 99.

Meredith, Peter. '"Nolo Mortem" and the Ludus Coventriae Play of *The Women Taken in Adultery*'. *Medium Aevum* 38.1 (1969), pp. 38–54.

—— 'The York Cycle at Toronto: October 1 and 2, 1977'. *RORD* 20 (1977), pp. 112–14.

—— 'The Two Yorks: Playing Toronto and York'. *Early Theatre* 1 (1998), pp. 160–3.

Mills, David. 'The Chester Cycle of Mystery Plays at Chester'. *METh* 9.1 (1987), pp. 69–76.

—— 'York Mystery Plays at York'. *METh* 10.1 (1988), pp. 69–70.

—— 'Reviving the Chester Plays'. *METh* 13 (1991), pp. 39–51.

—— 'The Chester Mysteries 1992'. *METh* 12 (1992), pp. 120–3.

—— 'The 1951 and 1952 Revivals of the Chester Plays', *METh* 15 (1993), pp. 111–25.

—— *Recycling the Cycle: The City of Chester and its Whitsun Plays*. Toronto: University of Toronto Press, 1998.

Muir, L. 'Women on the Medieval Stage: The Evidence from France'. *METh* 7.2 (1985), pp. 107–19.

Mulryne, R., and M. Shewring, eds. *The Cottesloe at the National: Infinite Riches in a Little Room*. Stratford-upon-Avon: Mulryne & Shewring, 1999.

Murdin, Lynda. 'Review of York Millennium Mysteries'. *Yorkshire Post*, 28 Jun 2000.

Nelson, Alan. *The Medieval English Stage: Corpus Christi Pageants and Plays*. Chicago: University of Chicago Press, 1974.

Neuss, Paula. 'God and Embarrassment'. *Themes in Drama* 5. *Drama and Religion*. Ed. James Redmond. Cambridge, Cambridge University Press, 1983, pp. 241–54.

Nicholson, Helen. *Applied Drama: The Gift of Theatre*. Basingstoke: Palgrave, 2005.

Nightingale, Benedict. 'Theatre'. *Harpers and Queen*, Sep 1977.

—— 'Review of National Theatre's *The* Mysteries'. *The Times*, 21 Dec 1999.

Nisse, Ruth. *Defining Acts: Drama and the Politics of Interpretation in Late Medieval England*. Notre Dame, Indiana: University of Notre Dame Press, 2005.

Non-Cycle Plays and Fragments. Ed. N. Davis. Early English Text Society SS 1. Oxford: Oxford University Press, 1970.

Normington, Katie. *Gender and Medieval Drama*. Cambridge: D. S. Brewer, 2004.

Northern Echo, 16 Jun 2000.

Oakshott, Jane. 'York Guilds' Mystery Plays 1998: The Rebuilding of a Dramatic Community'. *Drama and the Community: People and Plays in Medieval Europe*. Ed. Alan Hindley. Turnout: Brepols, 1999, pp. 270–89.

Oakshott, Jane, and Richard Rastall. 'Town with Gown: The York Cycle of Mystery Plays at Leeds'. *Towards the Community University*. Ed. David C. B. Teather. London: Kogan Page, 1982, pp. 213–29.

O'Connell, Michael. 'Extracts from the *Lincoln Mystery Plays*'. *RORD* 34 (1995), pp. 183–6.

Ottley, Margaret. 'Worsbrough's Mystery Plays'. *Dalesman* 45.8 (Nov 1983), pp. 662–4.

Owen, David. 'The Ethnic Composition of Coventry in 1991'. National Ethnic Minority Data Archive Information Paper 95/2, Aug 1995. Centre for Research in Ethnic Relations, Aug 1995. http://www.warwick.ac.uk/~errac/coventry.pdf. Accessed 29 Mar 2006.

Palmer, Barbara. 'The York Cycle in Performance: Toronto and York'. *Early Theatre* 1 (1998), pp. 139–42.

—— 'Recycling "The Wakefield Cycle": The Records'. *RORD* 41 (2002), pp. 88–130.

Parry, David. 'The York Mystery Cycle at Toronto, 1977'. *METh* (1979), pp. 19–31.

Paul, Sarah. 'The 1996 York Cycle of Mystery Plays: mirrors of the Community'. *The Month* (Sep/Oct 1996), p. 395.

Pawlowski, Roman. 'Teatr Biuro Podrozy from Poland: Mystery Plays for the Twenty-First Century'. *TheatreForum* 10 (Winter/Spring 1997), pp. 84–9.

Pearsall, Derek. 'The Visual World of the Middle Ages'. *The New Pelican Guide to English Literature 1. Medieval Literature*. Ed. Boris Ford. London: Penguin, 1991, pp. 290–317.

Peter, John. 'Acting in the Best Faith'. *Sunday Times*, 16 Mar 1997.

Phythian-Adams, Charles. 'Ceremony and the Citizen: The Communal Year at Coventry 1450–1550'. *Crisis and Order in English Towns*. Ed. Peter Clark and Paul Slack. London: Routledge & Kegan Paul, 1972, pp. 57–85.

Pickering, Kenneth. *Drama in the Cathedral*. 2nd edn. Malvern: Churchman Publishing, 2001.

Potter, Bob. 'The York Plays: University of Toronto, 20 June 1998.' *METh* 19 (1999), pp. 121–8.

Rastall, R. 'Female Roles in All-Male Casts.' *METh* 7.1 (1985), pp. 25–50. http://www.leeds.ac.uk/reporter/452/mysteryp.htm. Accessed 29 Mar 2006.

—— 'The Mystery Plays 25 Years On.' *The Reporter* 452, 22 May 2000.

Richardson, C., and J. Johnston. *Medieval Drama*. London: Macmillan, 1984.

Rogerson, Margaret. '"Everybody got their brown dress": mystery plays for the Millennium.' *New Theatre Quarterly* 17/2 (May 2001), pp. 123–40.

—— 'Review of York Mystery Plays 2002.' *RORD* 42 (2003), pp. 161–9.

—— 'Living History: the modern Mystery Plays in York.' *RORD* 43 (2004), pp. 12–28.

Roose-Evans, James. *Inner Journey, Outer Journey: Finding a Spiritual Centre in Everyday life*. London: Rider and Co, 1987.

Rubin, Miri. *Corpus Christi: The Eucharist in Late Medieval Culture*. Cambridge: Cambridge University Press, 1991.

Schechner, Richard. *Performance Studies*. London: Routledge, 2002.

Shepherd, Jack. 'The "Scholar" Me: An Actor's View.' *Tony Harrison*. Ed. Neil Astley. Newcastle: Bloodaxe Books, 1991, pp. 423–8.

Shuttleworth, Ian. 'Review of *York Millennium Mysteries*'. *Financial Times*, 26 Jun 2000.

Simeonova, Kristina. 'The Aesthetic Function of the Carnivalesque in Medieval English Drama.' *Bakhtin: Carnival and Other Subjects*. Ed. David Shepherd. Amsterdam and Atlanta: Editions Rodopi, 1993, pp. 70–9.

Sinanoglou, L. 'The Christ Child as Sacrifice: A Medieval Tradition and the Corpus Christi Plays.' *Speculum* 48.3 (1973), pp. 491–509.

Smith, Julia. 'The Rival Mystery Plays.' *Dalesman* 57.4 (Jul 1995), pp. 38–40.

—— '...To the Mysterious.' *Dalesman* (Jul 2000), pp. 32–3.

Spencer, Charles. 'Mystery Stripped Back to the Basics.' *Daily Telegraph*, 10 Mar 1997.

—— 'Review of National Theatre *The Mysteries*.' *Daily Telegraph*, 20 Dec 1999.

Sponsler, Claire. 'The Culture of the Spectator: Conformity and Resistance to Medieval Performances.' *Theatre Journal* 44 (1992), pp. 15–29.

—— *Drama and Resistance: Bodies, Goods, and Theatricality in Late Medieval England*. Minneapolis: University of Minnesota Press, 1997.

Staines, David. 'The English Mystery Cycles.' *The Theatre of Medieval Europe*. Ed. Eckehard Simon. Cambridge: Cambridge University Press, 1991, pp. 80–96.

Stevens, Martin. '"Processus Torontoniensis": A Performance of the Wakefield Cycle.' *RORD* 18 (1985), pp. 189–99.

Taylor, Betsy. 'The York Cycle at Toronto.' *Cahiers Élisabéthains* 55 (1999), pp. 55–63.

Taylor, Paul. 'Review of the York Millennium Mysteries.' *The Independent*, 26 Jun 2000.

Thomason, Ed. 'From the Director's Rehearsal Notes.' Programme, *Coventry Mysteries*, 1979.

Tushingham, David. *Live One: Food for the Soul*. London: Methuen, 1994.

Turner, Victor. *The Ritual Process: Structure and Anti-Structure*. Chicago: Aldine, 1969.

Two Coventry Corpus Christi Plays. Ed. Hardin Craig. Early English Text Society, ES 87. London: Oxford University Press, 1957.

Twycross, Meg. '"Places to Hear the Play": Pageant Stations at York, 1398–1572'. *REED Newsletter* 2 (1978), pp. 10–33.

—— 'Playing "The Resurrection"'. *Medieval Studies for J. A. W. Bennett*. Ed. P. L. Heyworth. Oxford: Clarendon, 1981, pp. 273–96.

—— 'Books for the Unlearned'. *Themes in Drama 5, Drama and Religion*. Ed. J. Redmond. Cambridge: Cambridge University Press, 1983, pp. 65–110.

—— 'Transvestism in the Mystery Plays'. *METh* 5.2 (Dec 1983), pp. 123–80.

—— 'The Left-hand-side Theory: A Retraction'. *METh* 14 (1992), pp. 77–94.

—— 'The Theatricality of Medieval English Plays'. *The Cambridge Companion to Medieval English Theatre*. Ed. Richard Beadle. Cambridge: Cambridge University Press, 1994, pp. 37–84.

—— 'Forget the 4.30am Start: Recovering a Palimpsest in the York *Ordo paginarum*', *METh* 25 (2003), pp. 98–152.

Twycross, Meg, and Sarah Carpenter. 'Purposes and Effects of Masking'. *Medieval English Drama*. Ed. Peter Happé. London: Macmillan, 1984, pp. 171–80.

—— *Mask and Masking in Medieval and Early Tudor England*. Aldershot: Ashgate, 2002.

Tydeman, William. 'An introduction to medieval English theatre'. *The Cambridge Companion to Medieval English Theatre*. Ed. Richard Beadle. Cambridge: Cambridge University Press, 1994, pp. 1–36.

Tyler, Mike. 'Review of York Mystery Plays 2002'. *RORD* 42 (2003), pp. 158–61.

The University of Leeds Reporter 71. 29 May 1975, p. 1.

Velz, John. 'The Coventry Cycle of Mystery Plays, 1978'. *Cahiers Élisabéthains* 15 (Apr 1979), pp. 125–6.

Vinter, Donna Smith. 'Didactic Characterisation – The Towneley *Abraham*', *Medieval English Drama*. Ed. Peter Happé. London: Macmillan, 1984; reprint 1993, pp. 71–89.

Walker, John. 'Promenade of "Passion" Gets Audience into Act'. *International Herald Tribune*, 23 Aug 1978.

Weimann, Robert. *Shakespeare and the Popular Tradition*. Baltimore: Johns Hopkins University Press, 1978.

Whitworth, Charles. 'Review of 1984 York Plays'. *Cahiers Élisabéthains* 26 (Oct 1984), p. 108.

Wickham, Glynne. *Early English Stages, 1300–1600*. 3 vols. London: Routledge & Kegan Paul, 1959–1981.

Wiles, David. *A Short History of Western Performance Space*. Cambridge: Cambridge University Press, 2003.

Willett, John, ed. and trans. *Brecht on Theatre: The Development of an Aesthetic*. London: Methuen, 1964; 2nd edn, 1974.

Williams, Raymond. *Keywords*. London: Fontana, 1983.

Winston, J. *Drama, Narrative and Moral Education: exploring traditional tales in the primary years*. London: Farmer, 1998.

Woodis, Carole. ' Review of RNT, *Mysteries*'. *City Limits*, 25 Jan 1985.

Worsbrough Mystery Plays 1998, Programme.

Yates, Kimberley. 'The Critical Heritage of the York Cycle'. Unpublished PhD diss. University of Toronto, 1997.

York Millennium Mystery Plays, Programme.

York Millennium Mystery Plays, *Yorkshire Evening Post*, 22 Jun 2000.

York Mystery Plays, review, *Guardian*, 16 Jun 1992.

York Mystery Plays, review, *The Independent*, 15 Jun 1992.

York Mystery Plays, review, *Northern Echo*, 1 Jul 1992.

York Mystery Plays, review, *Daily Telegraph*, 2 Jun 1996.

York Mystery Plays, review, *Financial Times*, 12 Jun 1996.

York Mystery Plays, review, *The Guardian*, 2 Mar 1996.

York: Records of Early English Drama. Ed. A. F. Johnston and Margaret Rogerson. 2 vols. Toronto: University Press, 1979.

Yorkshire Evening Post, 7 Nov 1991.

Personal Interviews

Brereton, Andy. Co-director, Chichester Mysteries. Interviewed 18 Dec 1999.

Cherrington, John Paul. Director, Lichfield Mystery Plays 2000. Interviewed 10 Apr 2001.

Fisher, Bob. Director, Worsbrough Mystery Plays 1994–2001. Interviewed 1 Mar 2006.

Hytch, Jane. Producer Belgrade Theatre. Interviewed 19 Jun 2000.

Leach, Robert. Director and Founder, Lichfield Mystery Plays 1994. Interviewed, 31 Jul 2001.

Meredith, Peter. Organiser, York Plays at Leeds 1975. Interviewed 27 Apr 2001.

Mitchell, Katie. Director, Royal Shakespeare Company, *The Mysteries*. Interviewed 15 Mar 1997.

Oakshott, Jane. Director, York Plays at Leeds 1975 and Guild Plays at York 1994. Interviewed 28 Apr 2001.

Pegg, Matthew. Education Officer, Belgrade Theatre. Interviewed 27 Jun 2000.

Ramsay, Keith. Director of Licoln Mystery Plays. Interviewed 17 Apr 2001.

Retallack, John. Director, Oxford Stage Company *Mistero Buffo*. Interviewed 14 May 1997.

Roman, George. Director, Chester Mystery Plays, 1997. Interviewed 30 Aug 2000.

Wroe, Julian. Chair, Worsbrough Mystery Plays. Interviewed 2 Jul 2001.

Public Interviews

Ossie Heppell, interviewed by Mike Tyler, 8 Sep 1999. http://www.yorkmysteryplays.org/index_highres.htm Accessed 15 Apr 2006.

Eileen Skaite, interviewed by Mike Tyler, 19 Aug 1999. http://www.yorkmysteryplays.org/index_highres.htm Accessed 15 Apr 2006.

Alderman Keith Wood, interviewed by Mike Tyler, 13 Dec 2001. http://www.yorkmysteryplays.org/index_highres.htm Accessed 15 Apr 2006.

Websites

http://www.artscouncil.org.uk/documents/information/HistoryACE_phpJGGeGy.doc Accessed 23 Mar 2006.

http://www.cofe.anglican.org/info/statistics/ Accessed 3 Sep 2006.

http://lichfield-mysteries.freeserve.co.uk Accessed 21 Jun 2000.

http://www.millennium.gov.uk/index.html Accessed 6 Oct 2006.

http://www.statistics.gov.uk Accessed 14 Sep 2006.

http://www.yorkmysteryplays.org/index_highres.htm Accessed 28 Apr 2006.

http://www.yorkstories.fsnet.co.uk/york_mystery_plays_2002/ Accessed 28 Apr 2006.

http://www.un.org/millenniumgoals/ Accessed 11 Apr 2006.

Performances

Chichester Youth Theatre. *The Mysteries*. Minerva Theatre. Dir. Andy Brereton. *Creation*, 23 Dec 1999; *Passion*, 30 Dec 1999.

Coventry *Millennium Mysteries*. Cathedral ruins. Dir. Pavel Szkotat. 21 Jul 2000.

Lincoln Mystery Plays, 2004. Lincoln Cathedral. Dir. Karen Crow. 28 Jul 2004.

Oxford Stage Company. Dario Fo's *Mistero Buffo*. Greenwich Theatre. Dir. John Retallack. 19 Apr 1997.

Royal National Theatre. *The Mysteries*. Cottesloe Theatre. Dir. Bill Bryden. *The Nativity*, 4 Dec 1999; *The Passion*, 11 Dec 1999; *Doomsday*, 16 Dec 1999.

Royal Shakespeare Company. *The Mysteries*. The Other Place. Dir. Katie Mitchell. *The Creation*, 14 Mar 1997; *The Passion*, 15 Mar 1997.

The Middle School Mysteries by Mich Martin. Salisbury Cathedral. 24 Mar 1999.

The Worsbrough Mystery Plays, 2001. St Mary's Church. Dir. Bill Fisher. 2 Jul 2001.

York Guild Plays, 1998. York Streets. Dir. Jane Oakshott. 12 Jul 1998.

York *Millennium Mysteries Plays*. York Minster. Dir. Greg Doran. 22 Jun 2000.

Videos

Chester Mystery Plays: A Live Performance Chester Cathedral Green, 5 Jul 2003.

Lichfield Mysteries 1994. Personal Archive, Robert Leach.

Lincoln Mysteries 2000. Personal Archive, Keith Ramsay.

The Mysteries, National Theatre. Channel Four Television, 1985.

York Guild Plays 1998. VPS-TV, 1999.

York Plays at Toronto 1977. See http://www.chass.utoronto.ca/~plspls/links.html.

York Plays at Toronto 1998. *Poculi Ludique Societas* archives.

York *Millennium Mysteries*. Video recording held by York Minster Library.

Index